BUGGIN'
A Brother's Tale

DONALD F. TAYLOR, JR.

Published in the United States of America

ISBN 978-1-962730-63-1 (SC)

Donald Taylor Publishing
222 West 6th Street
Suite 400, San Pedro, CA, 90731
www.stellarliterary.com.

Ordering Information and Rights Permission:

Quantity sales. Special discounts might be available on quantity purchases by corporations, associations, and others. For details, contact the publisher at the address above.

For Book Rights Adaptation and other Rights Permission. Call us at toll-free 1-888-945-8513 or send us an email at admin@stellarliterary.com.

CONTENTS

I dedicate this book to all my friends and family who have stood by me over the years.

I so hope you enjoy my work and find it not only fun to read, but also helpful as you navigate through some of life's ups and downs.

I also invite you to read the next book in the Jerome Mitchell series, <u>The Cave</u>.

BUGGIN'

A Brother's Tale

BUGGIN': (Noun or Verb)A state of mind or series of behaviors which confirm one is not thinking or acting in ways which could be considered rational by others, either in one's circle of friends or the society at large.

I

October, 1995

I glanced at the clock hanging on the wall behind the judge's bench. It indicated I had only been here for fifteen or twenty minutes, but I felt as if I had been sitting for hours. Ready or not, I was about to begin the final act of this play. The bailiff's raspy voice confirmed this current reality. This was not a play. This was real. This part of my life's drama was hurtling toward a conclusion.

"All rise!"

Standing, I checked out the courtroom. I noticed it did look somewhat like the ones I've seen on TV. All seats, as well as the judge's bench were stained a light mahogany color. I wondered who came up with that decorating plan.

A plain, thin woman with thick dark hair mixed with gray strands wearing a simple navy suit and what looked like a silk blouse, sat in an area that looked like a hockey penalty box next to the judge's bench in front of a small machine, her fingers poised over the keys.

Thinking back to my favorite *Perry Mason* episodes, I figured she was the court reporter. The one who read back witness statements just before Perry went in for the kill.

The seats in the courtroom were mostly empty.

My brother, Robert, an Atlanta attorney, sat on the back row as an observer of the process and a support to me. Up front, in the corner near the door where I supposed the judge would enter, were a few deputy sheriffs talking in hushed tones to each other. A few other people were scattered throughout the room talking quietly.

Judge Sarah Morris, a white female, entered with a flourish. Her gowns rustled as she moved. After ascending the steps to the bench, she stood surveying the courtroom. The deputy sheriffs' conversation along with other conversations in the room, ceased mid-sentence.

Judge Morris appeared to be in her early sixties. Her hair a little too blond, I thought. I also guessed she liberally applied hair spray to keep the intricate; but old school style in place. From my vantage point, she appeared to be rather short; but hefty.

I thought about a phrase which I had heard about a person shaped like the Judge, '*a four by four*.' In other words, four feet tall and four feet wide. It fit.

Standing next to my attorney, John Stiles, Esq., I adjusted my tie and smoothed my blue, double-breasted jacket.

I peered at the table just a few feet away, where my soon to be ex-wife and her attorney with the movie star good looks stood. Both were wearing gray suits. Akeba's knee length skirt fit her perfectly.

"Shit, I bet he picked out the suit he has on just to match Akeba's," I thought slowly shaking my head. As much as I hated to admit it, they looked almost like a couple standing there facing Judge Morris.

Akeba's jaw was set, her eyes firmly locked on the Judge. I noticed her attorney, Mr. Q'vin (pronounced Kevin) Lattimore, Esq. holding her arm. Q'vin. Damn, I bet his name really is Kevin. I'm sure he changed the spelling of his name to be some bullshit legal-eagle player.

"Why does he need to touch her like that?" I wondered.

Hell, I guess I could have answered my own question. Akeba was only minutes away from returning to single hood and her attorney was probably trying to move in. I had heard about divorce attorneys making a move on their vulnerable female clients and I was sure this pretty bastard was one of them.

"She's still my wife," I thought to myself as I tried to look at them, without looking.

Without a word, the Judge sat and busied herself with papers on her desk.

"Be seated and come to order, the Honorable Sarah Morris presiding!" the bailiff barked. Absently I sat, still trying to notice if pretty ass Q'vin was hitting on Akeba.

He and Akeba had their heads together. As he whispered to her, she nodded tightly a couple times. Q'vin looked over Akeba's shoulder right at me. I could have sworn he smiled at me.

"Punk," I thought to myself. That bastard is hitting on Akeba. I glanced back at Robert. He gave me a faint smile and a nod of support.

Since Akeba and Q'vin were whispering, I thought it might be a good idea to whisper about something to my attorney, so we could look like we had some strategy to discuss. I poked Attorney John Stiles gently on the arm with my elbow. He moved his head toward me.

Attorney Stiles' thinning brown hair was brushed across his head. His reading glasses were perched on the end of his nose. His short, stubby fingers were stretched out against the files piled in front of him.

"What's up?" he whispered, flatly.

"Uh, you think this judge will do what we asked?" I whispered back.

"Well, like I told you, we've done all the necessary prelim work."

"Your wife's attorney, Mr. Lattimore," Attorney Stiles glanced at Akeba's table, "has agreed to mostly everything, the rest will be a formality." I nodded.

"Anything else?" he asked.

"Uh, no."

It was time to end this conversation. Stiles' stale cigarette breath was irritating. I reached in my pocket, took out a packaged mint and slid it toward him. I didn't look at him, directly, but out the corner of my eye I saw him look quizzically, first at the mint, then at me. Without a word, he opened the cellophane package and popped the mint in his mouth. He reached out and squeezed my forearm.

I balled my hands up. My fingers were cold, but clearly, the room wasn't. No one else seemed to be reacting to a chill in the air. I felt myself holding my breath. Remembering my past yoga class, I took a deep cleansing breath. Damn, this is crazy. I wished the judge would just begin and get this over with.

"Mr. Mitchell?"

Attorney Stiles elbowed me. He indicated with his head I was to look at the Judge.

"Yes, your Honor?"

"Mr. Mitchell, Mrs. Mitchell, do either of you have anything you'd like to say before I end this?" I looked up at the bench. Judge Morris' voice was soft; but firm. It was clear that she knew she was in command. Absolutely no-nonsense.

I shook my head, slowly. No, I had nothing to say. I blew it. Just buggin'. I should have known better. Eleven years, gone…just like that; well actually twelve if I counted the North Carolina requisite one-year of separation. Wow! A whole year of separation. I briefly closed my eyes as this realization washed over me.

"No, your Honor," I responded.

I followed the Judge's eyes as she looked at the table where Akeba and her attorney stood. Akeba's head never moved in my direction. She continued to look up at the judge. Mr. Lattimore put his hand on her back as if to steady her. After taking a deep breath, she spoke solemnly, "No, your honor."

"Fair enough," the Judge said with gravity. She put round wire rim glasses on her round face. For a brief moment, I almost smiled in spite of myself. She looked just like the pictures I remembered of Mrs. Santa Claus.

"You can all be seated." We sat.

My stomach felt like it was doing back flips. I felt the beginning of a throbbing headache. I needed to get out of this courtroom.

The Judge asked a few questions.

"Mr. Mitchell, are you claiming ownership of the artwork?"

"Mrs. Mitchell, you are satisfied with the amount written for child support?"

"Mr. Mitchell, the visitation plan recorded here is satisfactory to you?"

"Mr. and Mrs. Mitchell, are you on one accord regarding the termination of this marriage?"

Judge Morris asked looking alternately at both of us and removed her glasses. I could feel the end coming.

Then, it was over. Based on me and Akeba's answers and the statements by our attorneys, Judge Morris approved most of the items we had discussed then quickly dispatched the areas in dispute. She banged her gavel. We all stood as ordered by the bailiff while Judge Morris exited the courtroom by the door she entered. I stole another look at the clock.

On Tuesday, October 24, 1995, eleven o'clock am, the marriage of Akeba and Jerome Mitchell, ended.

I studied my attorney as he began loading files and papers in his briefcase. I wondered if I should have gotten a female attorney. Not for any specific reason other than to give Akeba something to think about. Am I screwed up or what? Man, my headache was really gathering steam. Once Stiles finished filling his overstuffed briefcase, he turned toward me and shook my hand.

"I'm sorry about your marriage, but this went as well as it could," he said, releasing his hand from mine, then squeezing my shoulder.

I stared off into the air over his head before responding.

"Thanks for all your help, Mr. Stiles. Your expertise made this as simple as I guess it could have been. You'll send me the bill as we discussed?"

Attorney Stiles smiled. "You can count on that, Mr. Mitchell."

"Mr. Stiles, the case is over. You can call me Jerome, now."

"I'll do that after I get and deposit your check, Mr. Mitchell." He laughed, covering his mouth with his fist.

"Well, I have to go to another courtroom. Have a good day and get some rest, Jerome. You look tired."

"Ok, John. Thanks."

Attorney Stiles took off down the aisle toward the exit. He stopped to talk with another man at the door. The two of them left the courtroom together.

Watching Akeba and her attorney talking quietly to each other at their table, I thought her attorney was leaning too close to her, so I decided to walk over to their table. I wasn't sure what I was going to say, but I figured that would come to me once I got there.

"Akeba, I'm so sorry it came to this. I really loved you, in fact, I still do—"

Before I could finish, Akeba raised her hand and looked pointedly at me.

"Jerome, I know you did, once, but you…well never mind. This conversation would be pointless right now. Look, I'm gonna go home. Call me tomorrow so we can schedule your visits with Dani, ok?"

"Sure Akeba, sure."

I had almost forgotten how beautifully Akeba's almond brown skin glowed. Her thick, shiny black hair was pulled back and french rolled. I wanted to reach out, grab her and kiss her real hard, right in the courtroom. Was that fantasy my way of making my claim on her? Was it about Q'vin?

Akeba stepped past me and away from the table into the aisle. She looked at me with those piercing, sexy brown eyes that were beginning to moisten. Then she glanced at her attorney.

Q'vin Lattimore looked back at her, slid his brown leather briefcase off the smooth mahogany table and nodded his head in my direction. When I didn't respond, he turned to follow Akeba, who stiffly walked toward the exit. Once there, he pushed open the door for Akeba. He turned to look at me, his expression hinting at an unstated thought then strolled out of the courtroom.

"I should punch that pretty mutha out," I said to my brother, Robert who seemed to materialize next to me. "See, Robert. I knew her attorney was gonna hit on her as soon as this was over. I mean, look at him. You know he purposely wore that suit so they could match."

Robert put his arm around my shoulder.

"Calm down, Jerome. You aren't going to do anything. You might as well come on with me, have some coffee, get something to eat."

"Akeba looked good, didn't she, Robert?"

"Yeah, she did," Robert said following my gaze. He turned back to me.

"I'm sorry about all this, little brother."

"Thanks, Robert. This whole thing is so fucked up, but hell I'm glad you were here, though." Together, we walked out of the courtroom, through the side door toward the parking lot.

II

Once the case ended, Akeba left the courtroom with Q'vin walking quickly behind her. He pulled a large black phone out of his bag as he walked. He nudged Akeba, who stopped and leaned against the wall, waiting. From time to time, she glanced back at the courtroom, and peered down the hall. After making his call, he put the phone back in his bag and walked with her to the exit door.

Q'vin pushed open the door and Akeba stepped out into the warm October day. The warmth calmed her. She dabbed at her eyes with a finger, took a deep cleansing breath and walked toward the street.

"Hey, hey, hey!" Q'vin called to her as he rushed out of the building.

"Hold up, Akeba," he said just before he caught up with her.

He lit a cigarette and watched her as she watched him. Akeba marveled at how little movement he wasted. She had to admit Cynthia was right. He was by far the coolest man, not to mention the best looking man she had seen in quite some time.

Though she had made every effort to keep their relationship strictly professional, from time to time, she had allowed herself to wonder what type of lover Q'vin Lattimore might be.

"Probably a selfish, arrogant lover," she thought to herself. "I've heard it said gorgeous men usually are," she thought.

"We have to go back to the office to clear up some paperwork," Q'vin said as he slowly exhaled the blue smoke. His voice forced her to concentrate on him.

"I know, Mr. Lattimore. But can't we hurry? I don't want to be out here when my ex comes out with his brother."

"First of all, you need to call me Q'vin. The case is over and we don't have to be so formal. Is that ok with you?" Akeba slowly nodded. "Can I call you, Akeba, now?" Again, she nodded.

"As for your ex, don't sweat it, Akeba." Q'vin moved closer to her. "I saw them leave through the side door headed toward the parking lot. Besides, my man is coming with his cab to chauffeur us back to my office. Akeba took a deep breath and tried to relax.Just then a horn sounded close to them. Both looked toward the sound. Q'vin smiled.

"That's my man, Louis," Q'vin said as he ushered her to the curb.

Akeba looked at the shiny, blue cab emblazoned with the name *Southeast Royal Cab Company* on it.

The stocky driver in a tan linen suit and matching Kangol, worn backwards, hopped out, ran around the front of the car and opened the passenger side rear door for her.

"Thank you," she said as she got in. As Louis closed the door, Akeba noticed he and Q'vin exchanging a warm handshake. Louis and Q'vin went to the other side of the car. Louis returned to his seat behind the wheel and Q'vin got in the back next to Akeba.

Akeba looked around. "This has got to be the cleanest cab in Charlotte," she said to no one in particular.

"Well, to be honest, I think I own the cleanest cab in North Carolina," Louis responded, with obvious pride.

"That's for sure," Q'vin added. "My man Louis keeps the inside and outside spotless."

"It smells good in here," Akeba said. "I'd like to have this fragrance in my car. What is it?"

Louis pulled out from the curb. "Y'all headed to your office, Q?" He looked in the rearview mirror. Q'vin nodded.

"Well to answer your question, ma'am…"

"Oh please don't call me ma'am." My name is Akeba."

"Ok, uh, Akeba. The fragrance is my own concoction. I mix African Violet with Jasmine, a hint of spice and I spray it in the carpet, front and back.

"Very nice," she said, laying her head back against the soft fabric.

"You alright, Akeba?" Q'vin asked, touching her shoulder.

"You mean aside from ending my marriage today?"

"Yeah, aside from that."

Akeba looked out of her window. Though lost in her thoughts, Akeba felt Q'vin's hand on her arm. His soft squeeze felt good. At first she wasn't sure how to respond to his touch, so, she decided not to.

"Relax girl," she told herself. She forced herself to be still, focusing her gaze out the window.

Her daughter, Dani's, face filled Akeba's consciousness and she felt slightly panicky about how she would talk with her about the finality of the divorce.

Akeba stiffened when Q'vin touched her fingers. He rubbed the tip of his finger over her nails. For a moment, Akeba allowed herself to look down at his fingers as they traced hers. His nails were obviously well taken care of and she thought she detected some clear polish on them. She wasn't sure, nor was she sure how she felt about a man who wore nail polish, regardless of how good he looked.

Akeba turned again to look out of her window. She saw only blurry images. She found it difficult to focus. She wondered if it were Q'vin's insistent touch or the lingering emotions from the day's proceedings.

Out of the corner of her eye, she noticed that Q'vin's eyes seemed locked on her legs where they extended from under her skirt.

"No, he won't," she thought to herself.

Just then, Q'vin's hand moved from her fingers to her leg just beyond the hem of her skirt. The heat from his hand on her leg felt like a mini-sun, probing through her hose, spreading through her thigh. The warmth broke her out of her reverie. She looked at him, her mood darkening.

"Q'vin, what are you doing?"

"Just trying to relax you, Akeba." His words sounded practiced.

"I know this has been a tough morning for you but I want you to know that I'm gonna be right here for you."

"Q'vin stop," Akeba said.

"What's the matter, Akeba?" Q'vin asked, his expression all innocence.

"Like I said, I'm only trying to help you relax. I thought you liked my touch."

"Q'vin, I appreciate your concern, but touching my leg moves you from providing comfort to exploitation." She took his hand off her leg and moved it to his lap, accidentally touching his burgeoning erection. Now she felt herself becoming surly.

"Mr. Lattimore, you're my attorney and I do appreciate what you did; but right now, you don't have permission to touch me like that," she said, looking him directly in the eye. Her voice was brittle.

"You said 'right now.' Are you suggesting that at some point, I might have that permission?" Q'vin asked with a hopeful smile.

"Mr. Lattimore," she said, her eyes flashing, "do you really think this is the kind of conversation we should have? We just left a courtroom where my divorce from the father of my daughter, was finalized. Is this really what you want to talk about? You can't possibly be that self-absorbed."

Angrily, she looked out the window of the cab. She instantly knew that they were not anywhere near Q'vin's office.

"What's going on? She asked tensely. "And why are we way out here instead of at your office?" She looked into the rear view mirror. Louis was looking at her. She leaned forward.

"And you need to keep your eyes on the road and get us to Mr. Lattimore's office, right now."

"Yes ma'am, uh, Akeba," Louis said, sheepishly.

"No, you were right the first time. Call me Ma'am," Akeba said shortly. He nodded and turned his attention to driving.

"Sister Mitchell, calm down. I've found that a drive after a traumatic and emotional experience usually helps my clients relax," Q'vin said as soothingly as he could.

"Yeah, right," Akeba said frostily. "Get on your side of the car, ok?"

She looked out the front window and noticed that they were pulling into the parking lot of the building where Q'vin's office was located.

"Louis, that's my car over there," Akeba said pointing. Louis nodded, stopped the car and looked in the rearview at Q'vin.

"Why are you looking at him, Louis?" Akeba asked raising her voice. "Aww, the heck with this." She pushed open her car door and got out. Q'vin quickly followed her.

"Akeba, wait. What's wrong?"

Akeba found her keys and opened her car door, turned and leaned against the open door as Q'vin approached her. She noted the cab parked a respectful distance away.

"Akeba, what did I do that was so wrong?"

He stopped in front of her. His caramel colored skin glistened in the light. His sideburns were perfectly trimmed as was his short jet-black hair. His white teeth shined and the dimple in his chin reminded her of some wicked thoughts she had had about him. And that gray suit? It fit him perfectly. She gathered herself to say what she was thinking.

"Frankly, I resent feeling like I'm some stupid bimbo you think you can make out with in the back seat of a taxi cab."

"Akeba, it wasn't like that," Q'vin said reaching for her.

She shrugged her arm away from his grasp.

"Well, that's what it felt like and Louis looked like he was enjoying some dime peep show." She got in the car, slammed the door and rolled down the window and the engine roared to life.

"And on the day of my divorce," she said through clenched teeth.

"What about the papers you need to sign?"

She took a deep breath and looked up at Q'vin whose face was framed by the window.

"Mail them and your final bill. Now step back so I can go. I need some alone time."

Q'vin stepped back and Akeba moved her car away. She was determined not to look at him again, but she couldn't help it.

She stole a glance in her rearview mirror. She saw his hand go up in a wave. She ignored it, pulled into traffic and headed home. While driving, she thought how she was going to tell Cynthia about what just happened.

"Yep, they were right," she said out loud, "arrogant and selfish."

A couple hours after leaving the courtroom, I was sitting in my apartment with Billy, my life-long friend and my brother Robert. A western movie was on the TV, but I couldn't concentrate on it.

"Come on, Rome. Why don't you ride with us and get some air. You don't need to just sit in the house," Robert said with concern as he turned the TV off.

"Man, I was watching that," Billy whined.

"This ain't about you, Billy. Besides, you can watch an old western anytime."

"For your information, that was *100 Rifles* with Jim Brown and Raquel Welch. That was one of the best westerns ever made, man!"

Ignoring Billy, I responded to Robert, "No, I think I'll just stay here and chill. You two go ahead. Robert, I know you said you wanted to see some folks while you were here."

"Rome, you sure you want to be alone?" Robert asked.

I nodded in response.

"I'm not gonna leave until tomorrow morning," Robert continued. "So, I'll be back in a couple hours, ok? Page me if you need anything before then."

"You want me to stay, Rome?" Billy asked

"Nah. That's ok. I just need to be alone."

I stood as Robert and Billy headed toward the door.

Billy stopped and quickly paced back to me.

"Hey man, that Jim Brown movie was on AMC in case you're interested."

"Thanks, Billy." We shook hands.

"Much love, Rome," Billy said with sincerity.

"Thanks, man. Now go and let me chill out."

"Right. I'm out, Rome. Call if you need me."

Billy jogged back to the car. He got in and they pulled away. I could see Billy using his hands as he talked to my brother in the car. I smiled to myself thinking about Billy with his big bald head and Isaac Hayes chin whiskers.

I looked around. Strangely my two bedroom apartment didn't look any different. For some reason, I expected it would. Silly, huh?

The expensive abstract painting I bought because I was attracted to the artist, still hung over my chocolate-colored sofa. The mildly dusty ebony wood and soap-stone African sculptures I purchased at various festivals and art shows over the last couple years, sat in their places.

My pine colored entertainment center containing my 32" TV, 5 CD changer and VCR was where it always was. With Billy and Robert gone, I nestled back in my recliner, which I bought at an estate sale this past summer. On top of the TV tray, in front of the recliner was a paper plate, covered with another paper plate containing the remains of breakfast, and all three of the remotes lined up like soldiers waiting to be called to duty.

I grabbed the TV remote and punched the 'power button'. The TV leapt back to life and on the screen, Jim Brown grabbed Raquel Welch and kissed her. I hit the 'mute' button and glanced at my answering machine. I had two messages on it.

"Probably bill collectors," I thought, but I pressed play button anyway.

'You have two messages.' The mechanical voice said.

There was a 'beep', then my younger brother, Marcus' smooth tenor voice.

"Hey man, sorry I can't be with you today, but I'm thinking about you, though. Look, call me when you get in, let me know how you doing."

The next message was my mother, calling from Philadelphia.

"Honey, you ok? I'm so sorry about you and Akeba, but God never gives you more than you can bear. Dad says he loves you. Kiss Dani for us and make sure that child knows it's not her fault that her parents are apart. And smile honey. God loves you and so do we. Tell Robert that we're proud he came in from Atlanta to be with you. We love you. Bye."

I could almost see my mother holding the phone with the extra long cord walking around the kitchen as she talked with her favorite white apron on.She always seemed to have that apron on as far back as I could remember. I pressed the save button on the machine, picked up the CD remote and reclined.

Listlessly, I pressed the play button on the remote. Sade's smooth voice came out of the speakers.

"You give me the sweetest taboo," Sade sang.

"Yeah, taboo," I thought to myself. "Yolanda, my sweetest taboo."

I felt warm all over. For a few minutes, I found it difficult to breathe. My situation dawned on me all at once.

At 40 years old, I have an eleven year old daughter and I'm divorced.

III

Ninety minutes after leaving her attorney standing in the parking lot of his building, Akeba was in her bathroom, running hot water in her tub preparing for a long soak. From under the sink, she took out a box of vanilla scented candles.

"It's time to use these," she said out loud. The sound of the running water and the steam which filled the bathroom comforted her. She went back in her room, selected her favorite classical CD's and placed one of the speakers on a chair just inside the bathroom door.

Returning to the bathroom with a goblet of Chablis she had poured earlier, she lit the four thick candles, poured a cup of scented oil in the tub, dropped her robe and stepped into the steaming hot water.

The soft blue color of the walls glowed in the light from the thick candles. Flickering light highlighted the glossy ceiling of the bathroom. This combined with the fragrance from the candles had a hypnotic effect on Akeba. For the first time today, she felt herself relaxing.

The water was hot and it felt good. As she soaked, she pictured Jerome in the courtroom. He looked so handsome in his blue suit. His short dark hair, flecked with gray was neatly cut. His mustache was flawlessly trimmed, as always. She pictured his broad shoulders as he leaned over talking with his attorney. His brown skin was tight and clear.

"What happened to us?" she asked out loud. "How could things get so messed up?"

Over time, she and Jerome had been spending less and less time together.

***

They had even stopped going to church at the same time. Jerome had favored the early morning while she and Dani went to the mid morning services and Sunday School. Akeba wanted to know what was going on between them. She had decided to talk about the 'elephant in the room' topic, while they sat at the kitchen table.

"Jerome, what's happening to us? What's wrong with with you?"

"Akeba, you know, I get so tired of our 'discussions' ending with me as the bad guy. I know this is hard for you to believe, but you ain't so perfect yourself, Akeba."

"Look, Jerome. If you don't want to be with me anymore, just say so. I don't need this shit." She pushed his shoulder. "And don't act like you don't know what I'm talking about. Really, you can be such a dick sometimes."

"Say what you gotta say, Akeba!"

"Jerome, are you seeing someone else?"

"Aw shit, Akeba," he responded and walked out on the back deck.

Sitting in her tub, Akeba shivered. Lost in her memories, she ran more hot water in the tub as she remembered 'the day,' a few months later.

She had almost gotten to her job at the bank, where she works as manager of the commercial loan division, when she remembered she had forgotten some files for an important meeting. She decided to return home to retrieve them.

Arriving home, Akeba remembered thinking it was strange that Jerome's car was still in the driveway. She thought he had an early class that morning. But she was glad he was home.

She parked on the street and smiled as she thought about surprising Jerome at home. They hadn't made love in a couple weeks and Akeba hoped they might have time for intimacy and conversation before she returned to work.

Akeba remembered approaching the door but as she reached for the door knob she suddenly developed a feeling of dread. For a second, she thought about not going in. Her feet were glued to the front steps. She wasn't sure why she felt that way, she just did.

"This is stupid!" she said to herself. She put her key in the door and opened it. At first, the sound of the long beep of the security system was all she heard.

"Jerome?" she called out quietly. There was no response.

"Jerome?" she raised her voice.

There was a muffled sound over her head. She walked to the bottom of the stairs. Jerome appeared. He was out of breath and only half dressed.

"Akeba? What are you doing here?" he had asked. At first his face was blank, then a look of apprehension covered his face.

His breathing was shallow, but it was clear to Akeba that he was struggling to appear nonchalant.

"No, I think the question is what are you doing here? I thought you had an early class this morning? What's going on?"

"Nothing."

A one-word answer. Akeba felt anger rising in her, like an express elevator racing for the top floor.

"I'm just working here before I go to work. I've got some papers to grade," he said finally.

"When did you decide to do that?"

"This morning, why?" Jerome sat on the steps and looked down at her. "Do I need your permission to work at home, now?"

"Jerome, stop that…"

Jerome started down the steps, hurriedly. Just then there was a thudding sound which came from upstairs. He stood frozen on the steps, his eyes never leaving hers.

"Akeba…uh…I…" His voice faltered. As he began to talk, his eyes dropped to the floor.

A fully dressed woman stood behind Jerome on the stairs. Akeba stood. She looked at the two of them, her eyes blazing, her nostrils flaring.

"What's going on?" Akeba was finding it hard to breathe.

Jerome began to speak. "Akeba, I know what you're…" Akeba held up her hand in his face. She could not believe who was standing behind Jerome, almost cowering. Akeba recognized her right away. 'Miss Red Dress!'

"You don't know shit, Jerome…" She took a step toward them. The woman began to speak.

"Akeba…"

Akeba jerked her head up. "Bitch, don't say anything to me! Don't even let my name come out of your nasty mouth! Get out!"

The woman reached for Jerome's arm. The motion infuriated Akeba. Before the woman could touch Jerome, Akeba picked up the sculpture on the table, brandishing it like a weapon and screamed at them.

"Get out of my house! Both of you!"

Enraged, Akeba threw the sculpture at them. They ducked and the sculpture hit the wall behind them shattering. The pieces showered them as they cringed before Akeba's fury.

She then went into the first-floor bathroom and slammed the door. Yolanda Walker! Yolanda Walker! What the fuck was Jerome thinking? She heard the front door open and close. She waited until they left the driveway. Blind with fury, Akeba collapsed to the floor, pounding her fists against the carpet.

Akeba shuddered in her bath as the flashbacks came in waves. She remembered she and Jerome's wedding day and Yolanda's red dress careened across her mind. She knew he was buggin' then, but she paid very little attention to it. She thought about her best friend Cynthia's occasional stories about married men who cheated, but she never thought Jerome was or could be, one of those.

"I believed in you, Jerome!" she said loudly. The acoustics in the bathroom amplified her voice.

"I believed in you!"

Suddenly, she lifted her arm and slammed her fist into the hot bath water. She repeated the motion again and again as her voice rose to a scream, "You LIED TO ME!" Each motion of her arm sent water splashing out of the tub drenching the rug, sloshing against the walls. Exhausted, she sank back.

"Maybe you never really loved me, after all," Akeba said with her voice breaking. She sat up, bitterly weeping.

IV

In my solitude after my brother and my friend's exit, I found myself pondering my life from just before I married Akeba to this very moment, hours after our divorce was finalized in court.

I kicked off my shoes, closed my eyes and reflected as the jazz enveloped me. I knew this day could have been avoided, but over the last few years, I didn't make the kind of choices that would enhance our marriage. Even on my wedding day, I was 'buggin'.

What a wedding it was. We were married on the deck of a battleship in Norfolk, VA, the *USS Stars and Stripes*, surrounded by a hundred and fifty friends, relatives and well-wishers. Akeba's father, a retired Naval officer, arranged this for us. The ship was decked out with blue and gold ribbons and Akeba and I stood under an arch of white flowers to say our vows.

With the Chesapeake Bay as our backdrop, the day was perfect. At the moment we were introduced to the guests as Mr. and Mrs. Jerome Mitchell, the ship's horn was blown. Each guest had been given a blue or gold balloon which they let go into the clear blue sky.

After riding around in a white limousine, we arrived at our reception held at the Fireman's Union Hall in downtown Norfolk. There must have been over a hundred people there. Each was well-dressed, including the children. Based on the looks of most of those who attended our reception, barbershops and beauty salons in the area made some money this weekend.

We were sitting at the head table feasting on fried chicken and roast beef with all the fixings when I found my eyes drawn to a sister who sat at a table not far from ours. When she got up to get her meal, I did all I could to look at her without being caught.

I know, I know. That's really messed up. But you needed to see her. I mean she wore a perfectly fitted red dress.

Her stockings seemed to go up forever and her ass looked just like someone had drawn it. Her skin was the color of Nestle chocolate and her make up was impeccable.

Her long, thick black hair hung to her shoulders and framed her face perfectly. Her lips full and inviting.

Everybody seemed to know her. Or maybe it was that everybody wanted to know her. She moved effortlessly through the hall speaking to some of the guests and smiling like she was family. Damn, I was certainly curious who she was.

A little while later, while walking through the hall, I felt a tug at my sleeve. I turned and looked into the most beautiful pair of eyes I've ever seen.

"Congratulations, Jerome." Her eyes seemed to focus only on me and they sparkled like the champagne we had been drinking most of the evening.

"My name's Yolanda and I work at the same bank with your bride."

She held out her hand to me. I took it and gently shook it. Damn, her hands were soft. Her fingernails were painted to match her dress. I found myself running through the computer in my mind. I just couldn't remember ever meeting her before. But of course, why would Akeba introduce a sister looking like this to me? Duh!

"Well, thank you Yolanda. You know, I don't remember Akeba ever mentioning your name."

"Actually, I don't work in the same department as Akeba. I saw the announcement in the staff newsletter at work along with the generic invitation to attend.I've got some family living here, so I decided to come up." She looked at me coyly.

"After all, Virginia is for lovers, right?"

I let that statement slide. "I don't remember seeing you on the ship. And I'm sure I would have remembered."

With a slight tilt of her head in my direction, she lightly hit me on the shoulder. "Thank you, kind sir."

She took a quick glance around the hall before speaking again. "Well, I wasn't actually at the wedding. I got here only in time to attend your reception."

"So, you drove to Virginia to attend a wedding reception of a couple you hardly know, huh?"

"Well, to be honest," she started coyly, "I was planning to come here anyway for the christening of my cousin's baby, tomorrow. So, I figured why not attend this wedding as well. I just love weddings!"

"Oh, do you now? Are you married?" I looked at the ring on her ring finger.

Yolanda glanced down at the ring, then covered her left hand with her right fingers. A thoughtful look came over her face as she rubbed the ring with her right forefinger.

"No, I'm not married. I don't think that I'd make a very good bride."

She reached for my arm and gave me a playful squeeze. In the process, I caught a glimpse of the red bra under her dress. A shiver ran down my spine.

Yolanda looked pointedly at me and said, "I will get a dance later, won't I?" Before I could answer, Akeba was at my side. Damn, how did she do that?

"Oh, hello, thanks for coming. You are…?" Akeba asked.

Yolanda held out her hand. "My name's Yolanda Walker. Your reception is the greatest. And you look absolutely beautiful."

I nodded my head. The sister had style. Had to give her that. But I wasn't so sure I was out of the woods. When Akeba spoke again, her voice was noticeably icy.

"Are you a friend of Rome's?"

That was my cue. "No, Akeba. Actually, Yo works at the same bank you do, don't you, Yo?"

Did I just say *'Yo?'* Twice? Shit. I closed my eyes and hoped Akeba didn't notice.

"As a matter of fact, I do," Yolanda said smiling at me then looking back at Akeba.

"I work in the accounting department. I was just saying to Jerome, uh, your husband, that I noticed your announcement in the newsletter and since this was the same weekend of my cousin's christening, I decided to attend. I hope that was ok."

Akeba's momentary laser eye contact with me before she looked back at Yolanda, gave me a little chill.

"Sure. We've got plenty of food and drink. of course, you're welcome, Yolanda." Akeba, too, had style.

"Thank you. That is so gracious," Yolanda replied. She looked around and waved to someone in the hall.

"Well, Jerome, Akeba I see someone I know. Again, Akeba you are lovely and this is wonderful reception."

Yolanda smiled at me and held out her hand to Akeba. After she and Akeba shook hands, she turned and walked away. I wanted to watch, but I knew better. *'Yo'*? Shit.

With her hands on hips, Akeba looked at me seriously for a moment.

"How close a watch will I need to keep on you, Mr. Mitchell?" she asked with her head cocked and one eye partially closed.

I returned her look, smiled and shrugged my shoulders.

"Don't be trying to give me that innocent, little boy look, negro," she said. "You liked that red dress, huh?" Akeba looked toward Yolanda who was surrounded by a couple laughing men. Instinctively I knew to be quiet.

With a deep breath, she turned and took my arm.

"Rome, we need to greet people. Let's go." I silently exhaled. I guess Akeba didn't notice my calling Yolanda, 'Yo'. Thank you, Lord! But I was sure she wouldn't forget that red dress.

She didn't.

Eventually, after rounds, Akeba and I found ourselves back at the head table. My brother, Robert who was my best man, started the toasts. My brother was at least two or three inches taller than I and broader. His size and demeanor has always made me feel safe and confident when he was around.

Meanwhile, I was really downing the champagne. I had to admit I was nervous about this marriage thing, but I knew I loved Akeba. I really believed it would be all right. Guess I never figured in my own lack of maturity.

In my apartment, I squirmed as the memories flooded me.

The music at our wedding reception was really sounding good. The money we had spent on a DJ was worth it. As we looked out, folks were dancing, drinking and enjoying themselves.

As the funky sounds of George Clinton rocked the house, I surveyed the dance floor. There Yolanda was, dancing with that jubilant abandon people have when they are having a really good time.

My friend Billy, who was also in the wedding, came over and whispered in my ear.

"Hey, partner. Have you seen that sister in the red dress out there? Man, that girl could make a lot of my dreams come true."

I laughed and gave him 'five'. We both watched as she moved so smoothly and confidently on the floor.

My youngest brother, Marcus, pulled me away from Billy and motioned for Akeba to join us while he pulled me toward the dance floor. Marcus' short cut hair and clean shaven face always made him look even younger than he was. From the middle of the floor, he beat his a spoon against a goblet for everyone's attention.

Once people quieted down, he loudly proclaimed that it was now time for the traditional dance for and with the bride and groom.

Folks who had been doing the "dog" with P-Funk formed a circle around us began swaying to the smooth sounds of Roberta Flack, *The first time ever I saw your face,* Akeba's favorite Roberta Flack song.

Akeba said it was the first slow song we danced to. Guess she's right. I didn't remember. I only remembered that on a slow song I fell in love with her. Little did I think that she and I would marry. But on that June day, as I looked at her in her brilliant white gown, I was sure glad I did.

In real time sitting in my recliner, I shook my head as Sade continued to croon. I sure didn't want to start crying. I stared at the abstract painting over my sleep sofa and felt myself again transported back to our wedding day.

"Baby, this is the happiest day of my life. I've never felt so close to you as right now. When I get the chance, I'm gonna just tear this gown off you and rock your world!"

"Jerome, if you tear this gown, the only thing you gonna get tonight is lonely. But I do love you baby and I'm gonna try to make you happy."

"Akeba, I'm already happy. There's nothing more you can do to make me happier than I already am."

I turned and dipped Akeba. That's when I saw Yolanda over Akeba's shoulder looking at us intently. She was sipping a drink with a straw. Watching her and the way she worked that straw was really turning me on!

"Feels like you're getting ready for me already, baby. But you better get a grip," Akeba said with a laugh. I grinded a little harder on Akeba.

"Rome, stop!" she whispered.

As the last notes of the song faded into the air, separate lines had formed to dance with Akeba and me. The DJ played *Fire and Desire* by Rick James and I danced for a few moments with each female in line. First there was my mother, then my mother-in-law. Each lady took her turn dancing with me, mechanically with an *'I'm having such a swell time'* smile on their faces.

Just as Teena Marie began to sing, there Yolanda was, standing right in front of me with her arms up.

"Shoot, I thought my turn would never come!" she said with a slight pout. There was a rivulet of sweat running down the front of her neck and it disappeared into those beautiful mounds inside that red dress. Man, I felt like the whole world was looking at us.

With my right hand on her waist and my left hand holding her right hand gently, I was acutely aware that I needed to keep Yolanda at a respectful distance as we danced to Rick's song.

Akeba was right. 'Rome, get a grip,' I said to myself. I stole a glance at Akeba. She was dancing with one of my uncles sloppily trying to do a hand dance with her, attracting much attention.

Akeba danced as politely as possible, with him. But I didn't fool myself one bit. I knew she was watching me. I was sure of it.

"Sorry, I'm a little sweaty. Your DJ has been rocking the house, tonight," Yolanda said quietly as we danced.

"You know, you two look good together." She squeezed my hand little tighter, reached up and whispered in my ear, "Don't blow it, Jerome."

I looked down at her. Again I marveled at her looks and that hundred watt smile.

"I don't plan to. I'm a very lucky man!"

Yolanda looked intently into my eyes.

"Yeah. That I can believe." She smiled and it was time to move to the next person in line to dance with me, the groom.

Yolanda was gone, replaced by one of my mother's friends, Miss Maureen whose legs and feet were so big, she had to wear bedroom slippers.

"Child, I could dance with you all night. These old men don't know nothin' about dancing with no woman like she wants to be danced with. Awwwwww work it, boy!"

Man. The thought of dancing with Miss Maureen all night really chilled me. I silently laughed as I thought about what life would be like with those gigantic legs and crusty feet curled up against me. I guess she thought I was having a good time with her.

"Boy, you and me could turn this place out!" she shrieked.

I turned her around so I could locate Akeba in the crowded hall. She had finished dancing with the men in her line. She looked at me with a smile as Miss Maureen held me too tightly. I saw her laugh with several other guests as Miss Maureen swung me around the floor like I was a rag doll. I think Miss Maureen was oblivious to the fact that I had stopped holding her and instead was just holding on.

"Hey young fella, you can't be hogging all the women. I know it's your wedding day, but heck, save some for us men who ain't getting married."

I looked over my shoulder and saw my dad's friend who we called Uncle Web standing there. I gladly worked to extricate myself from Miss Maureen's death grip. Once I accomplished that, I turned her over to Uncle Web.

Uncle Web. He had on his favorite mint green leisure suit with the matching shirt and black tie. No matter what anybody said, Uncle Web wore that outfit with a white belt and white shoes. He was sure he looked good and nobody could tell him anything different.

After turning Miss Maureen over to Uncle Web, Billy, Marcus and Robert grabbed my arm and ushered me toward the door.

Akeba stopped us before we opened the door. "Man-time, huh?" she asked looking pointedly at me. I nodded. She looked at my brother.

"Robert, you're the only one of the four that has good sense. Don't let Jerome get lost, hear?"

"Don't worry, Akeba. We'll be back in a few minutes. We just wanted to have a guy moment with our newly-wed brother, here," Robert said in his deep attorney voice. Akeba smiled and walked away, joining her friends.

"Damn, Rome. Married." Billy said as we walked out.

"I know, Billy. Married," I said as looked back toward my new bride.

The night air felt almost tropical. Cars moved past the building but traffic was light. The sound of reggae music drifted through the air from a man with a portable radio across the street. The warm, breezy weather and the strains of the reggae music were almost hypnotic.

We moved toward the back of the building and bullshitted for a little while. Billy pulled out a joint and lit it, taking a deep drag and exhaling like he was sampling an expensive cigar. Then he pointed the joint at me.

"No thanks, man. I need all my facilities, tonight!" I said with a smile pushing his arm away.

"I know that's right!" Billy responded. All of us laughed. He continued.

"Rome, that sister in that red dress damn near stuck her tongue in your ear in there. So, what she say to you?"

Robert, Marcus and Billy all looked at me. Each face seemed to share the same question.

"Billy, Yolanda was just offering me congratulations and telling me how nice I danced. Ain't nothing to it. So don't be makin' up shit."

No one said anything. The silence felt almost accusatory.

"I'm serious. Just congratulations, that's all," I said looking from one face to the other.

"You know her, Rome?" Robert asked.

"Nope. She works at the bank with Akeba and came by on a lark."

Our conversation died down as we enjoyed each other's company. Every now and then one of us brought up some long ago memory and laughed together.

A car horn sounded from the parking lot across the street.

"Speak of the devil, man," Billy said excitedly. "That's the lady in red, uh, Yolanda." He looked at me and chuckled.

"One of us need to go see what she wants. Guess it needs to be me, the big dog."

He rubbed out the burning joint on a telephone pole and walked toward the car. We followed.

After reaching the car, I took careful pains to stand back.

"Hey Yolanda, I spoke from behind my 'body guards.'

"These are my brothers, Robert and Marcus and my best friend, Billy."

"Well, you Mitchell boys really look good." She looked at each of us separately. Then she turned her attention to Billy.

"You're not so bad either, best friend Billy." She looked past the guys at me.

"I heard your wife call you Rome. Is that your nickname?"

I nodded.

"As in roaming the range? Or is it Rome as in Romeo?"

For a moment I flashed on our dance. I decided not to answer that question.

"Well, it's been nice meeting you, Yolanda," Robert said. "We need to head inside."

"Oh no, the pleasure has been all mine. Four fine brothers talking to me? Wait till I tell my girlfriends."

Billy blurted out, "Damn, baby, I'd do almost anything to ride home with you, tonight!"

Yolanda focused her eyes on Billy. With her forefinger, she traced her bottom lip.

"I'm sure you would. But be careful what you wish for. You just might get it."

Billy smiled, bumping my brother's shoulders with his fist. I guess he thought he might actually 'get it.'

"Uh, Billy is that a joint in your hand?" Yolanda asked. Billy nodded, dumbly. "May I?" she asked holding out her delicate hand with the perfectly painted fingernails.

Yolanda waited while Billy re-lit the joint. He handed her the joint and we all watched as she took a deep drag.

After what seemed to be an eternity, she turned her head away from us and exhaled the pungent smoke. Turning back to us her eyes seemed to see all of us at once.

"Rome, this was an awesome reception and I'm sure you had a beautiful wedding. I would wish you the very best, but unfortunately, I am the very best."

Yolanda took another deep pull on the quickly disappearing joint.

"Y'all step back. I gotta go." With the roach clenched between her red lips, she moved her stick shift into gear. We stepped back, and she roared off with the sounds of Prince coming out of her radio.

"Damn!"

"What's wrong, Billy?"

"She kept my joint!"

Robert snorted. "Hell, Billy. You practically gave the sister your arm." We all laughed.

We walked back to the hall with our arms around each other's shoulders, laughing and bullshitting. As the door opened, we could hear the sounds of Brick playing. Billy started singing.

'Dazz dance-disco jazz. Dazz dance-Disco jazz.'

Robert started laughing. "You pothead, sucker. Don't start singing and messing the song all up."

Billy muttered, "Go to hell."

Just inside the hall, Robert grabbed my arm and pulled me close to him. He moved his smooth shaven face close to my ear.

"I love you, Jerome. I just want to tell you. Watch that Yolanda, man. Women like her can be real trouble."

"Robert, I'll probably never see her again." I looked at his face which was implacable as he maintained eye contact. I hit him in the chest with the back of my hand.

"Don't worry, man. Really."

After a few moments, Robert put his arm around my shoulder.

"Ok, man. Look, let's go celebrate."

With that, we each returned to our respective women.

Back in my chair, I could see my recently ended marriage unfold before me like an old road map.

The first two years after our wedding were wonderful years for Akeba and me. During that time, Danisha Renee Mitchell was born.

I was ecstatic. I was a father! It was awesome to look at that little human being and know that she was the product of our love.

I knew I would love being a father. I just knew it. My daughter and my wife were the most phenomenal females in my life.

During that time, I had also gotten a teaching position at the Charlotte State University. The position meant more money and finally we were able to prepare to move into a house. Akeba fell in love with a lovely red brick home not far from the campus. We moved into the house a year later.

I was sitting in my office when my mentor Samantha Carlton, whom I call 'Sam,' entered.

"How's it going, Jerome?"

"Not bad. I'm settling in. How are you?"

"Not bad. Just wanted to give you a heads up on something." I looked at her suspiciously.

"Don't worry. It's not that bad," Samantha said as she sat. Her blond hair was cut short and her tanned skin gave her a healthy, wholesome look.

"So what's the heads up?"

"As you probably know, the college sponsors a job fair each year." I had heard about it.

"Well," Samantha continued, "new faculty members are expected to spend some time there, so—"

"So, I got to plan to be there, huh?" Sam raised her eyebrows.

"That's right, my mentee." She handed me an envelope. "This has everything you need, so read it and sign up for some time. You only need to do a couple of hours." She reached over and patted my hand. Her hands were cool.

"Don't worry. It's painless. You'll hardly have anything to do." She stood and smoothed her skirt.

"Well, that's all. I have to go. Don't forget to sign up for your time and hurry before all the good times are gone." With that, Sam breezed out of my office.

Little did I know how this one event was going to change the arc of my life.

At the job fair, I wandered about and casually glanced over at the banking and finance area. To my surprise, I saw Yolanda standing there surrounded by students and answering questions. She really looked good. I hadn't seen her since the wedding. I walked over so I could get a better look, just to be sure.

Yolanda looked as fit as she did a couple years ago. Her navy blue business suit fit her well. She was animated while talking with the students that surrounded her.

Of course, many of the students were male. Just like the wedding. Everyone seemed to want to know her.

For a moment, my attention was pulled away due to some yelling between students in the hallway in front of the gym. As I watched, I could tell security was on it and the situation didn't require my attention. When I turned around, Yolanda was standing right in front of me.

"Excuse me," she said so sweetly. "I don't know if you remember me, but—"

"Of course, I do, Yolanda," I said, eyes glued on her. Man, she was still gorgeous.

"I'm impressed. You remember my name."

"I certainly do."

"Well, where do you remember me from?" she asked with a hint of challenge in her voice

"My wedding, two years ago, in Virginia. You had on a red dress that I know you must have sprayed painted on you."

"Was it that tight?" She put her fingers up to her mouth.

"No, no. It wasn't too tight. It's just that you wore it so well. In fact, you look like you can still wear it."

"I wish." She ran her hands quickly over her hips and thighs.

"I've picked up too much weight to put that on again. It will have to be spray painted on if I tried to get into it, now." She smiled as she looked at me.

"Yeah, right." I playfully waved my hand at her. I looked at her booth. "How did you get roped into this?"

"I'm in the marketing department at the bank, now. Actually, I'm glad I'm here. The students have been so responsive."

'I'll bet they have,' I thought to myself. "Well, welcome to the campus," I said to her.

"I didn't know you worked here, Jerome. What do you do here?"

"Teach."

"Really? A college professor? My, my. Are you a Ph.D.?"

"No, I plan to begin working on it in the near future, but I haven't begun yet."

"Still, that's impressive."

"Thanks. But you…you're impressive."

"Aw, that's sweet. Look, I really got to get back. Good to see you again."

"Same here, Yolanda." I knew I should have just stopped there, but I didn't. Without warning, Robert's warning the night of my wedding leapt to mind. I closed my eyes and forced his words away.

"Look, why don't we get together sometime and catch up with each other?"

"Ok. We'll do that. I'll look forward to it."

A couple hours after the job fair, I was sitting at my desk reading a text for class when there was a knock on my office door.

"Come in!" I shouted. The door opened and Yolanda came in.

"Surprise!" she exclaimed as she walked in.

"Well, don't I get a hug? It's been a long time," she said holding her arms out to me as she stood. I felt rooted in my spot. I wanted to so badly, but I could hear Robert's warning the night of my wedding.

"Jerome, I'm not going to rip your clothes off you, I just want a hug, silly." I shrugged and went to her. Her hug felt really good. As our hug broke, she ran her fingers down my arms slowly and smiled.

"What?"

"Oh, nothing." She did it again. I tingled all over. I collapsed into the chair I had cleared for her. Realizing my mistake, I jumped up and went behind my desk. Yolanda sat and crossed those long legs.

I raised my eyes from those legs and looked into her beautiful brown eyes.

"So, Yolanda what brings you here?"

"Well, you said let's get together and catch up, but you didn't tell me how to get in touch with you, so I had to find you." She looked around the office.

"A college professor, ain't you something?" She looked at the pictures on my desk.

"So, I see you and Akeba are still together."

I felt a little uncomfortable with the turn this conversation was taking, so I decided to change the focus.

"What about you? What's been going on with you?"

Yolanda gently placed Akeba's picture on my desk.

"Well I've been married and divorced already. We only made it a year. He decided he needed a woman with a much lighter complexion than me, so..." Her voice trailed off.

"I'm sorry, Yolanda. I really am. But I know you aren't just sitting at home, knitting."

"No, that's true. I'm not one for just sitting around, especially knitting," she said a little too cheerily. Her face belied her tone.

Obviously, this wasn't a subject she wanted to discuss. "So, what else is going on with you?" I asked.

"I took back my maiden name, Walker. I just couldn't imagine going through life with that asshole's name."

She covered her mouth with her hand, looking around. "I'm sorry. I know I shouldn't talk like that in your office."

Maybe she did want to talk about it. "No problem. These walls have heard a lot worse than 'asshole."

She laughed a humorless laugh. It sounded really forced. There were a couple moments of uncomfortable silence.

Yolanda sighed heavily. Her eyes focused on the picture of my daughter.

"Your daughter?" I dipped my head in confirmation. "Pretty girl," she said as she fingered the frame holding the picture of my young daughter. "How old is she?"

"She's a year and a half, going on twenty-five. You have any children?"

"No way! I'm not the motherhood type, you know?"

"Well, I don't know you too well, but I'd be willing to bet you'd be a good mother."

Yolanda got up and leaned over the desk. She kissed me on my forehead. Then she rubbed her finger across it, removing the lipstick.

"Don't want you getting in any trouble because of me," she said.

"And I truly appreciate that!" I added with a grin.

Yolanda ran her fingers through her hair. Her pearl-colored nails contrasted beautifully with her shiny black hair. She got up and walked around my small office looking at the pictures and degrees on the wall. I watched her. At times, she seemed sad. I guess beauty is only skin deep.

She turned and looked at me.

I wanted to get up, go to her and hold her, but I knew that if I did, it would be a step on a path I might not be able to control.

"I'll bet all the hearts of those young co-eds in your classes stay fluttering when you teach."

"I wouldn't know about that."

"Yeah, right."

Looking back, I'm sure that's where my marital descent began. I never felt as sexy and handsome as that moment. Robert's wedding night warning to me was now mashed under my foot. This beautiful, sexy woman was openly flirting with me and I liked it. I wanted it to continue. I didn't want this chance meeting to end.

I cleared my throat again before speaking. "Are you from here?" I asked.

"Born and raised in this area." She leaned forward in her chair.

"Don't meet too many natives," I said. "What do you do when you're not 'wowing' people at the bank?

"I date and I enjoy my single life, most of the time. Every now and then, I run into some not too stable persons, but overall my life's not too bad."

"Well, that's good, but a woman like you got to watch out for some of those unstable brothers, huh?"

"That's for sure. There's this one brother I've known a long time and he's been kind of after me forever.

"We've dated a couple times, but he's just not my cup of tea. Some people I know think he's gotten into drugs or something lately. Every once in a while, he'll stop by my job. Sometimes, he'll get a little obsessive about calling me, but mostly, he's harmless. Sometimes I feel bad for him and I'll agree to meet him for lunch or something."

"Better watch yourself, Yolanda."

She waved her hand at me. "Him? Like I said, he's harmless. I'm not worried he'll do anything."

I glanced at the clock on my desk. "Well, I hate to cut this short, but I've got a class to teach in a little while."

"I've got to go too." Yolanda turned to face me. "This has been so much fun. Maybe we can do this again sometime soon. What do you think?"

"Sounds good to me. Give me a call and we can schedule something."

She took a card from the card-holder on my desk slipping it into her jacket pocket while looking me in the eye. I shook my head.

"She's just teasing," I thought to myself. I slid by her and opened my office door.

"If you'll hold up, I'll walk out with you," I told her as she walked out in front of me.

"Absolutely, I'll wait," she replied, softly.

I gathered my books and supplies and walked out of the office with Miss. Yolanda Walker. Neither of us spoke as we walked. When we got to her car, she turned, hugged me and brushed her lips against my cheek.

"Lunch at Shynee's in a week or two?" She asked in my ear.

"Yes. I'll call you."

Without another word, she got into her car and cruised away.

Walking to class I again heard Robert's warning, "…a woman like that can be real trouble, Rome."

I knew I had crossed a forbidden line.

"Glad we could meet for a bite," Yolanda said as she settled in her seat at Shynee's.

"Me too, Yolanda." We ordered and after getting our meals and eating in silence, we looked up at the same time. Her eyes and face were so beautiful.

"So, you a native, huh?" I asked.

"Yes. I grew up in the Cherry neighborhood with my grandmother. Actually, I was fifteen when I was sent by my mother to live with Nana. Me and my brother, Gil, were raised in Monroe."

"Really? What's your brother doing?"

"He's dead. He joined the Army and died in a helicopter crash at Fort Bragg, two years after joining the military."

"I'm so sorry for your loss. Were you close?"

"Very. For years, I thought I had done something to earn my mother's dislike. Even before I went to my Nana's house, me and mom just didn't get along. She made me think I was in the way of her relationship with my stepfather. I didn't understand, but I was glad to get to Nana's house. Mom and Thomas, my stepfather, didn't seem to have that problem with my brother. While my mom was driving me to Nana's, Gil cried all the way."

"Sounds like you must have learned something different about your mom and stepfather."

Yolanda toyed with her salad before responding.

"Yeah, I did. After mom's death, me and Gil were going through her papers and found her diaries. Seems like she was scared of Thomas' interest in me and she sent me to Nana's for protection, not anger."

She took a napkin and dabbed at her eyes.

"Yolanda, I didn't mean to pry—"

"No, that's alright. I haven't thought of this in a while." She smiled a crooked smile and took a deep breath.

"Nobody ever knows what someone else is going through, right?"

"That's true. Thank you for trusting me with such a personal story, Yolanda."

"Thank you for listening." She stabbed at the lettuce on her plate and put it in her mouth. After swallowing, "can we talk about something more cheery?"

"Sure."

The lunch lasted almost two hours as we talked about a variety of subjects and our best friends, Tanya and Billy.

"Billy. That was your friend at the wedding who gave me a joint, right?"

"Damn, good memory. That's right. In fact, he still thinks you owe him a joint."

"Well, I don't smoke weed anymore, but if he likes wine, I can definitely hook him up."

"I'll tell him, but I think if you just showed up with an bottle, he'd be happy."

"Think so?"

"Yolanda, you take a brother's breath away. Your beauty, your femininity, and that smile. And that smile."

"Wow, Jerome. Thank you for that, but—"

"But nothing. Just accept what I said in the spirit I offered it and besides, I have no hidden agenda."

"No hidden agenda, huh?"

I shook my head and ate more salad as I watched the smile spread across her face.

"You know what? I think I believe you."

"Good."

The more we talked, the closer to her I felt.

V

Back in my apartment, in the here and now, I find myself staring at the framed print of The Banjo Lesson by Henry O. Tanner.

The intimacy of the painting was comforting. The old man and the little boy seemed so real, so connected even amidst the organized chaos of the room.

Out of nowhere, I felt like the walls were closing in on me. I went to my CD rack and pulled out my Roger Troutman and Zapp Greatest Hits CD. Hurriedly, I put it in the player and pressed play. Zapp's '*More Bounce to the Ounce*' filled the air as I paced the room.

I turned up the volume, hoping the music would drown some of the memories in my head of me and Akeba's arguments and how I allowed my feelings for Yolanda to unravel the feelings of love I had for Akeba. We became more and more uncomfortable around each other.

I went to the kitchen to get some wine as I listened to Roger sing, So Ruff, So Tuff." Yeah and stupid-ass decisions make everything even more ruff and tuff out here.

I poured myself more wine. After a swallow, I examined the glass and the bright red contents. How many glasses of red wine, Yolanda's wine of choice, had she and I shared?

In a sudden moment of fury, I threw the glass into the sink. The glass shattered and I jumped as a piece of glass stung my cheek.

The contents of my glass ran down the sides of the white ceramic sink like watered down blood. I touched my cheek and winced as my fingers came across a piece of glass lodged in my skin. It hurt, but I didn't care.

I needed the pain. I collapsed against the sink. I could barely breathe. I felt like exploding.

"Do it Roger, Do it!" the music exclaimed. *"Do it, do it!"*

It seemed the music was talking directly to me. Now I know I'm not crazy, but I had to do something and I had to do it now. Still in my dress shirt and slacks and with only socks on my feet, I grabbed my keys, bolted out the door, slamming it behind me and ran across the apartment complex to the workout room.

Using my key, I unlocked and thrust open the heavy door to the workout room and sat on the bench press machine.

Without another thought, I lay down and began lifting the weights already on the machine until the tears mixed with sweat running down my face blurred my vision and my arms went limp from exhaustion.

Soaked with sweat but feeling emotionally clearer and stronger, I returned to my apartment from the weight room, stripped off my clothes and threw them in a corner of my bedroom. I picked up the phone and pushed the speed dial button to ring my parent's home, stretching out on the carpeted floor as I waited for the call to go through. My mother answered on the first ring.

"Jerome?"

"Hi, mom. How did you know it was me?"

"I just knew, that's all. Are you ok, honey?"

"Well, kind of, but considering you and dad have been married forever and I didn't even make it 15 years kind of bothers me."

"Jerome Levi Mitchell. Don't you dare compare yourself to me and your father. We all do what we can. Your marriage didn't make it.

You and Akeba are good people, don't talk like that. You two are not us or her parents, you hear me?"

"I hear you, Mom. You're right, I know." She had used all three of my names. My mother was serious.

"Where's Dad?"

"In his study working on his crossword puzzles waiting for your call. Let me get him on the extension."

I listened as I heard her call my father. "Barry? Barry? Pick up the phone, it's Jerome." To me, she said, "Is it ok if I stay on the extension?"

"Sure Mom. That's fine."

"Hello, son."

I exhaled. My father's strong baritone voice had a calming effect on me.

There were times when he drove me crazy with his observations, but I had to admit, he was rarely inaccurate. I always knew he was a port in the storm for me. I was blessed to have him.

"Hey Dad."

"Tough day son, huh?"

"Yeah, pretty tough, but it's over now."

"Son, I'm sorry. I really am."

"Yes, son. We really are," my mom echoed.

I could tell that they were both genuinely struggling with what to say to me. Strangely, it was rather sweet and touching. I felt another tear run down my cheek. I swallowed hard before I could answer.

"Thanks, Mom and Dad. Your support through this has been my rock. Thank you.

"Well son. Don't you worry about it. We will always be there for you and your brothers. You know that, right? Have you talked with Robert and Marcus, yet?"

"Yeah, Dad. I know you're both there for us, for me. As for my brothers, I talked with Marcus and Robert is still here. He's staying until tomorrow."

"We are so proud of how you boys have stuck together," my mom said.

"What did you expect, CeCe?" My father said with obvious pride. "We raised them to stand by each other."

Mom said nothing, but I could almost see her sad smile and wet eyes.

"That's right mom. You and dad did raise us to stand by each other."

There was an awkward silence. Dad spoke first.

"Well, son. We won't hold you. Thanks for checking in. Call us if you need anything, ok? We love you. And remember, Son. What's done is done. We love you."

"That's right, we do," mom added softly.

"Thanks for being there for me, Mom and Dad. I'm gonna be alright. I'll probably spend a day or two with Dani, this week and then return to work. I love you both and I'll talk with you, next week."

"Fine, fine. Goodbye, son." My father hung up.

"Are you sure you're ok, Jerome?" mom asked.

"Yes Mom. I'm ok."

"Alright then. Talk to you soon. Love you!"

"Love you too Mom. Bye."

After hanging up the phone, I padded down the hall to the bathroom. The white bathroom appeared small, today. I turned on the hot water and stood at the mirror as I waited for the room to steam up.

While I waited, I brushed my teeth and shaved. I stepped into the hot shower and the stinging water felt good. After the shower, wearing a pair of shorts and a tee shirt and a towel around my neck I went into the kitchen to get something to drink.

Sipping on a large tumbler of ice water, I returned to my living room to listen to the radio as I slumped into my recliner.

What's done is done. So, now what?

VI

Guess I must have fallen asleep. The next thing I knew, my brother Robert was shaking me gently.

"Rome, wake up. You ok?"

I sat up, groggily. I was still in my recliner and it was dark outside. "What time is it?" I asked.

"Man, it's a little after nine. I got in about twenty minutes ago. But you didn't budge when I tried to wake you up, before. You ok?"

"Yeah, I am. It's nine already? Man I was out, huh?"

"Yeah, bro. You were out. But you've been through a lot today. Sleep is a normal thing. Look, I bought you some KFC and put it in the fridge. You want to talk for a while?"

I thought about that. "Yeah, I would like that Robert," I said quietly. "But before we get started, I talked with Marcus. He told me to have you call him when you get in."

"Yeah, I know. He paged me. We already talked." Robert pulled off his sweater and sat on the sofa. "What have you been thinking about, all day?"

"I guess everything, you know?"

Robert looked at me with concern in his eyes.

"Everything, like what?"

I took a deep breath. "You know, everything from day one. I don't even know where to begin." I shook my head. "Just buggin' I guess."

"Jerome, I got time. You're the reason I'm here. You're my brother and you were the first of us to get married. I admired that about you. I mean, I got so focused on my career that I just couldn't see the importance of marriage.

You and Akeba really made me think how nice it would be to have someone in my life."

Robert admired me? Now, that was something. Robert took a deep breath and I looked at him, expectantly.

"Jerome, when you told me you and Akeba were getting separated, I was shocked, you know?"

"I can believe that."

"Now that you've had some time to think, what happened?"

Robert looked at me intently. I wasn't sure how to answer him. Robert filled the silence between us.

"If it's too difficult for you to talk about, I understand. I don't want to be in your business. But I will listen, if you want me too."

His deep voice was soft and inviting. I imagined he must be a good attorney with a voice like that. I nodded my head. I wanted to talk and I trusted no one as much as I trusted my brother, Robert.

I thought that talking to him might help me make sense of what happened to my marriage.

"We did a few things, but she was so focused. Sometimes, I thought she only thought about school and work. In fact, I remember thinking a couple times that you and Akeba were more alike than me and Akeba." Robert said nothing. He just watched me as he swirled his cup of iced tea.

"The first few years were great. We had Danisha and life was good. Shortly after Dani's birth, we just didn't talk like we used to.

I know that having a baby required more of Akeba's attention, but I really thought she would loosen up, some. You know what I mean?"

"Well, to be honest, no, I don't know what you mean. Akeba worked outside the home on a full time job. She's in a city she doesn't know very well. She's recently married and now she's a mother. How did you think she could be 'looser'?"

"Damn, Robert. You sound just like her. See, I told you she and you were alike."

"Naw, Jerome. This lies squarely at your door, you know? I have learned that children have a way of changing a person's life, but what can you do. Jewell's children have really changed my lifestyle. I knew I was going to be more scheduled. But then I know we aren't talking about me."

"No Robert, that's ok. I know you took on Jewell and her two children and I got to give you your props for it. I don't know if I could have done the same. But as for Akeba, I just got tired of her trying to plan everything."

"Like what, Jerome?"

I got up and began to pace around the room.

"Robert, from the first moment of Dani's life, Akeba planned every little thing. Sometimes it seemed that even our lovemaking was on a schedule. Now don't get me wrong. Akeba still turned me on, but I didn't get that toes curling feeling like I used to with her."

I stopped pacing and stood in front of the TV with my back to Robert. "You know, sometimes I used to wonder if I ever had that 'toes curling' feeling with her."

"What do you mean by that?" Robert asked.

"I don't know," I said turning to face my brother. "I knew I loved her. I knew I would do anything for her she asked, if I could. She was the right woman to marry, I knew it."

"The 'right woman to marry?' What does that mean?"

I focused my eyes on a painting over Robert's head. That was a good question. What did I mean by the 'right woman to marry?' To Robert, I responded.

"She had all the qualities. Smart, pretty, focused, employed. How could I not marry a woman like that?"

"So, she was 'smart, pretty, focused and employed.' Except for 'pretty' and 'employed' sounds like she was a job applicant."

"Hm, I hadn't thought of that before. Interesting point of view."

"And so?"

"And so, what?"

"And so, how do you think this affected your marriage, Jerome?"

"I don't know, Robert. You know, once I thought that maybe Akeba was beginning to intimidate me.

She was making a lot more money than I was and it seemed that the opportunities on her job were outstripping my opportunities. I think that at some level I was afraid she wouldn't need me, anymore. You know, how mom needs dad."

"Like 'mom needs dad?' Where's that coming from, Jerome?"

"Well, it seemed that the whole time we were growing up, mom always deferred to dad. He was the breadwinner and the undisputed 'ruler of the kingdom.' I could never imagine mom handling stuff without dad's knowledge or approval."

We were silent for a moment or two. I stretched my arms, turned away from Robert.

"Then there was Yolanda," I said as 'matter of factly' as possible.

"Ah, yes. Lady Yolanda. I was wondering when you would get to her. But before you start, I'm gonna get a beer. You want one?"

I nodded. Robert got us two bottles of beer and returned. He sat on the couch with his legs outstretched.

"She was definitely a good looking sister, probably still is, but I had my concerns about her even at your wedding, if you'll remember," Robert said looking at the carpet.

"True, true. You said a woman like that could be real trouble."

"Well, in that outfit and knowing how she looked in it, on another woman's wedding day, I just thought maybe she was a little over the top. Akeba handled it well, though. There are some women who would have made a scene. I was just glad she left the reception early that's all. But I was surprised when you told me you had started seeing her a few years later."

"Robert, I thought she was everything Akeba wasn't." I sat.

"Yolanda was spontaneous, full of life, adventurous and she really loved being a woman. Around her, I felt sexy and desirable. A man's man. Around Akeba, I just felt like a husband."

"I'm sure you considered having Yolanda in your life full time and you must have rejected the idea. You're an intelligent man. You are a Mitchell and you must have had some peek into the future with Yolanda and decided against it, but still you refused to let her go."

"You nailed it, Robert. You did." I stood up and stretched. My brother was so wise. He had gone straight to the heart of what I was thinking and feeling.

"That's why my clients pay top dollar for my services," Robert said smiling.

"So, am I on the clock?"

"Always, my brother. Always."

"I do feel better having talked with you."

Robert stood. His eyes told me he understood we would go no further tonight. He approached me and we hugged. He kissed my cheek.

"Jerome, I'm sorry about your marriage. I really am. Keep working on yourself and know that I love you, little brother."

With that, he broke the embrace, took his empty bottle to the kitchen and headed toward the bedroom. He stopped and looked at me.

"You sure you'll be ok?"

"In time. Robert, you don't know how much I appreciated your being here."

"Yeah, I do. You're my brother. I love you and I'll stick by you. Now can I go to bed before you get any more mushy on me?"

"Mushy?" I asked with a smile. "You're the one who's hugging and kissing somebody." I threw a couch pillow at him, which he caught.

Robert turned and went into the guest bedroom and I headed to the kitchen.

I felt hungry again. I wolfed down a piece of chicken while standing at the open refrigerator door and washed it down with the last cold beer.

Closing the door, I thought about the conversation I just had with my brother. I wasn't sure I felt better. My brother's ability to prod information out of me was somewhat unsettling.

After turning off the lights, I went into my room, undressed and lay down on the cool sheets. I pushed the 'sleep button' on the clock radio and soft jazz began to play.

Tomorrow would be another day.

VII

"Wake up, Jerome. Wake up!"

"Huh, what's wrong?"

"Nothing, man. I'm getting ready to go." Robert was standing over me. I sat up. He was already dressed and looking good. I looked at my clock.

"Damn, Robert. It's only six in the morning. How long you been up?"

"A little over an hour. Got some bacon cooking and some coffee brewing. You hungry?"

"Man, I am never hungry this early. You're still getting up with the chickens, huh?"

"Yep. Got the car packed up and I'm ready to get out before the traffic heats up. Come on, man get up!" he yelled as he left the room.

I got up, went into the bathroom and looked at myself. Well, I didn't look any differently. This was my first day as a truly single man in twelve years. Ok, I did need a shave I guess, but I looked basically the same.

As I moved through the apartment to the kitchen, the smell of bacon frying and burning toast filled the air. Robert had the radio on. From time to time, a too jovial weather and traffic reporter barked out traffic and weather reports.

"Jerome, what station is Tom Joyner on, here?"

"Tom Joyner? I thought you were a NPR fan."

"Usually, I am, but I just thought I'd do something different today. So change the station for me, Ok?"

I changed the station. I've rarely heard the beginning of Tom's show before. When I'm up this early, I've usually got an early morning class to teach or I'm going to work out. The phone rang.

"Dawg, who could be calling here, this early?" I said out loud.

"Probably Jewell," Robert said.

"Oh, ok." I picked up the phone. Robert was right. It was Jewell, his wife.

"Hi, Jewell. Yeah, he's right here dressed, eating bacon and listening to the radio."

I gave Robert the cordless. I watched him walk around the kitchen as he talked with his wife. He was so smooth. I liked his relaxed voice tone and the effortless way he maneuvered around the small kitchen.

"Yeah, he's feeling better, I think," Robert said into the phone, *looking at me. "Yeah, I'm glad I was here too…yeah, I told him to come down for a couple days… yeah, I think I'll be leaving within the hour…I just wanted to talk with Jerome for a few minutes before I left…I'll page you with our code when I get to town, because I'll be going straight to my office…yeah, he's here…ok, love you too. After you talk to Jerome, just hang up. I'll talk with you when I get home."* Robert held out the phone to me.

"Jewell wants to speak with you, if you're feeling up to it," he whispered with a questioning look on his face.

"Sure," I whispered back. I took the phone from Robert and plopped into my recliner.

"Hi, again…yeah, well thanks, but I'll be ok… thanks for loaning me Robert…that is so nice, thank you, Jewell…ok…I will take you up on it…ok…well, have a good day…tell the kids, I said 'hello…' ok… have a good day."

Robert had settled down on the couch near the end of my conversation with Jewell. "You got a couple minutes, Jerome?" he asked watching me.

"At this hour? What could be so important that you got to talk with me before you head back to Hot-lanta."

Robert cleared his throat.

"You…ah, we, that is, talked about Yolanda just a little last night. I was just wondering if you've given any more thought to where she'll fit in your life now that you're officially single."

"You mean '*is she is or is she isn't,*' huh?" Robert nodded still watching me intently. "Well, I got to be honest with you," I continued. "I have been thinking about her, but I just don't see her as my future, you know?"

I shifted in my chair. "Don't get me wrong. For the short term I think I would really like to be with her, but I don't think I'm her 'cup of tea' either. She likes excitement and unpredictability. She likes the 'high-life.' She runs 'hot' or 'cold.' Sometimes, I'm not sure what spigot is on."

Robert half-smiled. "Seems like the things you wanted from Akeba are the very things that make you uncomfortable with Yolanda. How interesting."

"Oh don't go Mr. Attorney on me, Robert," I said smiling.

"Is that what I'm sounding like? I thought I sounded more like a male Dr. Laura myself."

"Nope. You sounded like you had a vulnerable witness, and I'm the witness. So don't even try it, *Perry Mason.*" I stood up. Is that all you wanted to ask me, Counselor?"

Robert stood as well. "Yep, that's it. I guess the prosecution rests. Look, I gotta go. Give my niece a kiss and a big hug, ok?"

"I will, Robert. Thanks for coming. I don't know how I would have made it through this without you." We hugged.

Robert looked at me pointedly. "Look, Jerome. Don't just sit in this house and obsess."

"Naw, I ain't gonna do that."

Robert looked at me a little longer. Then he grabbed his sandwich and moved toward the door. "Look. Don't beat yourself up. Remember, like dad always says, '*what's done is done*'."

He held out his right hand to me. I nodded and shook his hand with both my hands. We then hugged each other.

It felt pretty warm for an October morning, but that's Charlotte. Tom Joyner and his crew were laughing insanely. I looked at the clock. It was 6:50. I wondered what could possibly be said so early that would be that funny. I turned off the radio, the lights and went back to bed, laying in the darkness. I was just drifting off to sleep when the phone rang.

My bedside clock said 7:25. I figured it was Robert who had forgotten something.

"What you forget, shithead?"

"Daddy, it's me!"

Oops, it was Dani, my daughter. "I'm sorry, honey. I thought you were your Uncle Robert."

"You call him that?" she asked with that innocence that made me smile.

"No, honey. I don't call Uncle Robert, that. I—well never mind. How are you this morning?"

"I'm ok, daddy. I guess. I'm still sad about you and mommy. Are y'all mad at each other?

"No, sweetie. We're not mad at each other and we're certainly not mad at you. What makes you think that?"

"Well, on TV, divorced parents are always mad about something with each other. Then they fight and fuss all the time. You and mommy won't do that will you?"

"Honey, we had fights when we lived together, remember? That's gonna happen, but we don't want you to think that we only got divorced so we can fight. We didn't do that. And it had nothing to do with you. We both love you very much. Nothing is ever gonna change that. You hear me?"

"Yes, Daddy. I hear you."

"Good. Now what did you call me about? This is a surprise call."

"I was just wondering if I was gonna see you today."

"Maybe. What is your schedule?"

"I got dance class after school. Can you pick me up?"

"Hey, that's a good idea. Maybe we can get some ice cream and some McDonald's. Is your mother there?"

"Man, daddy. That would be so cool. Yeah, mom's here. I don't think she's going to work today. I'll go get her." Then she yelled.

"Mom? Daddy's on the phone, pick up!" I was slightly surprised at how nervous I felt waiting for Akeba to pick up the phone and talk to me.

"Jerome?"

"Good morning, Akeba."

"Hang up the phone, Dani," she yelled. I heard the other receiver click as our daughter hung up.

"Good morning."

I tried to guess at what her tone of voice meant. But actually, there was no real tone. She sounded neutral. Maybe that was the problem. Maybe I expected more reaction than a somber *good morning*.

"Well, Dani called me. That wasn't a problem was it?"

"Not really. It's just that she needs to be ready to catch that bus, not call you or anybody. She misses that bus too regularly."

"Oh," I replied. There was an awkward silence. I think we both sensed that by talking about our child, we were on more solid ground. Well, at least, I did.

"I told her I might pick her up from dance class, tonight. Hope I won't cause a problem."

"No, actually, that would be great. I was hoping I could finally take a day of pampering and relaxation I owe myself. In fact, today would be a good day. I certainly don't plan to go to work. I'm glad you are willing and available to pick her up."

"Now am I psychic or what?"

"Good question," Akeba replied. "Look, I need to get her out of here. Can we talk after she gets on the bus?"

"Sure. I'm gonna go workout. Takes me about 30 minutes and we can talk then, if that's ok."

"Hold on, Jerome." I heard her talking to Dani in the background. "Come say good bye to your father. You better not miss that bus!"

"Daddy?"

"Hi, again, sweetie."

"I gotta go. Mom is starting to trip about the bus again."

I listened as Akeba talked in the background. "You miss it, you walk."

"Bye, Dani. I'll pick you up from dance class, this evening. We'll have ice cream if you want."

"And McDonalds?"

"Ok, baby. Mickey D's, too. Now get out to that bus stop."

"Ok, Daddy. Bye!"

"Jerome?"

"Yes, Akeba."

"Thanks. I'll call you right back, once she gets on the bus."

Ten minutes later, the phone rang. It was Akeba.

"That was quick," I said.

"Well, the bus was coming when I finally got her out there. I swear, that child just tries to aggravate me about catching that bus. Now where were we?"

"I'm going to pick her up from dance class and then do what with her?"

"You can just bring her home. If I'm not here, would you take her to Dot's house at the end of the block?"

"I could, Akeba, but I'd rather just take her home and wait with her until you get home, if that's ok?"

Akeba audibly exhaled. "Jerome, maybe you shouldn't be at the house waiting for me. I don't think I want to come home to you and Dani. It would feel too weird, you know?"

"Not really. I mean I am planning to stay real honest with her."

"Ok, Jerome."

"We are a family, Akeba."

"No, Jerome. We're not a family anymore. We're parents. We share a child. We're not a family."

"Ouch."

"I don't mean to sound mean. I just want us to keep everything straight."

"Well, excuse me, Miss 'keep track of everything'," I said tersely.

"Jerome, are you getting angry?"

"No."

Akeba exhaled. "Ok, Jerome. Ok. It's too early to go through all this. If you want to stay until I get home, go ahead, but once I get home, I really need for you to leave. Agreed?"

"Agreed."

"Alright, then. I gotta go. Tell Robert that I apologize for not speaking while at court, but I wasn't feeling real sociable. Will you do that?"

"No problem. Have a wonderful time, today."

"I will. Bye."

"Bye, Akeba." We hung up. I put on my running clothes and did my jog.

Forty-five minutes later, I was standing in my bathroom looking in the mirror. I wanted to change something. But what?

I found myself looking at my mustache. I have cared for and trained my mustache for the last ten years. I've kept it trimmed and off my top lip. There was no gray in it and each hair seemed to know exactly where it belonged.

Impulsively, I grabbed my trimmer and without another thought, I removed my mustache.

I then got out my Edge gel and shaved the rest of my face as I usually do. I rinsed the foam off my face and slowly looked up in the mirror to see my "naked" face.

The difference was striking. I looked at the hair in the sink, mixed with the puddles of sweat that dripped off my body onto the faux marble sink top.

A beard. That's what I wanted, a well shaped, manicured beard. I vowed to shave my entire face on my regular schedule for the next week, then I would begin to grow a beard. Pleased with my decision, I took one more look at my "new" face and got in the shower.

It was 10:30 by the time I got dressed and went out to the living room. I went to the kitchen to fix some toast and I decided to call Billy.

"Technical assistance, Truesdale speaking. How may I help you?"

"Oh my. Don't you sound professional, '*Truesdale speaking. How may I help you?*'" I laughed as I munched on my toast. "What up, Billy boy?"

"Rome? What you want? Don't you know I'm a busy man?"

"Busy, hell. They got you answering the phone. That doesn't sound too busy."

"Rome, I got a phone on my desk. You called my office number. You ain't the only brother who got those kinds of conveniences. Don't mess with me this morning."

"Yeah, right. Don't start buggin' on me."

"Rome, how you doing?"

"I'm ok, today. I already talked with Dani and Akeba. I'm gonna pick up Dani tonight and take her home."

"I hear that, my man." How's Danisha?"

"She seems ok, I guess."

"Good. I'm going to go to Club Premier for the Karaoke night, eat some twenty five cent wings and drink some dollar drafts. You want to join me? I mean after you drop off Danisha."

"I don't think so. I'm gonna just chill for the rest of the week. Maybe we can go next week. How does that sound?"

"You know me, this week, next week, next month, works for me. But don't forget about the game on Saturday, Woodson against my alma mater."

"Absolutely. I haven't been to the Classic in a couple years. Should be real fun, even though this year, your boys gon' get spanked."

"Ain't gonna happen, Rome. A&M has won five years in a row. That is not a streak to be broken. And next year, the game moves back to South Carolina. And you know Woodson ain't gonna go to A&M and win."

"Twenty dollars? You got that much confidence in your Wolves?"

"You're on, Jerome. Twenty dollars and a full tank of gas to the winner."

"We'll stay in touch, Billy. Look I gotta go."

"I hear that. Peace, bro."

VIII

After the early morning chat with Jerome, Akeba hung up and called her friend, Cynthia.

"Hello?"

"Cyn, this is Akeba. You ready for our day of pampering?"

"You know it, girl! Are you driving or am I?"

"Cyn, I got a million things to do afterwards. Why don't we just meet at *Your Way*?"

"Sounds good.

"Cool, girl. See you, there."

Akeba and Cynthia had met about three years ago at a shoe exhibit at the Mint Museum. They found themselves discussing the shoes on exhibit and wondering what type of women wore some of the shoes in exhibit. Later, they had wine together and have been friends ever since.

Two hours later, Akeba arrived at the salon. She scanned the parking lot, looking for Cynthia's white Camry, but she didn't see it.

Akeba knew that Cynthia would be there in Cynthia's time. That was Cynthia's way. She went in, checked in and waited.

"Hey girl!" Cynthia breezed in. They hugged. "Are you ok?"

"I will be after today's pampering," Akeba said with a smile.

"I know that's right, Akeba."

"We're ready," Akeba said to the receptionist.

"Very well. Your host for the day is Henri," the receptionist told Akeba, pronouncing the host name as '*Aun-ree*.'"

A tall, slim but muscular white male approached them. Both assumed that he was Henri. They were right.

"Ladies, will you follow me?"

A couple hours later, after the massages, facials, pedicures and manicures, Cynthia and Akeba were sitting at the small, indoor pool when they finally got the opportunity to really talk.

Cynthia watched as a young girl approached them. "Looks like we're gonna be offered some more wine."

Akeba followed Cynthia's gaze. A young dark haired girl approached them. "May I get you something?"

"Can I get some bottled water? I don't want the carbonated kind, just regular bottled water," Akeba said.

"Will *Evian* be alright?"

"That'll be fine. Thanks"

"And for you?" The server looked at Cynthia.

"I'll have the same, thanks." The waitress smiled and walked away.

"Ok, Akeba, talk to me. Are you really ok?"

Akeba sighed. "I think so, Cyn. You know, I did think we would somehow work it out, but I guess it just wasn't supposed to happen. Cyn, let me tell you, though. Jerome looked good at the courthouse.

"I'll bet he did." Cynthia kept her eyes focused on the glimmering water in the pool.

Cynthia turned to face Akeba.

"You know what you need? A divorce party."

Akeba shook her head as she sipped her water.

"A divorce party, Cynthia? A divorce party?" Akeba dangled her feet in the water.

"Girl, they are the rage, now. In fact, I read about throwing one in *Essence*."

"Cynthia, please."

"You just leave it to me."

They lapsed into silence for a moment.

"Akeba, can I tell you about somebody new in my life?"

"Do tell, Cynthia. Who is he?"

"Don't laugh, ok?"

"Moi? It is a 'he' isn't it?"

"I'm serious, Akeba."

"Ok, Cyn, Ok." She looked at Cynthia.

Cynthia cleared her throat. "It's a principal of one of the schools I'm responsible for overseeing."

"So what's so wrong with that, Cyn? I don't know why you're trippin' so hard. What's the big deal?"

"Girl, he's white!" Cynthia said with a loud whisper.

"White?" Akeba looked incredulously at Cynthia. "Not Ms. *'No white man can do anything for me*'?"

Cynthia nodded slowly. "Nuts, ain't it? But girl I really like him. He's fun and he doesn't pressure me for sex all the time. I'm just worried about how my sons will take it. I know their father is gonna' trip real hard."

Akeba and Cynthia talked through the rest of the day, Akeba listened intently and shared in her friend's excitement over a new love.

IX

"Damn, I'm gonna be late!" I thought to myself as I wove in and out of traffic. I glanced at my car clock and it was already 5:45 and I wasn't even to Third Street yet. Traffic was terrible and it seemed that every car was headed in the same direction I was. I knew Charlotte traffic was bad, but I thought I had left my apartment with plenty of time to spare.

It was already close to six o'clock and I was just getting on 277 headed toward Freedom Drive when my pager went off. I didn't recognize the number, but I did recognize the two-digit number at the end of the 7-digit number. It was my daughter, Danisha. I stopped at a nearby gas station to use the phone. I dialed the number on my pager. Danisha picked up on the first ring.

"Daddy?"

"Hi, honey. I'm on my way. How did you know it was me?"

"Miss Lahti said that this is a private line and no-one uses it without her permission, so I knew that it had to be you. And see? I didn't forget to put in my code, either."

"That's good, Dani. Where's Miss Lahti?"

"In her office. Wait, I'll get her."

I listened as I heard her yell for her dance instructor. Meanwhile, I was feeling impatient. I don't like standing at a pay phone at a gas station. In the background over the traffic noise, I could faintly hear approaching footsteps. The phone was picked up.

"Hello?"

"Miss Lahti?"

"Yes, this is Lahti Pearl. Is this Mr. Mitchell?" Her voice sounded throaty, yet refined.

"Yes, ma'am it is. I want to apologize for being late, but I'm in a pay phone just a few blocks away. Can you wait for me? I'd really hate for Danisha to wait outside."

"No problem, Mr. Mitchell. I've got plenty of work to do. I can wait a little while longer. See you when you get here."

"Thank you. Can I speak with Dani?" There was a slight pause as the phone changed hands.

"Yes, Daddy?"

"Dani, I'll be there in ten to fifteen minutes. Hang in there and be good."

"Sure, daddy. Oh, Daddy?"

"What, Dani?"

"Will you get me some McDonalds to bring with you?"

"No, I won't get any McDonalds to bring with me, Dani. Miss Lahti is waiting on me and I need to get you right away. We can get that after I pick you up."

"But, I'm hungry Daddy!"

I sighed. "Goodbye, Dani." I hung up the phone and raced to my car. Kids. About fifteen minutes later, I finally saw the sign for the dance school. Danisha was standing at the front door. She came running out as I pulled up.

"Daddy!" She hugged me and looked up.

"What happened to your face? "What?" I touched my face self-consciously. Then it dawned on me.

"I shaved off my mustache. I'm thinking about growing a beard. What do you think?"

She shrugged. "Mom's not gonna' like it."

"Think not, huh?" I rubbed my finger over my 'naked' top lip.

"What do you think?"

Dani shrugged. "I guess I'll get used to it. It's your face, daddy."

"You are one smart young lady. But then you're my daughter. What can I say?" We both laughed and hugged again.

The door to the school opened and Miss Lahti, director of the Pearl's School of Dance stood in the doorway. I had forgotten how good she looked. In the twilight, she looked almost regal.

Lahti Pearl was tall and shapely. I guess dancing did that for a person. Her skin was a little darker than corkboard and her hair was dark, thick and pulled back from her face.

Lahti's silhouette in the doorway was fascinating and intriguing. I guessed her age to be between thirty-five and forty-five. Most younger women would love to look as good as Lahti Pearl.

I released my hold on my daughter, and told her to get into the car. I approached Lahti and shook her hand.

"Thank you for allowing me to be late. I'm so sorry I kept you waiting."

"No problem Mr. Mitchell. Danisha is a wonderful student and someday she'll make a wonderful dancer. I didn't mind waiting for you at all." Her hazel eyes bored into mine after she spoke.

Am I crazy or what? Did she just say 'waiting for you' like she was interested in me? Most likely, I read more into it than she meant. It wouldn't be the first time. Me. Just buggin'.

"Well, I appreciate it, anyway. By the way, do you have a card with your number on it. I would have called sooner, but I didn't have the correct number."

"Sure, I do. Will you follow me to my office?"

Following Lahti Pearl was a pleasant experience. Her body gently swayed as she walked. She moved with the grace of a dancer and she looked to be in fantastic shape. I could faintly hear the material of her calf-length dress. It sounded like the sound of a drum brush softly playing a high hat cymbal. I wondered if she were aware of how intently I was watching her.

After getting to her office, Lahti sat behind her desk, keeping her eyes down as she appeared to look for some business cards.

"How is Mrs. Mitchell?" she asked off-handedly.

"She's fine. We're, uh, divorced. Just finalized. But don't worry, we plan to keep Dani coming. She really likes your school."

Lahti looked up. "Well thank you, Mr. Mitchell. Sorry to hear about your divorce. I'm divorced myself. Have been for seven years." Lahti stood.

"I started this school shortly after my divorce. The hardest part for me was the emotional adjustments I had to make. But over time, I adjusted." She motioned around the room with her hand.

"And I dare say, you shouldn't have any problem adjusting." She looked at me, intently. She handed me a couple of her business cards.

"Well, Thank you. I'd better get back to my daughter."

"Of course, Mr. Mitchell. Have a good day. And call me if I can help in any way."

After shaking her hand, I walked to the car wondering if calling her would ever be a good idea. Occupied with my thoughts, I didn't notice Lahti watching me from the tinted windows of her studio.

"You were in there a long time, Daddy. I'm hungry."

"Sorry sweetie. Just wanted to make sure all was well with your dance classes. I hear you're doing quite well."

"I like dancing. I just don't like to practice. Ms. Lahti makes us go over the same stuff again and again. It gets boring sometimes."

"I'm sure but repetition is vital for perfection."

That was the last thing I said for a while. I nodded as I listened to Dani. It was clear she had a lot to say, so I settled down and drove.

Even after we stopped to pick up her favorite fast food, she barely stopped talking. She took a breath, ate some more, took a breath and continued talking.

Dani talked about school, dance class, why she likes McDonalds better than Burger King. I learned that BK's fries are too hard, her dance class is preparing for a recital in December, a boy named Rashad likes her in school and she still doesn't get along with Debbie Richards. According to Dani, she is the best speller in her class andher teacher lets her lead the line a lot in school while walking down the hall. I listened as attentively as I could.

"Daddy, are you listening?"

"Sure, honey. You really got a lot to say, tonight."

"Well, I haven't seen you in a couple days daddy, so I got to catch you up."

"You are certainly doing that, honey."

After a few more minutes of talking, Dani was quiet, sipping on her drink. I glanced over at her. She looked so grown up. When did that happen?

Her feet reached the floor of the car. I remembered when her feet didn't even reach the edge of the seat. She was looking out the window. I got nervous. She was too quiet, too suddenly.

"You alright, Dani?" She nodded, but kept looking out the window. "You sure? You wouldn't kid your old man, would you?"

When she turned to look at me, I sharply caught my breath. In that instant, she looked just like her mother. Her dark eyes and loose dark hair were fully her mother's. Funny, I never noticed that much of a resemblance before. I mean, I always thought Dani looked like her mother, but not that much.

"Honey, you are as beautiful as your mother. You know that?

"Thank you, daddy." She then sat quietly looking out the window.

For the remainder of the ride to the house we used to occupy together as a family, Dani was quiet. The only sounds was the radio and thenoise of disappearing liquid through her straw. Sometimes she would drum her fingers on the seat in time with the music.

Eventually, we arrived at the house. I pulled even with the mailbox on the street leaving the driveway clear for Akeba. I waited as Dani gathered her bookbag and other belongings.

"You need any help, honey?"

"No, thanks, Daddy. I got it," she replied. We got out of the car. We closed our doors at the same time. Dani walked to the house and stood at the front door waiting for me to open it.

"Dani, I don't have a key. Don't you have yours?" She put down her book bagand rooted around in her purse. She got out her key and gave it to me. I unlocked the door and we went in. Dani took the alarm off the house and went directly upstairs.

"Dani, where are you going? Don't you want to watch TV with me until your mom gets home?"

"No thanks, I have homework to do."

"Dani, come here. I want to talk to you." I picked up the phone and paged Akeba.

Dani sat in the chair opposite me. With her face in her hands she looked intently at me.

"Dani, I know all this is crazy. Honey, we got to keep talking. Things are already bad enough, you know?"

Dani's eyes filled with tears and she put her head in her lap and covered her head with her arms. I kneeled next to her with my arm around her shoulder. I didn't know quite what to say at first, so I just stayed quiet and held her. Her body began to shake as her tears became sobs. I knew what she was crying about. And much of it was my fault.

"Honey, it's got to be tough on you. Me and your mom are divorced and I know it hurts you. Hurts us, too. We tried, but we just couldn't stay together. But we both still love you. Nothing is ever going to change that. Just don't ever think that there was something you did to make this happen.

"What happened is solely between me and your mother. The best thing that we ever did was to give you life. You have been a joy to both of us, all your life." I took a deep breath. I was close to tears myself.

"Dani? Dani? Look at me. Come on. Look at me." She held her head up. Her eyes were swollen from crying and tears still streamed down her face. I reached out and held her soft face. I tried to wipe the tears away, but they just kept coming.

"Honey, you do understand that you had nothing to do with our decision to divorce each other, right?"

She nodded. "Daddy, it's just…that…uh…never mind!" She put her head back down.

"Dani, finish what you were going to say." I needed her to finish. In fact, I was almost panicky that she wouldn't finish. What the hell had I done? I said a silent prayer for the right words in this situation. Just then, a horn blew outside.

"It's mom," Dani said simply. She slowly stood up, wiping her face and went to the front window. She opened the blinds to watch her mother come in the house. I got the feeling that this was a regular routine.

"Hi, Dani, Jerome," Akeba said as she entered, carrying a brown bag of groceries. She looked from Dani to me. A look of concern clouded her face.

"What's wrong?" she asked. She dropped the bag on the floor. Dani burst out crying and ran up to her room. We just looked after her.

"Rome, what happened?" Akeba's voice was rising

"Calm down, Akeba. Dani and I were beginning to talk about the divorce when you pulled in. She's been crying for a while now. How was your day at the salon?"

"It was good, but what about Dani?"

"Akeba, you and I have talked about this before. We knew this was coming. We went to that child psychologist and we both did the reading she suggested. This was bound to happen. We're divorced. Separation was one thing, but this—this is another."

"Damn it, Jerome. This was not supposed to happen. We were supposed to be married forever. We were supposed to grow old together." Her voice began rising. She massaged her forehead.

"Jerome, I could really kick your ass!" she hissed.

I walked to the couch and sat down to avoid her blazing eyes. Akeba followed, stood in front of me, looking down on me.

"Look, Akeba. I'm willing to take responsibility for my part of this. I expect you to take responsibility for your part as well."

"My part? Now what part is that? My daughter—"

"Our daughter, Akeba. Our daughter," I said, tightly.

"Our daughter wouldn't be up there," Akeba pointed up toward the second floor of the house, "crying her eyes out, if we were still together." She put her hands on her hips and moved closer to the couch I sat on.

"Akeba, move back," I said.

"Move me."

I stood up and we were now face to face. "I've had enough of this shit. I'm out of here, so will you move so I can leave?"

"I knew it. You two are just gonna argue and be mean to each other," Dani yelled from the top of the stairs. We both looked up. "I told you, daddy. I told you!"

"Honey, it's ok," Akeba said softening her voice. She walked toward the steps.

"Leave me alone!" Dani screamed and ran in her room, slamming the door behind her.

Akeba turned to look at me. "Now what, Jerome. Now what?" She sat and put her head in her hands. She looked up with tears in her eyes. I looked down on her and shook my head. I didn't know what to say.

"I'm really sorry, Akeba. I really am. We may not be living together as a family, but we're Dani's family. We don't need to fight in front of her, that's for sure. Can we at least agree on that?"

Akeba stood. "Yeah, I can agree to that. You want to go upstairs with me and talk with Dani?" I nodded.

Together, we went up to talk with Dani.

After talking with Dani, we returned to the first floor.

"You did a good job talking with her, Jerome," Akeba said.

"We did a good job, Akeba."

"Yes, we did a good job," Akeba confirmed rubbing her temples as she sat on the loveseat. "I need to apologize for my behavior earlier. This whole thing has got me all off-center."

I nodded. "Yeah, me too," I said sitting next to her.

We sat in silence for a few minutes, each of us lost in our thoughts. I broke the silence first.

"What are we gonna do?"

"Do about what?" she responded

"Everything."

"I don't know, Jerome. I would imagine we just keep taking it a day at a time and if necessary, one hour at a time. And we keep talking and being there for Dani."

I nodded my head and we sat in silence again. After a while, Akeba stood.

"Well, Jerome," Akeba started.

I stood up. "I get it. Time to go. You sure you ok?"

"Yeah. You?

I nodded and followed Akeba to the door.

Akeba smiled, thinly. Then she looked at me with a slight frown. She opened the door.

"Thanks, again for picking up Dani and helping me with her tonight."

We hugged, quickly. I turned and walked out into the night air. I was surprised Akeba had said nothing about my missing mustache.

Walking to my car, I said a silent prayer for Dani, Akeba and myself. What an evening this had turned out to be.

X

The next morning, I woke up refreshed. I had papers to grade and I was determined to get them done today. It was a beautiful day so I decided to do my work on the patio. I was listening to Spyro-Gyra and making good headway when the phone rang. It was Billy.

"Que pasa?" he opened the conversation.

"Just getting some papers graded and grooving on some jazz. What about you?"

"Man, I'm on my way to a late lunch. Wondered if you wanted to join me?"

"Lunch? What time is it?"

There was a momentary pause. "Man, it's two o'clock."

"Two o'clock?" Dawg, I've been kicking it, today. And all of a sudden, I did feel hungry. "You buying?"

"Your first post-divorce lunch. Of course, I'm buying, Rome. Where you want to go?"

"Well to be honest, I was hoping we could go over this way. Can you?"

"No problem. What about that Chinese Restaurant on Carmel?"

"Yeah, I know which one you mean, but there's a better one on Fairview near the movies. You know what I'm talking about? I don't know the name."

"You mean in the new development near Southpark?"

"Yeah, that's the one. You game?"

"Cool, meet me there in about 45 minutes, ok?"

"Yeah, that's good, Billy. See ya, then."

I hung up and gathered my papers, which were spread around the patio. I went inside and put on a pair of dress blue Savanes and a white short sleeve Van Huesen. I liked the feel of a crisp shirt just out of the cleaners. I ran a brush through my short hair.

I took off my glasses and put on my contact lenses. I finished my 'makeover' with black wing tips and grabbed my silk jacket. After a quick glance in the mirror, I left the apartment, headed to meet my friend.

My car was dirty and I wondered if I had the time to run it through a car wash before I met Billy. I didn't, but I did make a mental note to have my car cleaned after lunch. I pulled into the lot and parked a little away from the door because of my dirty car.

I sprayed on some cologne before going into the restaurant. As I opened the door and stepped in, I could see Billy waving from a table. I walked over.

"I must say, Rome, you lookin' relaxed today."

"I feel better, Billy. I really do," I said as I removed my jacket. Billy was looking at me quizzically as I sat down. "What?" I asked him.

"Not the 'stache, man. Not the 'stache. Man you took care of that hair on your upper lip like it was human. When'd you do…Wait a minute. What happened with you and Akeba last night?"

"We had some tense moments, last night. Dani had a rough evening and we all spent some time talking about everything that has happened."

The waiter appeared and handed us menus. We looked at the menus while our waiter rattled off the lunch specials.

Billy held up his hand halting the waiter's monologue. "I'll have the Sa-cha chicken platter. That comes with egg roll, right?" The waiter smiled and nodded. He then looked at me.

"I'll have the vegetable fried rice platter." The waiter nodded again and smiled.

"Drink?" he asked with a smile.

"Two ice waters," Billy said. I nodded in agreement.

The waiter took our menus and walked off in the peculiar light stepping way those Chinese waiters all seem to have.

Billy looked after him. "Man, how do you think they remember those orders without writing them down. Shit, if that was me, I'd have them all wrong." Our waiter appeared with our water, fried noodles and dip. Then he disappeared again.

"I know what you mean," I said as I nibbled on a few of the noodles.

Billy pointed to my face with a noodle, "So, what gives with the 'stache, man?"

"I just decided to do something different. I'm gonna grow a beard. What do you think?"

"But why'd you shave your 'stache, if you're going to grow a beard?"

"Dawg, Billy. I've just chosen to shave it off," I touched my lip, "then let the whole thing grow in together. So, what do you think?"

"I think, 'whatever' man. Whatever." He waved his hand at me. "I tell you, Rome when you 'bugg' you 'bugg'." He laughed. Then he got serious. "Rome, you my man. You know that don't you?"

"Yeah, I do Billy. I do." For a couple minutes, we just looked at each other and munched on the fried noodles. The silence was broken by the reappearance of our waiter.

"Sa-cha chicken?" he asked. Billy raised his hand. Our waiter put the plate in front of him. Billy bowed his head and breathed in deeply.

"The vegetable platter?" the waiter asked as he looked at me. I nodded. He put the plate of steaming food in front of me. Man, it smelled so good. "Anything else?" the waiter asked. Billy and I shook our heads 'no' and the waiter quickly left the table.

We ate in silence for a while. Billy looked up. "So, what's on your mind, Rome?"

I took a deep breath. "I was just thinking about my conversation with Robert."

"Yeah, how'd that go?"

"You know how Robert is."

"Yeah, solid, reliable, predictable Robert," Billy said between forkfuls. "Of course that ain't all bad. All of us have counted on him for his wisdom, even if he does get preachy every once in a while."

"That's true," I said slowly chewing on the crunchy vegetables from my lunch.

"So, was it good he was here? I mean, I was surely glad to see him. Robert doesn't get here too often."

"Yeah, Billy it was good to see him. And no question, having him here was really good for me. But I got to admit, Robert will hold a person to a standard." I ate a little more, then continued. "I didn't want to face a lot of shit, but Robert just wouldn't let me get away with that."

Billy pointed his fork at me, shaking it gently as he spoke, "You know that was the attorney in him. Robert cuts through bullshit better than a hot knife through butter." He ate a little more. "But, you and I both know that there isn't anybody better to go to when trouble strikes. He's been really helpful to me, over the years."

"Yeah, you're right about that, but I still felt spanked after I talked with him about everything."

"Everything like what?" Billy asked.

"Me, Akeba, Yolanda. You know." I paused as our waiter reappeared. He refilled our glasses with water, then discreetly disappeared. Once the waiter was out of earshot, I continued. "The divorce, my 'thing' with Yolanda and all the other bullshit."

Billy leaned forward in his chair, toward me. He took a long swallow from his glass, wiped his lips and fixed his eyes on me. "I told you not to tell Robert about your thing with Yolanda, didn't I?" I nodded. Billy continued. "Were you just kind of pushing her in his face, you think?"

"What do you mean by that?"

"You know what I mean, Rome. You've always had this funky little attitude about your relationship with Robert. Over the years, you've put him on this pedestal and then you act like you're mad he's up there.

"Me and Marcus have told you that, before. You've competed with him yet you never seemed to understand that it is damn near impossible to compete with a person on a pedestal.

"Besides, I think you have nothing to compete with him about. You've been very successful in your own right. But when it comes to Yolanda, as fine as she is, I'm wondering if you didn't want to show him the trophy you had."

I shook my head.

"Hear me out," Billy continued. "All four of us from the first day couldn't help but notice her. Then you got kind of taken with her and y'all started this thing a few years later. When one of my partners had a bachelor party and Robert came up, you decided to have Yolanda meet us at Club Premier, the night before. You and her were all huggy, huggy and then you practically made her dance with Robert. I told you that night, that was wrong, remember?"

I did.

"So, that's what I meant by you kind of saying to Robert, 'look what I got'. You know what I mean?"

Billy was right. He was right that night and he was right now. I did like the look on Robert's face as he looked at Yolanda that night at Club Premier. And I also remembered the lecture Robert gave me later that night about being 'careful' and not losing my perspective. It pissed me off and I was going to tell him, but I never did.

"Are you training to be a shrink, man?" I asked Billy.

"Naw, I just know that you've always respected Robert's take on shit. That's got to be kind of confusing for you."

"Yeah, you're right about a lot of stuff, Billy. I guess this is my week to be slammed about my behavior, huh?"

"Hey man. That's not what I was intending, Rome." Billy paused as the waiter reappeared.

"More water? Noodles?" I held out my glass for water, which the waiter refilled. Billy put his hand over his glass.

"Can I get some coffee?" he asked the waiter.

"Sure," the waiter responded and disappeared. He quickly returned with a cup, saucer and a hot pot of coffee. He poured. "You like?" he asked Billy.

Billy opened a pack of sugar and poured in the coffee stirring rapidly. He took a sip and looked up at the waiter. "Very good. Can you leave the pot?" The waiter nodded quickly, put the pot on the table and walked away.

Billy took another sip of coffee. "Where were we?"

"Talking about Robert, but before you start, let me run to the men's room, first." I left and quickly returned, dreading the remainder of this conversation. "Go ahead."

"Look, Rome we don't have to talk about this anymore. I didn't invite you to lunch for this. You've been through enough for this week. I just don't want you beating yourself up, anymore. You let Robert do that for you. He's good at it." He started to laugh.

Despite myself, I started to laugh with Billy. Soon, we were both laughing almost uncontrollably. As the laughter subsided, I wiped my eyes

"Man, I don't know what we were laughing about, but I sure needed a good laugh. Thanks, man."

"No problem, I think." Billy drank some more of his coffee. "Look man, I got to make a run, then I get back to the plantation."

"Cool. I'll wait till you get back, just to make sure you pay the bill." Billy snorted and walked away.

Billy returned, took his seat and studied the bill for a moment.

"Rome, I got to go. You ready?"

"I'm ready. Let's go."

As we headed toward the cashier, I heard my name called. "Mr. Mitchell?" I turned and looked in the direction of the somewhat familiar voice. It was my co-worker and mentor, Dr. Samantha Carlton.

"I thought that was you. How are you? You look good," she said.

"Hi, Sam. You look good yourself."

Sam's short blonde hair was styled beautifully. Her blue eyes seemed bluer than usual. She was wearing a peach blouse with a light colored jacket. The color of the blouse seemed to highlight the soft, whiteness of her skin. I couldn't see her legs, but I knew how nice those looked.

"This is a surprise. I'm ok. How are you?"

"Good. I, uh, we that is, all miss you at school." She looked at Billy.

"I'm Samantha Carlton and I work with Jerome."

"Ouch, forgive me," I said quickly. "Billy, this is Samantha, I call her Sam. Sam, this is my best and life-long friend, Billy." I looked down at Sam.

"Hello, Billy," she said. They shook hands.

"And hello to you, uh, Sam. You are certainly a lovely woman and that would add to my excitement about going to work," Billy replied with an arched eyebrow.

Samantha smiled. "Oh, Jerome. You have a smoothie for a friend. Actually, I'm surprised he's not mentioned me. After all, I am helping him with his doctoral studies."

"You're having a late lunch. Are you eating alone?" I asked

"No I'm not alone. My girlfriend is meeting me here in a few minutes."

We chatted a couple minutes then Billy and I turned to leave. I promised to call Sam later that evening to catch up on what's been going on at the school during my absence. Once outside, I turned to Billy.

"Don't say nothing, man."

"What?" Billy looked back at me. His shoulders hunched, the palms of his hands turned upward. "Oh, you mean about Samantha, uh Sam.

That woman looks good, man. Certainly you don't think I'm gonna say anything about the fact that when you mention Sam you conveniently forget to mention that Sam is a woman. A gorgeous white woman at that. Brother holding out on a brother. Ain't that somethin'?"

"What does her being white got to do with anything?" I asked.

"Don't even go there, Rome. You know a woman's skin color don't mean nothing to me. It's just when you mention the help that Sam is giving you with your studies, you always seem to say it without letting on Sam's a 'she'. Now I wonder how that happened?"

"Man, you are imagining things. Look, I thought you needed to go."

"Don't be trying to cut me short, Rome. That might make me think there's more to this Sam situation than you're letting on." He looked at me. "Is there more?" I looked blankly at him.

"Rome, don't get me wrong. Hell, man from what I could see, she looked real good. We know she's educated. And the way she checked you out…" He let the sentence just hang out there.

I shrugged. "I don't think there's any more to it than what you saw." But I had thought about it from time to time.

"Well, look Rome. I understand. You know I love you, right?" I nodded. We hugged. After the hug, he stood back and looked at my face. "Damn, your 'stache, bro? What in the world were you thinking?"

"You know, you really need to get a life."

Billy smiled. "Might not be bad," he said slowly. "Gon' take some getting used to though. But, look I got to go back to the plantation. Call me later. That is, call me after you call Sam." He emphasized the name 'Sam', laughed and walked to his car.

"Hey Billy!" I called out to him.

"What?"

I hurriedly walked over to him. "I've been meaning to ask you where you and Robert went after leaving my place yesterday."

"Robert drove around to some law firms where he knew people and visited for a while. After a couple places, I was bored. I had him drop me off at the house of the guy I told you about that works as a security guard in our building. He had a ladyfriend visiting so I didn't stay long. I picked up a sack from him and left. I've been meaning to introduce him to you."

"Robert knew you made a purchase?"

"And listen to his speech on the sins of 'king weed'? I don't think so. Not only that, you know he would have rolled out that shit about being an officer of the court and I was in no mood to hear that. When he picked me up, I just got in the car and kept my mouth shut."

Billy unlocked his car door, opened it and got in. He started his car and rolled down the driver side window.

"Then we stopped at KFC, he dropped me off at my crib and headed to your place. At least that's where I thought he was headed. Why?"

"No particular reason, I was just wondering, that's all."

"Well, that was it. Anything else?"

"Nope. Look, drive safely and we'll get together this weekend, right?"

"Right, Rome. Peace." Billy took off and I walked to my car.

As I walked to my car, I looked at the restaurant and toyed with the idea of going back inside to talk with Sam, but I changed my mind.

Two females walked past me. We made eye contact, one of them smiled at me, I smiled back but we continued in our opposite directions.

I wondered if one or both of them were meeting with Sam. Once I got to my car, I looked at it and shook my head. My car definitely needed a good wash and wax.

XI

"Your friend, Billy, who stopped by the other day, seemed nice," Melody said as she rested her head on the passenger seat back of Bernard's new truck.

"Glad you liked him, but he's not really a friend. He's just someone I know from my part time security guard gig. He only comes over when he wants to make a purchase. But who cares? I don't want to associate with the people from that job, especially a job I hate."

"Well, he was nice anyway," Melody said softly. Bernard just grunted.

"Whatever, Mel. What store did you want to go to?" he asked impatiently.

"The beauty shop in Freedom Mall."

Without another word, Bernard pulled out and headed toward their destination. Melody tried to engage him in conversation, but when it was clear he wasn't going to talk, she remained silent until they arrived at the mall.

Once there, Bernie parked in a secluded area of the parking lot facing the beauty shop and rolled a joint for them. Melody ran her hand over the dashboard in front of her.

"Damn, Bernard. I really like your new car. It's so manly," she purred.

Bernard massaged his temples with his fingers. "How many times I got to tell you, Melody. This is a truck. You drive a car. You're sitting in a truck. Shit."

"I know you ain'tbuggin' about whether this is a truck or a car," Melody retorted.

"Damn right I'm buggin'. Shit. You keep calling this a car and it obviously ain't a car."

"Whatever. Just pass the joint," she said holding her left hand in the air with the palm facing Bernard.

Bernard blew air out his clenched teeth. He turned to look at Melody as he passed her the joint. Her dark skin was pretty. He always thought she wore unnecessary make up and way too much weave. She made a big deal about flipping the honey brown fake hair out her eyes and that irritated him.

Melody's nails were long and painted various colors. Her tight black jeans and white top clung to her body. Looking closer, he could see the rolls of skin held in place by her tight white top. He shook his head and leaned his head back after Melody took the joint from him.

"What's wrong with you, man?"

"What are you talking about?"

"You're all quiet and shit. You in a bad place?"

"Look, why don't you just smoke and be quiet. Your voice is starting to get on my nerves."

"Whatever." Melody took another deep pull on the joint. "And don't be thinking I'm giving this back to you. I don't have to take no shit from you or no man."

"You really think you're all that, don't you?" Bernard sat up, twisted in his seat and looked at her intently. "Don't you?"

"Whatever."

"Is that all you have to say?" He leaned toward her. Melody flinched as he moved.

"Girl, I ain't trying to do nothing to you." He reached across her and opened the large glove compartment and pulled out a brown envelope.

Melody eyed the envelope as she smoked the last of the joint. She opened the window, threw out the roach and waved the smoke out with her hand. After she closed the window, Bernard opened the envelope.

"You want to see a real woman?" he asked.

Melody said nothing. Her eyes narrowed and her glowering look focused on his hands as he reached in and pulled out the photograph.

"Now, this is a woman who would know she was sitting in a brand new red Dodge Ram truck. And she wouldn't even use the word, 'whatever'."

Melody looked at the 5x7 picture. The woman looking back at her from the photo had pretty brown skin. Her eyes seemed to jump right from the picture. Her black dress fit her perfectly. She stood in front of one of those cheesy backdrops night club photographers carried around with them. This one was red with the words *'Hot Mama'* emblazoned above the woman's head.

"Who's this?" she asked, making every effort to control her growing fury. Bernard's smug smile only infuriated her more. "Who is that bitch?" she asked again.

"Her name's Yolanda. She's my future."

"Your future?" Melody raised her voice. "Your future?" She shook her head. "We've been kicking it for a couple months now and all of a sudden you show me a picture and tell me she is your future? Why you wanna say some shit like that to me?"

"I'm just trying to be honest with you, Melody. We never said nothing about a long term thing. This woman," he pointed to the picture, "is who I'll be with in the future. That has no impact on us, right now."

"Fuck that. You can begin your future now, nigga. I was your present, but now I'm your past and I'm gone." With that, Melody opened the door of the truck and sprang out. Once out, she slammed the door as hard as she could.

The passenger side power window slid down. "Don't slam the door on my new truck, Mel," Bernard said with a menacing voice. "You know I just picked this bitch up yesterday."

She held up her middle finger and stalked away as fast as she could. Once she was a safe distance away, she turned to look at the truck. It hadn't moved. The passenger window was closed and the dark tinted windows were impossible to see through. She marched away, toward the entrance of the beauty shop.

Bernard watched Melody stalk away through the tinted passenger window, then with a snort, he pulled out a bag of marijuana, a couple rolling papers and rolled himself a joint. He glanced across the parking lot, but he couldn't see Melody anymore.

"Stupid ho," he said as he lit another joint, inhaling deeply, then adjusted the air conditioning.

"Oh well, Yolanda," he said as he looked at her picture on the seat beside him, "guess the future will have to begin sooner than either of us thought." He took another pull on the joint. "And the cook out on Friday will be a good place to get our future together, started."

With that, he turned on the powerful engine and slowly pulled into traffic. He never gave Melody Williams another thought.

XII

An hour after I left lunch with Billy, Archie an employee of the car wash was finishing my 626. The champagne color was gleaming and the tire gloss set off the blackwalls.

"What you think, bro?"

I looked inside. "Looking good, Archie. Thanks. With a ride looking this good, I might even be able to get a date."

"Brother, that's a car a woman would be proud to be seen in. Have a good day!"

After giving Archie a five dollar tip, I got in and prepared to leave.

A part of me was feeling a little tired thinking about the rush hour traffic I was about to face to get home. Dawg, where does the time go? I've got more papers to grade and I was determined to finish grading them before I did anything else.

Tomorrow, I was scheduled to talk at a youth program on the importance of young people considering college in their future.

At home, I had four messages on my machine. The first two were telemarketing schemes, which I quickly deleted and the next was my brother, Robert. He was safe in Atlanta and very busy. The last was a voice I hadn't heard in a long time.

"Mr. Jerome Mitchell, bet you don't know who this is." The voice was female, playful and sexy.

"Give up? My first three digits are 801. Does that help? Call me, baby."

I smiled. I knew the voice well, but I was determined not to return that call until I finished grading my papers. I put on some music, opened my briefcase and began reading with my ever-present purple marking pencil.

But it was difficult to keep focused on the papers in my lap. My mind kept going back to that phone call.

"Stop it, Rome. Get your work done," I said to myself.

After finally finishing my work, I sat looking at the phone tapping my cheek with my forefinger. I wanted to call that number right away, but I decided to just cool it and make my other calls first. Picking up the phone, I dialed the first number. It was answered on the second ring.

"Hello?" The voice on the phone sounded young, but deep.

"Hey, Joe. This is Uncle Jerome. Is my brother there?"

"What's up, Uncle Jerome? Naw, he isn't here. He's still at work. You ok?"

"Am I ok?"

"Come on Uncle Jerome. Mr. Rob told us he was at your house because of your divorce this week. I was just checking to see if you ok. But if I'm just being nosy, my bad."

"Easy, Joe. I'm ok. Thanks for asking. When do you think my brother will be back?"

"I don't know. Want to talk to mom?"

"No, that's ok. Just tell her I said hello and tell my brother I got his message. No need to call back, ok?"

"Cool, Uncle Jerome. Later."

"Bye, Joe. Have a..." He had already hung up. I needed to have a conversation with Robert regarding his stepson's phone etiquette.

I took a deep breath while dialing the familiar number from my recent past. The second ring ended and I prepared to hang up, but I listened all the way to the receiver. The phone was picked up just as the third ring started. I knew that voice instantly...

"Hello?" The soft voice said

I could feel my heart beating faster, just from her 'hello'.

"Well, hello yourself. This is—"

"Jerome, sugar. I wondered if you would call. Been a long time. Bet you were surprised when you heard my message, huh?"

I was impressed and flattered that Yolanda recognized my voice so quickly.

"I sure was. How long has it been?" I asked as if I didn't know.

"I guess close to a year. How are you?"

"Considering my divorce was finalized this week, I guess I'm not doing too badly. Your call was a pleasant surprise."

"I'm sorry about the divorce. I know being with me didn't help any."

"Look, Yolanda. You weren't the one married, I was. I was responsible for my own choices. I should have made better decisions, but I didn't."

"Rome, let's not go down that road. I didn't call to reminisce. So, let's not do it, ok? I called to find out what you were doing tomorrow night."

"So far, me and Billy talked about getting together, then going to the Woodson, South Carolina Classic on Saturday. Why?"

"I'm having a little set at my house. I'm planning to get started about six o'clock. We'll cook some stuff out on the grill, listen to some music, play some cards and just fellowship. How does that sound? I really want you to come. I'd really like to see you."

"Do I need a date?"

"A date? If you can come, I was hoping you would be my date. You interested?"

"Well, can I get back to you?"

"No, I need to know right now." Yolanda paused, then her voice took on that sickening sweet sound that I knew wouldn't take 'no' for an answer.

"Come on Romey. Hang with me tomorrow night."

I was determined to make it difficult for her. "I heard you were dating an NBA player. That true?"

"Rome, that's out of line. I called you. What do you say?"

I thought for a minute. Right at that moment my call-waiting indicator clicked on the phone. "Yolanda, let me get this call. Can you hold on?"

"Ok, go ahead," she said quietly.

"Hello?"

"Que pasa, bro? What you doing?"

"Billy, I'm on another call, can I call you right back?"

"Wait, man!" Billy yelled into the phone. "I just wanted to tell you that I got a date tomorrow night, so you'll have to get along without me. Are we still on for the game, Saturday?"

"Saturday's cool. Have a good time tomorrow night."

"I will. But look, I got to get to a meeting. Talk with you tomorrow or early Saturday."

"Right on, bro. Later!" I clicked back to Yolanda. "Sorry, Yolanda. Hey, tomorrow is fine with me. What's the plan?"

"Perfect, Rome. Just be casually dressed and come to my house. I'm still living in Indian Trail at the same house and I'll look forward to seeing you. Be there about six or six thirty. By the way, don't make any other late night plans, ok?"

"Sounds good, Yolanda. I'll be there. Thanks for inviting me. I need a good party and I'll keep my night open."

I could almost see Robert standing in my living room looking at me shaking his finger.

"Just a party, Robert" I said. "It's just a party."

Yolanda hung up the phone with a smile. Jerome Mitchell is coming. "Damn, you sound good, man!" Yolanda said out loud.

She lay back on the couch and closed her eyes. She could see him in her mind. His brown, flawless skin, his clear light brown eyes, jet-black hair and his ever present, well trimmed mustache. She wondered if he had begun to gray at all.

She smiled as she thought about how distinguished he would look with a little gray in his hair and mustache. Yolanda could almost feel his large hands on her body. She could almost smell his ever-present POLO cologne, which smelled so good on him.

Yolanda pictured his broad shoulders and big chest. She knew Jerome liked working out and she was certain he hadn't let himself go. She wondered if he looked any differently after so many months. She was sure he didn't change too much, but she was curious.

The ringing of the phone startled her out of her reverie. She took a deep breath before she answered the phone on the third ring.

"Hello?"

"Hey Puff! What's up? I was about to hang up."

Yolanda sat up. "Hi, Claude. What's up with you?"

"Nothing. Just thinking about you and wanted to hear your sexy voice. Coach gave us tomorrow off and I wondered if you and I could get together tomorrow night."

Yolanda chewed on her bottom lip before answering. She really wanted to spend some time with Jerome.

"Sorry, Claude. I've got other plans."

"Who with?"

"What do you mean by that? You don't own me Claude Boozer. What's with this 'who with' shit?"

"Damn, Puff. Ease up. I was just kidding."

"No, you weren't Claude. I know you."

"Puff, Puff. Ease up. We were together for close to a year and I'd rather be with you than not be with you. Why are you so upset?"

"Claude, we're not together remember? We've been apart since August. You're too possessive. I told you that. Right?"

"Ok, Puff. You're right. But it's October, and I want us to talk about getting back together. I do understand more about what you've been saying and I can be more supportive.

You do deserve someone in your life who can be more like the person you want. I do want to change my ways. Can't we meet and talk about it?"

Yolanda took a deep breath and exhaled slowly. "Claude, you agreed to wait until I called you. Remember?" A part of her still longed to be with him. That annoyed her.

"Ok, ok, Puff. Whatever you're planning on doing, have a good time. But I don't know how you will without me."

"Ok, Claude. I'll try, anyway. Bye."

"C'ya," Claude responded quietly and hung up.

Yolanda hung up. She looked at her bedroom wall where she could see the images of Jerome and Claude standing side by side. Jerome was dressed in a shirt and tie with the long sleeves unbuttoned and partially rolled up. His smile was radiant. Claude had on his uniform, holding a basketball. His bald head gleamed.

"I got to do something different, I really do," Yolanda whispered to herself. She looked at the wall again. The image of Jerome shrugged his shoulders and faded away, while the Claude image looked back at her and smiled as his fingers played with the basketball. She smiled shaking her head and slowly Claude's' image faded away as well.

"I'm either buggin' or crazy, or both" Yolanda said to herself as she looked at the wall.

XIII

The alarm clock beeped loudly at 8 o'clock. I pushed the snooze button and lay back down. Man, I was horny. It had been a while since I woke up with a woman beside me.

I dragged myself up and padded down the hall to go to the bathroom.

My plan was to do my speech, get over to the school to do some catching up and then spend some time with Yolanda. This should be a good day and I fully expected my 'drought' to end.

Twenty minutes later, I was ready for the street and my jogging course. I set the security system, grabbed my timer and headed for the door. The phone rang.

I decided to ignore the ringing phone.

I returned home forty minutes later. I really liked how I felt after jogging. I sometimes tried to convince myself not to work out, but I was almost always glad I did it, anyway.

I first went to get my jug of water. Then I checked my messages. There were none. The red '0' in the message box on my machine looked back at me. I remembered that the phone was ringing when I left.

"Oh well, whoever it was will call back, I guess," I said to the phone.

I took my vitamins and got myself prepared for my shower. Afterwards, I chose to wear blue Slates and a blue striped Hilfiger long sleeved shirt with a blue patterned silk tie. I shined my black loafers and stood to look at myself in the full-length mirror.

"Well Rome, you look as good as you can look. May as well get on with your day," I said to myself. As an afterthought, I grabbed a Charlotte University tee shirt, for 'just in case.'

Since I didn't think I would have time to return home after leaving the school and heading to Indian Trail, I also chose a white FUBU golf shirt and my recently pressed carpenter jeans to wear to Yolanda's along with my Nike's and a pair of white socks.

It was time to head toward the site of my speech and I was excited. This should be a good day. And I hoped a good night. I needed to get laid in the worse way.

May as well be with someone I felt comfortable with. I took a quick look in the mirror. All was in place and I was ready. Time to go.

I looked at the address on my confirmation letter and the address on the building. They matched. As I looked around the parking lot I noticed several yellow school buses, there.

"Dawg, I was told there would only be about thirty-five to fifty kids here," I said to myself.

I parked as close to the building as possible. I was about twenty minutes early. I turned down the radio and leaned my head back with my eyes partially closed. I was feeling pretty nervous. After a few minutes, I sat up.

"Ok, Rome, let's go do this," I said a little too boldly and stepped out of the car.

As I approached the building, I could hear young people's voices and the bouncing of basketballs. The door closest to the parking lot was propped open with a thick rug. I peeped in and took a deep breath. There must be a hundred kids in there.

I pulled my head back, leaned against the brick wall of the building and closed my eyes again. I looked at my handouts. I have fifty-five. Not only that, I had never spoken to a group that large before. Now I was really nervous.

"Every knuckle head and round the way girl in the school system must be in there," I thought to myself.

After taking another deep breath, I went inside. Directly across the open door from where I entered the other door was propped open as well with a couple chairs. The two propped open doors provided a slight cross breeze.

I found myself in a large gymnasium. Both sides of the bleachers were partially extended toward the basketball court. There were four baskets down and each had a pick up game of half-court ball going on.

One game was all female. Teen-age brothers and sisters were playing ball, talking or laughing loudly. Out of the din, a voice carried, directed at me.

"Hey mister. You the speaker?"

I turned and looked at the source of the young voice. He had a bald head and I guessed him to be about fifteen. He was fashionably dressed in the latest urban gear.

"Yes, I'm one of the speakers. My name is Mr. Mitchell and you are?" I held out my hand to him. He took it and squeezed it gently. I guess that was his handshake.

"I'm Reece, man."

"Good to meet you, Reece. You know who's in charge in here?"

"Yeah. It's the woman in the African clothes."

I followed his gaze across the gym. There was a full figured sister seemingly talking to everyone at the same time in several directions.

"Thanks, Reece," I said, but he had already moved away. I watched him as he sauntered over to the bleachers, taking a seat at the very end. He was immediately surrounded by a group of giggling girls.

"Reece is a player, huh?" I said to myself, smiling. I then walked over to the sister in the middle of the gym Reece had indicated with his look.

"I told y'all not to start this with each other, didn't I?" The sister was saying to group of girls who were obviously upset about something. "We're gonna start soon and y'all need to get along, ok?"

Some of them nodded. Others just stared at her. I cleared my throat, not wanting to interrupt.

"Oh, hello!" The sister turned to look at me. She did a quick, slick up and down scan then her large, dark eyes met mine.

"Excuse me for interrupting. My name is Jerome—"

"Brother Mitchell! Good to meet you." She looked at the girls surrounding her. Several of them gave me the same up and down scan as their leader.

"Y'all go on, now. I need to talk with this brother. He is our speaker today. Go on, now."

After eyeing me, in that curious way teenage girls do, they moved away. I knew girls this age, could be brutal fashion police.

"I'm sorry, Brother Mitchell. As you can see, we got our hands full today." She held out her hand to me. "I'm NaLa Garvey the Director of SOCA.

I shook her hand. Her fingers were a little chubby, but they were soft. Her handshake was firm. I noticed that her fingernails were perfectly painted a muted earth tone and each nail had a soft glow.

"NaLa. What an interesting name. How's that spelled?"

Ms. Garvey's smile was as broad as her face and as inviting. "It's spelled capital N, little a, capital L, little a. It means caring and strong."

"That's beautiful. And the Garvey name has a nice historical ring."

Her colorful African dress and matching crown fit her well. Her light colored skin seemed to shimmer. Her lips were painted the same color as her fingers. A quick glance down revealed that her wide feet were covered by a pair of hemp sandals and her visible toes were also painted to match her lips and fingernails. She smiled again and looked down. Only then did

I notice that we were still holding hands. I released her hand quickly, somewhat embarrassed.

"Garvey, of course is a name I took on for myself just like NaLa. Marcus Garvey continues to be one of my strong black heroes." She was still smiling as I nodded my head. Then she pushed my shoulder gently.

"I'm just kidding. I did change my name from Karen to NaLa, but Garvey is my married name. However, I always have admired the work of Marcus Garvey."

Mrs. Garvey. I wanted to make sure I didn't mess that up in the future. I was feeling rather overwhelmed by the number of kids in there.

"Uh, I was told to expect thirty-five kids today. I see there's a lot more than that here, huh?"

"Your appearance was set up through Rasheed, right?"

"Yeah, uh…" I looked on my confirmation letter where I had written the name of my contact person.

"Yeah, Rasheed Harris. Is he here? We've only spoken on the phone a couple times." I took out my handkerchief and wiped my face.

"It is kind of warm in here, isn't it?" Mrs. Garvey asked me.

"Yeah, it is. Glad you got those doors propped open." Actually, I was getting warm with nervousness thinking how I was going to talk to all these young people at the same time. Plus I was wondering where the other speakers were.

"Honey, go over there and get Mr. Harris for me, ok?" Mrs. Garvey was speaking to a tall, pretty girl who seemed to appear out of nowhere.

"Oh, that's alright. I'll just walk over there with her, if that's ok," I said.

"By all means, Brother Mitchell." Mrs. Garvey turned away from me and put a whistle in her mouth. I quickened my step. I didn't want to be too close when she blew that whistle. Unfortunately, I was only a few steps away when the whistle went off. Sister NaLa can sure blow a whistle.

"Mr. Harris, Miss Garvey wanted me to bring this man over here to you," my escort said to the young man standing in front of me. She glanced back at me and then began to walk away.

"Thank you, sister," I said to her. "What is your name?"

"Tasha and you're welcome. You the speaker, huh?"

I looked at her. "I am one of the speakers, yes."

"I like your tie," she said with an appraising look.

"Thank you, Tasha. "Ah, approval by one of the fashion police.

"You're welcome." Her eyes never left my face. Then she turned and ambled off.

"Mr. Mitchell. So glad to finally meet you." Rasheed came over and smiled as he shook my hand. Rasheed was a young man, I guessed to be between twenty three and twenty five years old. He was light skinned and thin.

He sported a small Afro that was neatly combed. He also had a razor thin mustache, which looked like the one Teddy Riley sports.

His shirt was slightly damp and there was a thin sheen of perspiration on his forehead. His handshake needed some work, but he seemed to be a pleasant young man.

"Good to meet you as well, Mr. Harris."

"Please, call me Rasheed."

"Ok, Rasheed."

He smiled and we both looked at the herding job Mrs. Garvey was doing on the youth attending this program. Other young adults were assisting.

"Big crowd, Rasheed. Larger than I expected," I said as I watched the bleachers on one side of the gym filling. One of the last people to move was Reece, surrounded by his harem.

Rasheed's smile faded. He looked at me somewhat dismayed. "You didn't get my e-mail then?"

I shook my head. "Probably not your fault. I've been out of the office most of this week. Had some stuff to take care of. Actually, I feel pretty bad for not checking my e-mail before now."

"No problem. I e-mailed you to let you know that the schools kind of flipped on us about this program. They decided to," he made the 'quote' sign in the air with his fingers, "offer this type of program to more than the students we chose for it. We were told that since school time was being taken we needed to have more than thirty five kids participate."

He turned to look at the crowd. I did as well. "So therefore, we now have a hundred and ten students here. Sorry."

I shrugged my shoulders. "What else could you do?" We watched as the herding continued. "Now what does SOCA stand for again? And what is your role with this?"

Rasheed smiled broadly. I could tell he was about to enjoy what he was about to say. "SOCA stands for Students of Color and Achievement. I am the Program Coordinator. This is my first job like this before. Mrs. Garvey has been teaching me the ropes and I am learning all the time."

"Very good. Constant and consistent learning is real important, Rasheed. Where'd you go to school?"

"Benedict in Columbia. I graduated a couple years ago. Then I started working with young men in a youth halfway house. That's where I met Mrs. Garvey who told me about this position. I've been here about seven months."

"Who are the other people helping Mrs. Garvey?"

"Staff members of the agency and college interns. We only have three paid staff so far, but we'll grow, though. I'm here for the long haul," Rasheed said emphatically.

I nodded. "The school really filled y'all up, huh?"

Rasheed looked around the gym. "You got that right." We both watched Mrs. Garvey work and listened to what she was saying.

"…and we will agree to be respectful to each other and our guests, right?" There was little response. "Right?" Her voice was much louder the second time and the response was louder and stronger. She turned to look at us.

"Now let's welcome our Program Coordinator, Brother Rasheed Harris." She began clapping and many of the participants joined her.

"Guess I'm on," Rasheed whispered to me as he walked toward the center of the gym.

"Go get 'em, young brother," I whispered back to him. As Rasheed moved toward the middle of the floor, I moved toward the bleachers.

I took a seat on the empty front row and watched as Rasheed worked the crowd. I had to admit, he was pretty good. He seemed to have most of the students attentively listening to him. He talked about SOCA, its importance and SOCA's goals. I glanced at NaLa who stood behind Rasheed. She beamed as she looked at him. She almost looked like a proud momma. I found that rather touching.

I glanced over my shoulder at the sheer number of students on the bleachers. I found myself looking for Reece or Tasha. Perhaps they would be allies when I found myself stuck. I couldn't locate them from my vantage point. I turned around when I heard my name.

"…and Brother Jerome Mitchell will talk with you about the power of education. He teaches at Charlotte University and he'll give some information you can use. Stand up Brother Mitchell."

I stood and faced the bleachers and gave a little wave. Some of the students were clapping; others looked at me with disinterest.

As I sat down, I wondered if I was the only speaker. I hadn't heard Rasheed mention anyone else. I steeled myself for the possibility that I was the only game in town.

"You can do this Rome," I said to myself over and over. "Just calm down and do your thing."

I looked up again. Rasheed was talking about someone. "…so he will be able to talk with you about making it in the corporate world. Let's welcome Brother Kirk Alexander."

I silently said a prayer of thanks and waited for Kirk Alexander to speak. I turned to see a tall young man in a white shirt and red tie coming down the bleachers. I guessed that this was Mr. Alexander. I was right.

Rasheed sat next to me and NaLa sat next to him. Kirk stood at the half court line and began to speak. Kirk was a tall brother. I figured him to be at least 6-4. I guessed he was in his early thirty's. He was about my complexion and he also was bald. It looked like partially by choice, partially by nature.

I settled back to listen to him. He started his speech with a list of what he owned. House, car, lots of clothes, latest computer, cell phones, beepers, blah de blah. The house cost over 100K, his car is a Mercedes, his computer Japanese and so on. His point? What it took for him to amass these things.

Out of the corner of my eye, I could see Rasheed shaking his head almost imperceptibly. NaLa had her arms crossed over her chest, and seemed to be almost glaring at Mr. Alexander.

About 20 minutes later he finished. He asked for questions. All of the questions were about his possessions. *Where's your house at?* University area. *What color is your Mercedes?* Black on black. *You have a girlfriend?* Not really. *You want one? No answer but a smile. How much was that ring on your finger?* About a thousand.

There was a lot of stirring on that answer. That's when Rasheed got up and stopped the Q&A session.

None of the students had asked questions regarding corporate competence, which was the original theme of Mr. Alexander's speech.

"We're going to take a ten minute break before Mr. Mitchell begins." Rasheed said. "Ten minutes, ok?"

NaLa got up. "I'll blow this whistle when it's time to come back. Now get up and stretch."

Kirk came over to us. He was smiling while dabbing at his face with a silk handkerchief.

"I think that went well. What did you guys think?"

"Well, they heard what you said alright," I said. Rasheed nodded as did NaLa, although she did so, less enthusiastically.

"I would have liked them to more fully get your message about how you got the stuff you got. But it seemed to me they only heard about what you got," NaLa said looking pointedly at Kirk. It didn't appear she was happy.

Kirk shuffled a little and dropped his head. "Well, it might have been a little heavy on the possessions part, but I wanted them to aspire for the better things in life, you know?" He looked at Rasheed and me for support. I could only nod.

"Yeah, well maybe they got it. They need to hear that we all can go for the good life. Not make excuses," Rasheed said, looking at NaLa. He seemed to have some hidden communication going with her.

"Yeah, that was my point. Look, I'd like to stay, but I got an important meeting this afternoon." He shook hands all around and gave each of us his business card.

"Thanks for the opportunity and I'll look forward to working with SOCA again. I do believe I can teach these young brothers and sisters something." Kirk took off rather quickly. He stopped only long enough to show students his ring or to give them a business card. By the time he walked out of the door, his hands were of business cards.

"Meeting, huh? He probably got to get his Mercedes detailed," NaLa said grumpily. "I don't believe he got up there and bragged about what he owned for 25 minutes. Rasheed…?"

"I know, I know Mrs. Garvey. No more Mr. Alexander unless he changes his message. You better blow the whistle and get every body back in here." She did. Hard and strong.

It took another ten minutes to get the students settled back in the bleachers. Rasheed introduced me. I shook Rasheed's hand and gave him a one-armed hug as I approached the place he was standing just a few feet in front of the bleachers. Man, was I nervous.

I began by admitting that I was not as materialistically fortunate as Mr. Alexander, but I could talk to them about gathering other assets besides things. Before I knew it, Rasheed was giving "the cut across the throat" sign for me to stop. I took a quick glance at my watch. I had spoken for twenty-five minutes.

I asked for any questions. Several hands shot up into the air.

Could I get somebody a scholarship? No, but I can help with information and a recommendation. *How many black students go to the school?* About 15%. *You married?* No. *You got any kids?* One, she's eleven. *What job pays the most money?* Good question. Hard to answer that. *How much you make?* Enough. *Is it hard to teach in college?* Sometimes. *Is it true you can do what you want in college?* Yes, if you're willing to pay the consequences for your behavior. *Are there a lot of girls in your classes?* Yes, there are a lot of young ladies in my classes.

Rasheed stood and began to clap. "Let's thank Mr. Mitchell for his talk. If you want, maybe we can go in small groups to the University and sit in on one of his classes, someday." He looked at me. I nodded.

Rasheed shook my hand. He then turned to the students and talked about another activity. NaLa came over to walk me out.

"That was really good. Thanks. We'll certainly want you back. Would you consider it?"

"Absolutely. Just give me plenty of notice." I handed her the printed information I was going to give to the students. "I don't have enough, but I do want the students to have these.

"These are about the upcoming High School to University program for early admission, I talked about."

"I'll take care of it. Thanks again. Do you have another card?" I reached in my pocket and pulled out my card case. I handed her one. "Thanks. I'll be in touch, Brother Mitchell. Count on it."

"I will. Have a good day and thanks for the opportunity. Bye."

The fresh air felt good. My shirt and tie were wet from perspiration by the time I got to my car. I was glad I had brought the University tee shirt with me.

I looked around to be sure none of the kids were outside. Once I was sure I was alone, I hurriedly stripped off my shirt and tie, wiped down with a towel and put on the fresh shirt before I headed to the school.

Afterwards, I'd be off to Yolanda's.

Just as Yolanda prepared to leave her office, there was a knock on her partially open door. "Come in," she said softly. She cursed silently as she bent to pick up items off the floor that fell from her desk during the day.

"I'm in, good lookin'. Oh, please don't get up on my account." Yolanda quickly stood and turned to face the source of the voice.

"Oh hi, Bernard. I was just getting ready to leave, so I can prepare for tonight."

He looked at his watch. "It's only a little after noon."

"I know. I wanted to already be gone. I've got so much to do before everyone gets there."

"Well before you go, I gotta tell you, you sure looked good bent over like that."

"Out the gutter, man," Yolanda replied with a half-smile. "You still gonna come over and cook tonight?"

"I said I would didn't I? My boy, Rick is gonna help. You remember him, right? Rick Manzetti?" Yolanda nodded. Bernard pushed the door closed and walked over to her and took her hand.

"For you, I'd do almost anything. And you know I've felt this way for a long time." Bernard looked deeply in Yolanda's eyes.

Yolanda looked down at her hand in Bernard's. She felt mildly uncomfortable with his look and his closeness. She really didn't like the door being closed. She gently turned herself around, removed her hand from Bernard's and reopened the door to her office. She stood by the door as she talked to him.

"Bernard, you offered to cook because you want to, right? I mean, you know I'm not promising anything in return. I asked an old friend of mine to come and he agreed." Bernard said nothing. He just looked at her.

"Bernard, I can just get a caterer, you know? It's not too late."

His silence was irritating to Yolanda. All of a sudden his face broke into a grin.

"Chill out, girl. I said I'd do it and I will. Me and Rick will get there about five o'clock. I'm just glad to get the chance to spend some time with you."

"Bernard…" Yolanda began with a sigh.

Bernard put his finger to her lips. "Hey, look I'm out. See you later, ok?" Before walking out, he kissed her on the forehead as he squeezed past her out the door.

Once he was gone, Yolanda took a deep breath, gathered her things and left her office to begin her weekend.

"I think I made a bad mistake," Yolanda said to herself as she walked to her car.

XIV

Curtis Mayfield was sounding particularly good. As Yolanda cleaned up, she found herself singing along with the CD, *'Fred is dead, that's what I said...'* She was having a house full of people later and she wanted the house to look good, real good.

While she cleaned, she continued singing and dancing. Yolanda was so immersed in the music and the cleaning she was doing, she didn't hear the doorbell ring. She turned around and jumped. Her girlfriend Tanya was standing there.

"I didn't mean to startle you," Tanya said.

"Well you did, but that's alright. I'm just glad it was you. Was the door unlocked?"

"No. I used my key after I knocked then rang the bell a couple times. I could hear you all the way outside singing and messing up Curtis." They hugged. Tanya sat in a chair and relaxed while Yolanda continued singing and dusting. Before the song ended, they were both singing, *'Fred is dead.'*

Yolanda collapsed on the couch opposite her friend. "So, what's up Tanya? Don't say you came to help me clean 'cause I know better." She laughed.

"No, really. I did come to help you. I brought my stuff so I can change afterwards. That way I won't have to go back home."

"Great plan. Thanks for coming."

"No problem. I'm sure this is going to be a good night."

Tanya got up and walked to the kitchen. "What you got to drink?"

"I got some beer that somebody left here and I think there's some wine in there, too. Help yourself."

Tanya got a large goblet out of the kitchen cabinet and filled it with red wine. She sipped it and then returned to the front room with Yolanda and sat down.

"Durn, T. Did you leave any wine in the bottle?"

"Yep, but once I finish this I'm gonna finish the rest of it, smart ass." She looked around. "Looks good in here. Smells good, too."

"Thanks T. I've already gotten a lot done."

"What are you going to wear?"

"I'm just gonna wear a pair of black jeans, and a top."

"Oh, your 'bad girl' jeans?"

"And you know it."

"Good. I brought jeans to wear, myself. I made sure I brought the pair that shows off my ass- sets."

They gave each other 'five' and hugged as they collapsed on the sofa.

What about a date?" Tanya asked.

"I'm bringing back a flash from the past." Yolanda then laid her head back on the couch.

"Who, Claude?"

Yolanda sat up. "No, not quite."

"Well, who then?"

"Tanya, why you all up in my business?"

"Cause my love life sucks. But don't avoid my question. If not Claude, then who?"

"T, don't even mention Claude to me. We're on the 'outs' and for now that's just how I like it."

"Well, let's see…" Tanya clicked off her fingers as she spoke. "He's 6-8, built like he's cut from stone, nice round ass, he's a pro athlete, got a bomb crib at the lake and a smile that will melt a ho's heart. Yeah, I can see how all that could piss you off."

"Like I told you a few weeks ago, I need something more real, you know?"

Tanya took a deep swallow from the goblet. "Oh, damn. You ain't talking about that college teaching brother, are you?" Yolanda avoided Tanya's look.

"YoYo, why don't you leave that man alone? You and that nigga got busted by his wife in their house. He's lucky all she did was divorce him. You lucky she didn't try to end both of your days." Tanya took another swallow of wine, eyeing Yolanda as she swallowed.

"Ease up, T. We aren't getting married. We both been there, done that. We just gonna kick it tonight."

"Yeah, I got your 'kick it, tonight'. YoYo, Since you got this job at the magistrate's office, how many women have you seen with this story? I thought you had sworn off of him almost a year ago. I told you before, that man is like a drug to you. I have a cousin who quit smoking crack easier than you two quit each other. Hell, actually my cousin has quit smoking crack as often as you two have quit each other. What is it with him and you, anyway?"

"Let me get some wine before your wino ass drinks it up." Yolanda said as she got up and went to the kitchen. She got the matching goblet to Tanya's and poured herself about half a goblet full of the deep red liquid. When she returned to the front room, Tanya was changing the CD's. She pressed play and Chaka Khan's strong voice filled the room.

Yolanda sat back on the couch. "What were we talking about?"

"Shhhhhhheeeit…Girl you know what we were talking about. What is it with you and the Professor? Is he all that?"

"T, I don't know how to explain it. It's not that he's all that, but he has a way of talking to me and looking at me that makes me tingle, you know?"

"Girl, you too old to be tingling. Don't get me wrong, Jerome's a nice guy and he's intelligent, but what does he have to offer you?

You got a house, he lives in an apartment. You drive a Mercedes. He's in an old 626. You've both been married and both of the marriages ended for similar reasons. You know he don't have too much money. He's a college teacher. The last I checked, they weren't on the top ten paid list.

"Come on YoYo, you've been in an 'on again, off again' relationship with Claude Boozer. He's a pro basketball player, he's got mad love for you. And he's fine."

Yolanda nodded slowly as Tanya talked. "Claude is fine, you're right about that, girl. And money ain't everything. I'm surprised to hear you even bring that up. But a relationship has got to be more than money and looks, T." It just has to be. And as far as looks go, Jerome ain't exactly dog food, you know."

Tanya nodded in agreement. "Yeah, that's true. He's not bad looking. In fact, there are those that might say he's good looking, but he ain't no Claude Boozer, girlfriend."

"T, everything you said is right. I know it here." She pointed to her head. "But here," she pointed to her chest, "knows something else. I know it's crazy. Me and Rome's paths have crossed for years. I don't know." She shook her head.

"T, I just wanted to see him and so I acted on my impulse. And don't say you haven't done that."

"Guilty as charged, girl." Tanya got up and walked over to Yolanda. They gave each other a high five. "We're just two hopeless bitches, I guess." She smiled and looked at her friend.

Yolanda turned in her seat to face Tanya. "T, I really have missed him. You know what I mean, don't you?"

"I'm sure you have, sweetie, "Tanya said smoothing her friend's hair.

"I know when we were messing around while he was married, it was wrong. There was no way to make what we did right, I mean, for most of my life, to other women, I've been considered a bottom-feeder when it comes to men. That always hurt me.

"Because of that I never really was able to get along with other women. They were always threatened by me. I'm not saying that I didn't earn that reputation at times, but I really wanted to have girlfriends." Yolanda's eyes filled with water. Tanya put her arm around Yolanda.

"Some of that is your mother's fault. Don't you think?" Tanya said softly. Yolanda shrugged her shoulders.

"I'm your friend, Yolanda and I'm proud to be."

"Thank you, T. I mean it."

Tanya smoothed the hair out of her friend's face. "Poor, misunderstood Yolanda. I'm with you and you know it. When the professor gets here, I'll be gracious. Actually, it'll be good to see him again."

"Thanks, T. I appreciate it."

They sat in silence for a while. Yolanda looked off into space while Tanya continued smoothing her hair. Tanya broke the silence first.

"YoYo, what do you need me to do?"

"Do you mind cleaning the two bathrooms, while I do the kitchen?"

"No, I don't mind." They got up and went to separate parts of the house lost in their own thoughts. Tanya decided to call Glenn and see if he wanted to be her date for the evening. He had been asking her to go out with him for a couple weeks.

"YoYo, can I use your phone?" Tanya yelled out.

"Sure honey. Go ahead," Yolanda yelled back.

Tanya got her address book out of her purse, found Glenn's number and called. He answered on the first ring and readily agreed to be her date for the evening. Satisfied, Tanya hung up and moved to the bathrooms to clean.

Yolanda began rinsing dishes preparing them for the dishwasher. As time went on, she realized she was really becoming excited about seeing Jerome again. Right then, she decided not to wear her jeans. She decided on a patterned sundress she had which hugged her body in all the right places. She smiled to herself.

"Should be an interesting evening," she said to herself.

Just as Yolanda finished wiping down the counters and sweeping the floor, Tanya came out. "I'm finished in the bathrooms and I lit potpourri candles in each. Anything else?"

"Can you help me with the lawn chairs?"

"Sure."

"Thanks, T. I mean it. You're such a good friend. In fact, you're like a sister to me. I've wanted someone in my life like you for so long." They hugged again.

"On another note. You mentioned dates. Are you going to have one?"

"I will. There's a guy that has been asking me to go out for a while now and I just called and invited him. He said he'd come. Hope I'm not bringing sand to the beach," Tanya said laughing.

Yolanda shook her head. "I don't think so. But who's this guy?"

"His name is Glenn Tragg. He's a chef at Caswell's."

"A chef? How in the world did you meet a chef?"

"I met him at one of those 'kitchen parties' one of my neighbors had. He did the food."

"Is he good?"

"You've eaten at Caswell's right? How's the food been?"

"Good point. That is some good food in there. So, what's he like?"

"He's just a big old country boy. But he seems to be really nice. People I know who work at the restaurant tell me he's just as nice as he could be and so I guess I'll find out tonight."

"Well, good. I'll look forward to meeting Mr. Tragg. Oh, by the way, I decided to wear a sundress tonight instead of my 'bad girl' jeans."

"Of course you'd change your mind."

"T, you can wear a skirt of mine if you want."

"No. I'll think I'll stick with my jeans. In those jeans, Chef Tragg is gonna be mind blown."

"This should be an interesting night, T. "

"I bet it will, YoYo. When will Bernard get here?"

"He said he and his friend Rick will get here around five. He came to my office today."

"Oh really? What's up?"

"Just more of the same shit. I don't quite know how to get through to him that I don't want a relationship with him."

"Don't worry about it. He'll get it sooner or later. I know he'll get it when the Professor gets here."

"I hope he won't start buggin', T. I don't want any of that shit tonight. I just want a smooth, fun evening."

"Stop worrying Yo. We're gonna have a great time tonight. We need to start getting dressed though."

"You're right. You can use the shower in my bathroom. I'll go upstairs."

They split up and began preparing for the evening.

What a day it had been. After the presentation to the students of SOCA, I went to my office and answered voluminous e-mails. I also went through the stack of snail mail, signed forms and coordinated appointments with our departmental secretary, Edna, turned in grades from my most recent exams and recorded all grades from the papers I had graded on my patio.

The faculty lounge shower felt good. I stepped out and toweled off. At the mirror in the locker room at the college, I looked at my face again. I wondered what Yolanda's response to my no-mustache look would be. As I dressed in the clothes I brought with me for Yolanda's cookout, I realized how glad I was that my workday was ending. I was really looking forward to tonight for a host of reasons and I wanted to see the university fade into my car's rearview mirror.

The grill was already going when I got to Yolanda's house in Indian Trail. I could see the blue smoke and smell the aroma of cooking meat and I was hungry. But more than that, I was excited. I hadn't seen Yolanda in months.

There were several cars in the driveway and I parked mine on the street in case I had to get out. I hated to be blocked in a driveway, especially at a party. I sprayed on some cologne, checked my hair in the visor mirror, and grabbed the vegetable tray, the bottle of Yolanda's favorite red wine and a bottle of cognac I picked up on the way and went to the door.

Yolanda's friend, Tanya Willis answered the door. "Well, well Jerome Mitchell. Haven't seen you in a while. Here let me help you." I handed her the tray and followed her in the house.

There were a few couples there listening to music and talking. "Everybody, this is me and Yolanda's friend Jerome."

There were various *'hellos'* and I responded. "Hi everybody." Tanya put the tray in the refrigerator and came back to me.

"Don't I get a hug?" Tanya asked. We hugged. "Oh, Jerome. You smell good. What are you wearing?"

"*Polo* and thanks. You look great Tanya. "Haven't seen you in a while." Tanya really looked good. Her light brown, shoulder-length hair shined. Her light colored skin looked healthy and her green eyes sparkled. She looked slimmer and the jeans she wore really made her look especially sexy. But something else was different.

"Tanya, did you lose weight or something?"

"Actually, I did drop a few pounds since I last saw you. How long ago was that?"

"At least six or seven months, I think. I ran into you at the movies, remember? I think that was the last time I saw your girl, too."

Tanya said nothing. I couldn't get over the feeling that something else was different about Tanya. "Now, Ms. Redbone," I said as I looked at her, "what else is different about you?"

"Yeah, I got your 'redbone', chump." Tanya said as she playfully punched me in the shoulder.

I held her chin up with my fingertips. "I know what it is. "Where are your glasses?"

"Contacts," she said. "You've got a good memory, professor. I'm impressed."

I lowered my voice, put my head close to hers. "So, are those your real eyes or store-bought ones?"

"These are real, man. Real."

"Go on gurl. You know I'm single now and me and you can…" I put my arm around her and pulled her close.

"Nigga, don't even think about it." Tanya pushed me away from her, laughing.

"Oh, well. Your loss, sexy." I looked around then turned back to Tanya. "What are you doing with yourself?"

"Nothing different. Still working downtown. I did start photography classes though."

"Well, that's good." I looked at some of the people sitting around, drinking or grooving to the music.

"Speaking of Yolanda, where is your girl?"

"I don't believe we were speaking of Yolanda. Actually, I think you were hitting on me." Tanya laughed. "But don't feel bad."

She stood on her toes and whispered in my ear, "It's the jeans." We both laughed.

"But Yolanda ran to the store to get some more charcoal and lighter fluid. You know she left the bank and is now on track to be chief magistrate in the county."

"Really? No, I didn't know that. Wow, life just keeps on moving, huh?"

"Sure does," Tanya agreed with a smile. She then took my hand, pulling me with her. "Let me introduce you to my date."

"Oh, no wonder you're buggin'. You came with a date, huh?"

"Shut up, professor and come on. Tanya walked me over to a tall, heavy-set brother sipping on a water tumbler of brown liquid. It looked like pure liquor to me. I made a mental note to hide my cognac from this big brother.

"Jerome, this is Glenn Tragg. Glenn, this Yolanda's friend, Jerome."

I held out my hand. "Pleased to meet you, brother."

Glenn did the same. We shook. My hand practically disappeared in his. "Same here man," Glenn said in a deep, but almost musical voice.

"So, Jerome. What did you bring in that bag?" Glenn asked, pointing.

"Oh, this is some red wine Yolanda likes and some cognac for me."

"I'll take the bag, Jerome," Tanya said. I gave her the bag.

"Wine? Cognac? You need to have a man's drink. Let me fix you some Jack Daniels. You do drink JD, right?" Glenn reached for a bottle of Jack Daniels.

"I have, it's just not my favorite. But I'll have some." I figured if he made the drink, I could hide my cognac. At the rate he filled a glass, he would finish his bottle quickly and then begin eyeing mine. Shit, cognac is expensive.

Glenn got up and moved to the kitchen. He rambled through the cabinets until he found a glass as big as his. He put in two ice cubes and then filled the glass with liquor. The ice in the glass promptly melted.

"Ease up, Bro. I can't drink all that!"

"Oh no?" Glenn then put the glass to his lips and drained at least a quarter of the liquid. He then handed me the glass. "How's that?"

I looked at Tanya for assistance. She just shook her head and looked away. "Well, there is less than there was. Thank you, but I'll just wait until I get some food, then I'll join you and this JD."

Just then, Yolanda walked in. Her cheery 'hello everybody' got my attention. Boy, was I glad. I had a hard time picturing Tanya with this big brother and damn, drinking out of a glass and giving it to me? What the hell was he thinking? I turned and looked at Yolanda. Tanya and Glenn began an animated but muted conversation. I just hoped Glenn wasn't a mean drunk. He was too big to be drunk and mean.

Yolanda looked good. Her sundress went just below her knees. The dress fit her perfectly and set off her skin tone. The flare in it was perfect and made me almost swoon.

Her hair was shorter, but it still framed her face in such a lovely way.

The straps of her dress seemed to slither up her body, over those round breasts and magnificent shoulders then disappear down her back. The white top under those straps fit her nicely and hugged her body. Not too tightly, just right.

Yolanda's smile continued to be her most magnificent feature. Though her face was a little fuller than I remembered, that smile seemed to take up her whole face. God help me, I still love that face.

"Romey-O! You made it. I'm so glad!"

"Of course, Yo. I said I would." I walked toward her, carefully measuring my steps. As I got closer, I opened my arms and Yolanda slid in like an airplane gliding into its hangar. Lastly, I closed my arms around her. Oh, man. She smelled so good.

"Yo, you feel good. And you look great," I told her as I stepped back still holding her around the waist.

She looked at me and smiled. "Thank you, Jerome." She looked at my face, curiously. I could tell she was looking at my bare upper lip.

Suddenly she pulled me close and kissed me. A hard, tongue-less kiss. A kiss of promise. I held her tighter. I only let her go when I felt her struggling to get loose.

Once I let her go, Yolanda took my hand and pulled me toward the two guys who came in with her. Only then did I even notice them.

"Jerome, I want you to meet Bernard Fox and Rick Manzetti. They are our cooks today and in their other lives, they are deputy sheriffs." I held out my hand to them. Yolanda took her thumb and wiped her lipstick off my lips as Bernard, Rick and I shook hands.

"Jerome, come talk to me!" Yolanda said before I had barely finished shaking hands with the 'deputy cooks.' She pulled me by the hand toward her room. She looked back at the guys at the door.

"Bernard and Rick, can y'all take over for a moment?"

"Sure, Yolanda. We'll handle everything for you, ma'am," Bernard said, but there was a noticeable testiness in his voice. He and I made eye contact for a brief moment. His gaze was steady. His face held no emotion. For a moment, I wondered what that was about. Then I felt the insistent tug on my hand by Yolanda. I forgot about Bernard and followed her.

Once in her room, she kicked the door closed with her foot and kissed me again. This time our tongues explored each other's mouths, hungrily.

I slid my hands down her body, my hands closing on her round, firm ass. I felt the thin material of her panties through her dress. Yolanda moaned as she kissed me.

"You miss me, baby?" she asked while still kissing me.

"You can't tell?" I responded while still kissing her. Her hand slid down my arm to my fingers, then to my legs. Her warm fingers found my stiffening manhood and she rubbed it gently.

"Yeah, I can tell." Yolanda moaned again as I kissed her harder and pulled her tighter against me. Just then the door burst open. It was Tanya.

"What are y'all…oops, sorry!"

We broke apart. Both of us were breathing heavily. Tanya looked from Yolanda to me and back again.

"YoYo, in case you forgot, you are hosting a party. Can't y'all cool it for a few hours?" Tanya turned to me with a half smile.

"Jerome, go in there," she pointed to the bathroom, "and get yourself, uh, together. And get that lipstick off your face." She turned to Yolanda.

'And you, you sit down on this bed with me. Don't move until he leaves this room." Yolanda sat.

I went into the bathroom, splashed cold water on my face and wiped off the lipstick with some Noxzema face cream I found in the shower. I took a deep breath, looked in the cabinet and found some creamy after-shave, which I used. I briefly wondered who it belonged to. I also saw some Royal Crown, which I used on my hair. I had a hairbrush in my car. I decided to slip out and brush my hair. I came out and stood in front of the ladies.

"Well?" I looked from one to the other.

"You look fine Rome," Yolanda said as she began to stand up. Tanya restrained her.

"Uh-uh. Sit woman sit," she said. "Stay." Tanya wiped her brow. "I tell ya. You two, I just don't get it." She shook her head as she looked alternately at both of us.

"Jerome, what happened to your mustache?" Tanya asked.

"I shaved it off after the divorce. I decided to grow a beard. What do you think?"

"Ooh, a beard, Rome?" Yolanda stood up. "You will look really good with one. I can't wait to see how it looks on you!"

Tanya got up between us. She placed her hands on each of our chests.

"Out, Jerome, out!" She said with authority. I smiled, nodded and left the room. I then went to my car, brushed my hair and returned to the house. As I stepped in the house, my name was called.

"Jerome!" It was Glenn.

"Yeah, what up Glenn?"

"Come on out back with me and have a seat. Where you been?"

"Just ran out to my car for a moment. Now I need a drink."

"Want some JD?"

I laughed. "Glenn, brother. You're better than the Bud frogs and lizards. You working for the JD company?"

He laughed. "Naw. I just know what I like, you know what I mean?"

"Yeah, I do." We went to the kitchen. "How much JD did you bring with you?"

"Man, I bought two half gallons. One in here and one in the car, if it's needed." He held out his hand for 'five'. I gave it to him.

"That's a lot of liquor, bro." I watched as he poured JD in a fresh glass. "Yo, man add some 7-UP in it for me, Ok?"

"Cool. No problem." Glenn did as I asked and handed me the glass. I tasted it. It was a little strong, but it did calm the fire Yolanda had ignited.

"Not bad. You missed your calling. You could have been a bartender."

Glenn smiled. He shrugged his large shoulders and shook his oversized head. "Yeah, right. I'm no good hearing people's problems. Bartenders hear that shit a lot. I think people just whine for no good reason." He looked at the sliding glass door then back at me. "You ready to go outside?"

"Yeah, I think so," I said following Glenn out on the deck. Bernard and Rick were cooking up a storm. They looked like a true Mutt and Jeff combination. Rick was over six feet tall. His blond hair was covered by a *Pittsburgh Steelers* hat. Rivulets of sweat rolled from under his hat as he worked.

Bernard stood about five-ten. He was stocky and muscled. He had a slight potbelly covered by a black tee shirt and a long white apron. His short brown hair was covered by a *Charlotte Checkers* hat turned backwards. His legs were muscled and hairy as they extended from the bottom of his white, denim shorts.

Glenn and I peeked at the meat while the tops of the two grills were lifted.

"Wow, you guys are kicking it!" I said to them.

"Thanks man," Rick responded. Bernard said nothing. So I spoke to Bernard directly.

"Brother Bernard, I know you're jamming on those ribs, huh?"

"Yeah, right man. Right." He never looked up. I continued to look at him for a moment. Bernard then opened the sliding glass door and went in the house. He closed the door behind him.

"Hey, Rick. What's wrong with your friend? Did I do something to piss him off?"

"Naw man. Don't worry about it. Bernard just gets moody sometimes. He's ok. Just kind of quiet with people he don't know."

"Cool. Thanks for the heads up."

"No problem, man. You having a good time?"

"I will when I get some of that food you cooking."

"Well, we got some burgers ready. Y'all ready for a couple?"

Me and Glenn walked closer to the grills. On the table outside were plates, utensils, buns and napkins. We grabbed a plate and a couple buns and waited for the clear sign.

"You brothers want some cheese on these burgers?" We both nodded.

After a few minutes, Rick opened the sliding glass door. He announced that there were some burgers, hot dogs and baked beans ready. He also yelled for Bernard to bring the steaks and chicken out.

Folks in the house came out. Me and Glenn got our food and took up residence in a couple lawn chairs in the back yard while we ate. In between mouthfuls and running back and forth for cold beer and more food, me and Glenn talked.

I learned that Glenn is a chef at Caswell's, a well-known uptown soul food restaurant. He learned his chef skills at Meck Tech, a community college here in Charlotte. I shared with him that I taught at the university.

"Carter G or the white one?"

I smiled at his characterization. "The white one."

Glenn continued chewing slowly before he spoke.

"Oh. I went to CG for a couple years on a football scholarship, but I just wasn't ready for college, so I dropped out. I bummed around for a while doing odd jobs and some illegal shit. I always liked to cook, so my friends convinced me to go to Meck Tech and learn how to cook 'right'.

I did my apprenticeship at some of the uptown hotels and I got hired on my first interview at Caswell's. I've been cooking there for a couple years. While I don't like to blow my own horn, I've won a few awards for my creativity in the kitchen."

"Man, that's great, congratulations. Yolanda should have let you cook."

"Man, I cook all the time. I don't want to cook on my time off, you know?"

"Makes sense." We lapsed into silence while we ate and drank a little more. I was beginning to like Glenn. But I did wonder how a man his size maneuvered in a kitchen.

"Hey Jerome?" He cleared his throat, took a deep swallow from his glass of JD wiped his mouth with a balled up napkin and looked at me.

"Look man, I'm sorry I drank out of that glass, earlier. It was a stupid thing to do and I don't know what I was thinking. Forgive me, brother."

"No problem."

"Tanya was not a happy person. She said it made me look country, among other things."

Tanya was right about that. "Well, don't worry about it. No harm, no foul. All's well my brother."

"I don't know, man. This is my first date with Tanya. I've been after her ever since I met her, to go out with me. I don't want to embarrass her. Cause then, she'll never go out with me again. See I ain't got it like you got it with Yolanda." He pulled his chair closer to mine, lowering his voice.

"That sister is absolutely fine. You are one lucky brother, Jerome."

"Lucky about what?"

"Man to man?" Glenn asked in a low voice. I nodded. Intrigued with what would come next.

"Man, there ain't a brother here that wouldn't want to be with her." He took another drink. "Well, all except for me." I chuckled at the sheepish look on his face. He looked up on the deck. I followed his gaze.

"You know," he continued, "I think that's what may be bothering the cook. He probably was planning to be with her tonight. I saw his face when she kissed you. Damn, I bet that's it."

Glenn was probably right. In my excitement, I hadn't noticed the look on Bernard's or anyone else's face once I saw Yolanda walk through the door. I looked up at the grills, focusing my eyes on Bernard, but he never looked up. He seemed to be glued to whatever he was cooking on the grill. I hoped Bernard wasn't planning on blocking this evening.

All of a sudden, my head started spinning. Probably too much alcohol. I decided to drink water for a while. I got up and went to the house for a pitcher of water.

"What you got there?" Glenn asked when I returned.

"Water. I think I've had enough alcohol to drink for a while."

"You plan to drink water the rest of the night?"

"Yep, at least most of the rest of the night. Glenn, you play bid whist?"

"Hell, yeah. Why?"

"They got a game going on in there. Let's go spank somebody."

"Cool. But you gotta drink with me. I can't play cards with a water drinker."

"You got to, Glenn. I've had enough, but if necessary, I'll find another partner.

Just then Yolanda and Tanya came over to us. Yolanda bent down to kiss me on the cheek.

"YoYo?" Tanya said with a warning in her voice.

"What?" responded Yolanda.

"That's right. Leave them alone and bend down here and give me some sugar, Tanya," Glenn said. As if on cue, each of them bent down and kissed us.

"Girl, you have no idea how fine you look in that outfit," Glenn said.

Tanya looked at Yolanda and they both smiled. 'Mind blown.'

I whispered in Yolanda's ear. "When the time is right…"

She whispered back in my ear. "The time is almost right. Soon we'll be alone. We have some catching up to do." She stood up. "Ooh, it's getting chilly out here. We're going in. And there's a bid whist game going. You still play, Rome?"

"I sure do. You?"

"Nobody better. I'll bet me and Tanya can put a hurting on you and any partner you choose."

"Shit, then let's go and see what y'all got."I got up and holding Yo's hand walked up to the deck and in the house. I made eye contact with Bernard along the way.

"Bernard, you and your partner put your foot in this food today. I need to get you two to cook at a barbecue for me sometimes. "Bernard looked at me.

"We don't hire ourselves out, brother." He practically spat the word 'brother' at me. "I did this for Yolanda. She frequently comes to me for stuff I can do for her. So, don't even think about it."

The smile left my face. He and I stared at each other for a moment.

"What's up with you two?" Yolanda asked, looking from me to Bernard.

"Nothing," I said. Bernard just shrugged his shoulders and turned back to the grill. He took off his hat, wiped his forehead with the back of his hand and put his hat back on, still backwards.

"Bernard, Rick. You've done enough. Just take the rest of this stuff off when it's done and come inside and hang with us for a while. I think you've cooked more than enough for everyone. Ok?" Yolanda said quietly.

Rick spoke up. "Yeah, sure Yolanda. We'll get this finished and come right in. Right, Bernard?" Bernard just grunted.

"Alright y'all. Just don't stay out here too long." Yolanda walked in followed by Tanya, Glenn and me. Bernard glared at me briefly, then looked away slamming the top of his grill shut.

"Man, what's up with you?" Rick asked Bernard.

"Nigger think he all that. He ain't shit. Talking about hiring us to do barbecue for him."

"Damn, B. He was just bullshittin'. Chill out. Look, man. I know you buggin' about Yolanda, but this dude is her choice for the night. You need to chill, ok? I mean we got some hot little sexies waiting for us later tonight anyway. Right?" Bernard did not respond.

"Right?" Rick asked again lightly punching Bernard in the shoulder.

Bernard smiled. "Yeah, we do. Fuck it. Let's get all this meat off the grills, get cleaned up and get out of here.

I got my clothes and Yolanda said we could use her shower before we left. You got your shit?"

"And you know this, B. Let's get a shower. Get this barbecue smell off us and then go hook up with our honeys. Ok?"

"Yeah, that's cool." Bernard looked inside at Yolanda. Rick came over and followed his eyes. He elbowed Bernard.

"Man, forget about her tonight. You see her almost every day and there's always another time." He grabbed the roasting pot filled with grilled meat and corn on the cob wrapped in aluminum foil.

"Let's go." They went inside.

"Everybody give it up for our wonderful cooks today!" Yolanda said loudly over the music. Everybody clapped and whooped. Rick smiled broadly and bowed at the waist. Bernard dipped his head in acknowledgement.

"Yolanda we got some other stuff to do. Can we use your shower to get the food smell off us?" Rick asked.

"Sure. Get your stuff. The towels are…"

"I know where everything is," Bernard said looking directly at me. He turned to Rick. "You take the shower upstairs and I'll use the one down here." He looked at Yolanda. "Is that cool?"

"Yeah, that's cool. Just make sure y'all clean up after yourselves, hear?" Rick laughed and Bernard half-smiled. Bernard and Rick went out the front door, returning minutes later with hangers of clothes.

While Rick and Bernard showered, there were three tables of four playing bid whist or spades. Others were watching the quartets play, hooting, laughing and calling 'next.' Still others were listening to music as they watched a muted basketball game on TV.

Just as Rick and Bernard were about to leave, Bernard asked if he could use the phone. When Yolanda gave him permission, Bernard looked at me for a long moment, then went into the bedroom and closed the door.

"This was supposed to be our night, girl," Bernard said to a picture of Yolanda, with her arm around Tanya, sitting on her dresser.

Bernard opened the top drawer in the nightstand by Yolanda's bed. He picked up a green spiral book with the words 'My Contacts' written on it. He stared at the door of the room, listening intently. The sounds of the card games in the other room continued unabated.

Satisfied he had a few minutes to himself, he opened the book. He looked for his number. Finding it with a question mark next to his name caused his eyes to narrow. Then he found Jerome's number with a smiley face near it.

"You bitch," he said to the closed door. Going through the book, he found a number he was sure would cause some trouble.

"Bastard think he all that, huh? Let's see how Mr. Smiley Face deals with this." He smiled wickedly as he wrote the number on some paper he found in the drawer, stuffing it in his pocket for later. After putting the spiral book back where he found it, he left the room.

The night continued on. Around eleven, people started leaving. By eleven forty-five, only Tanya, Glenn, Yolanda and I were there. We were cleaning up when the doorbell rang.

"Who is that?" Tanya asked.

"Probably somebody who left something," Yolanda responded. We all stood in the living room looking toward the door as she looked through the peephole.

"Shit," she hissed.

"What is it, Yo?" I asked. She didn't answer me. The doorbell rang again. I was glad Glenn was still here.

The doorbell rang again. This time the bell was followed by a thumping on the door.

"Yolanda, it's Claude, open the door!" The male voice on the other side of the door said loudly.

"Oh shit," Tanya said.

"Who's Claude?" Glenn and I asked simultaneously.

"Yolanda's ex." Tanya responded. She looked at me briefly then averted her eyes.

I took a deep breath and shook my head. I should have known. I sat shaking my head.

Yolanda turned and looked at me. "Rome, I didn't—"

"Just open the door Yolanda," I said interrupting her plea. She did. Claude Boozer breezed in like he owned the place. As the door closed, none of us noticed a pair of headlights attached to a red pickup truck with darkly tinted windows gliding down the street.

"Hey Puff!" he said kissing her cheek. "Hi Tanya."

"Oh shit! You're Claude Boozer, right?" Glenn asked, excitedly. I put my head down. Leave it to Glenn to be impressed at a time like this.

"Yeah that's right." He held out his hand. "You are…"

"I'm Glenn Tragg. Man, you got a wicked jump shot."

"Uh, Glenn…" Tanya shook her head looking at him. Glenn got the hint and calmed down.

"Claude, what are you doing here?" Yolanda asked tightly.

"What am I doing here?" Claude asked looking at Yolanda with surprise on his face. "I got a call from one of your girlfriends to come over because you wanted me join you in your little cookout. I admit I was surprised, but glad. But how come you didn't just call me yourself?" He walked over and attempted to hug Yolanda.

"Uh, Claude." She looked at me, while avoiding Claude's embrace. I stood up.

"Claude, I'm Jerome Mitchell. Good to meet you."

"Good to meet you, Jerome." He looked from Glenn to me.

"If either of you want tickets to a game, let Puff know and I'll hook you up. They may not be on the front row, but they'll be pretty good seats."

Glenn smiled and nodded, "That sounds good. Thanks, man."

Tanya cleared her throat looking at Glenn. Again, he settled down. He busied himself with his glass of JD.

I stretched my arms and stood.

"Yeah, ok. Look, I'm leaving and I'll talk with you later Yolanda." Still I hoped Yolanda would send Claude packing.

"You don't have to go, Jerome." She turned to Claude. "I didn't have anyone call you, Claude. Maybe you got a call, but you didn't get a call from any friend of mine. And you know that. I don't operate that way."

Claude looked around. He seemed to ignore Yolanda's statement.

"So this was your 'other plans' for the evening. Pretty sneaky, Puff. That's must be why you had your friend call me."

"Claude…" Yolanda rubbed her forehead. I looked from one to the other. I wasn't for any drama tonight. Damn. Yolanda had to give me some type of clue as to what she wanted me to do. Claude walked toward the kitchen asking for food.

Tanya looked at me and shrugged her shoulders. She seemed to be as confused as I was about what to do. Yolanda took one look at me and then followed Claude to the kitchen.

I guess that was the clue. "Look, I'm gonna go. Thanks for everything and the set was really nice."

Glenn and Tanya got up to leave. Glenn wouldn't make eye contact with me. It was an awkward situation. Tanya put her arm around me and squeezed.

"Don't be mad, Jerome," she whispered to me. I could only purse my lips in return.

"YoYo, we're leaving," Tanya announced.

Yolanda came out of the kitchen. She walked over to me.

"Don't leave yet Rome," she said quietly.

"Why not?"

"I'll figure this out. I didn't invite him here."

"Yeah, right." I sat again. I really didn't know what to do.

"You ok, honey?" Tanya whispered. Yolanda nodded. "Ok, we're gone." They left.

With a solemn look at me, Yolanda returned to the kitchen. A few minutes later, she and Claude exited the kitchen. Claude had a large plate of steaming food and a huge mug of beer. I stood.

"Hey man, I didn't know you were still here. I'm not interrupting anything am I?" Claude said looking from me to Yolanda.

"Nope. I was just waiting to say good night. Good to meet you, man." Claude didn't respond.

"Thanks for the invite, Yolanda."

"You're welcome. Thanks for coming," she responded. Her face and voice were crestfallen.

I opened the door and walked out into the cool night air. As I got to my car, headlights came on and a car pulled up even with me. The window rolled down. It was Tanya and Glenn. Tanya was driving.

"Jerome, we decided to wait to make sure nothing would go down. You ok?" Tanya asked.

I nodded. "Thanks, Glenn, Tanya. I'm fine. Just a little pissed that's all. Who called that guy?"

"Tanya is just as confused about that as you and me are. But she'll talk to YoYo tomorrow and find out," Glenn said, somberly.

"If it's any consolation, Jerome. She didn't want to be with him. She's been excited about seeing you all day," Tanya said.

"No. It's no consolation. I'm out here. He's in there. Oh well, I need to go home."

"You want some JD?" Glenn asked holding out the bottle.

I smiled in spite of myself. "Ok, Glenn. Give me the bottle." He did and I took a healthy swig from it.

"Easy, partner. That ain't your poison," Glenn said.

I handed him back the bottle and got in my car.

"You're cool?" Tanya asked. I nodded. They pulled off. I started my car and sat there for a few minutes. Yolanda's door never opened, so I took off.

On the way home, I stopped to buy a six-pack of beer. By the time I pulled into my apartment complex, I had consumed three of them and thrown the cans out the window. Boy, was I pissed. I dragged out of my car and trudged into my apartment. I sat in my chair, sipping my fourth beer trying to think of what to do.

My answering machine indicated I had four messages. I listened and fast-forwarded shortly after I was able to identify the voice or the person said their name. None of the calls were from Yolanda.

Mr. Basketball. I bet that was his after stuff I used in Yo's bathroom. Aw hell no! I went to my bathroom and scrubbed my face.

'If you want tickets, I'll hook you up,' I said mimicking Claude Boozer's voice as I dried my face with a hand towel. I know I'm buggin' but the heck with it. How dare that fool offer to 'hook me up' with tickets.

"I can buy my own tickets, thank you!" I said out loud to the mirror. Besides, it's not like the team's winning anyway.

I turned on the television and watched one of the true crime shows while getting more and more steamed at what just happened.

'What's done is done', I said to myself.

I pulled out my address book. If ever I saw a time for a booty call, this was it. I called an old flame, Karyn Lawrence.

"Hullo?" a groggy female voice answered.

"Wake up, Karyn, it's Jerome."

"Who?"

"Jerome. Wake up Karyn. I know it's been a while, but don't act like you don't know who I am. Wake up."

"I'm awake, but I'm not Karyn. I'm her roommate Iris. Karyn's not here."

"Well, just tell her I called, ok?" I prepared to hang up. Oh man. This just wasn't my night. I felt so pitiful I wanted to laugh.

"Wait, wait. Don't hang up," Iris said.

"Why?" I sensed an interesting turn of events.

"Pretty late to call somebody, isn't it? It's after one in the morning."

"And so?"

"And so," she drew out the word 'so', "what did you want with my roommate at this hour?"

Don't tell me this woman wants to play detective, I thought to myself. To Iris, I said, "Just wanted to see how she was doing."

Iris laughed. "At almost one in the morning? Come on, Jerome, you didn't even recognize that my voice wasn't hers."

"And so?"

"And so, we're both adults. This is a booty call isn't it?"

"Not anymore. Karyn's not home."

"No, but I am."

"What are you saying?" My heart began to beat a little faster in my chest.

"What do you think I'm saying?"

I took a deep breath. "Sounds to me like you want me to come over, anyway. That right?"

"You're pretty smart, my man." Her voice was enticing.

"What about your roommate?"

"When was the last time you and Karyn spent time together?" I was silent as I tried to remember.

"That long, huh?" Karyn asked interrupting my recollection. I could have sworn I could almost hear her laughing to herself.

"Well, it is true it been a while. I've been busy—"

"Brother man," Iris said cutting me off, "that ain't none of my business. But one thing's for sure. Y'all ain't in a committed relationship. Right?"

"That's true," I responded slowly. What was she getting at?

"Jerome, me and Karyn are roommates and we've been friends since college. She and I wouldn't let a man get between us. Besides, she doesn't have to know everything. You coming?"

I was quiet. I had to think. What kind of woman would just invite someone over she didn't know? Maybe she thinks I'm a safe bet because her roommate knows me. Maybe, she's just crazy. Maybe, she just honestly wants some company. What to do. What to do.

"Hello? You still there?" Iris asked.

"Yeah. I'm still here. I'm just thinking about your offer."

"What's there to think about? You want some company and so do I. So I'll ask you for the last time, you coming?"

"We've never seen each other. I know Karyn has described me to you. Why don't you describe yourself to me."

"No honey, don't be thinking you all that. Karyn has never described you to me. In fact, I don't think she's ever mentioned you. As for me, you come for potluck or you stay home. That's the deal. Personally, I like potluck."

Maybe it was the beer. Maybe it was the JD. Maybe it was an unconscious desire to 'get back at Yolanda.' Maybe, it was just my ego. I don't know. I knew just what to do.

"I'm on my way. Thirty minutes, max."

"See you, then, sugar," she responded.

I hung up, gulped down my beer, grabbed my keys, a couple condoms and went out the door. Before I got to my car, I decided to go back inside and grab the last two beers and take them with me.

Heading back to the car, my pager buzzed. I decided not to let anything interrupt the groove I was on, so I turned it off without looking at the number. Once in the car, I tossed the pager in the glove compartment and headed to Karyn and Iris' house.

XV

At five am, I was parking my car at home. I sat at the wheel for a moment. Dawg, I was tired. Iris was a waste of time. She spent most of the time talking about her problem relationships, then wanting to engage in sexual teasing all night. I grabbed my pager and dragged myself to my apartment.

Back in my apartment, I checked the answering machine. There were two messages, both from Yo. I decided not to call her back, at least not for a couple of days, anyway. I took a shower and fell into bed, pressed the sleep button on my clock radio, so I could sleep to jazz.

It seemed that I had only been sleep for a minute when the phone rang. I let the machine answer it until I heard Billy's voice. I decided to answer.

"Billy?"

"Man, you sound like you still sleep. Wake up, it's after ten."

"Brother man, I just laid down. I'm beat. Long night."

"Long night, huh? Where you been?"

"I went to a set at Yo's and…"

"Yolanda's? Man, what were you doing over there?"

"Man, I'm just too beat to get into this with you, right now. Let me get some sleep and I'll tell you all about it tonight."

"Tonight? What about the Classic? You change your mind about going to the game?"

"Shit, the Classic. I did forget. What time is kickoff?" Please be a late kickoff, I prayed.

"Let me look at the tickets, hold on." I put the phone on my ear and held it with my shoulder wedging the head set against my pillow as I closed my eyes. I could hear Billy fumbling around. "Ok, I'm back. Let's see, uh, four o'clock. How's that?"

I silently exhaled. "That's good, I need some sleep first. So, what's the plan?"

"It's my turn to drive. I'll pick you up around two. How's that?"

"Billy, can you make it three?"

"Three's cool. Man, I can't wait to hear about last night. Alright, I'm out. I'm going to the lake with a new sweetie I met. Tell you what, I'll hit you on your pager with 911 just before I come, ok?"

"There ain't much to tell," I mumbled.

"That's alright. I still want to hear about it. Ok, then. Sleep tight, Rome. Don't forget about our wager, though."

"I won't. Just don't forget your wallet. Peace."

I hung up and reached over to set my alarm clock for 2:00. I turned off the ringer on my phone and pulled the sheets up. It was 11:20. The jazz music was soothing. Next I knew I was out.

The knocking on my door and the continued bell ringing woke me. "What the hell?" I sat up working hard to orient myself. The knocking on my door became more insistent. I glanced at the clock, it was 1:00. "This better not be Billy," I said to myself as I gathered myself to walk toward the door. I grabbed my robe and slow walked to the door to see who was so fired up to get in my house.

"Oh, shit," I whispered as I looked out of the peephole. I took a deep breath, then opened the door. My visitor rushed in, already talking. She and I never got past the foyer.

"Rome, before you say anything. I'm sorry about what happened. I mean I didn't expect Claude to come over. In fact, I'm pissed off that he did. I really wanted to be with you last night. You believe me don't you?"

I sat in the foyer with my back against the wall. "Yeah, Yolanda. I believe you. You came all the way here just to tell me that?"

"Well, I called and paged you, but since I didn't get a response, I decided to come in person." She looked around self-consciously. "I'm not interrupting anything am I?"

"Why would I let you in, if you were?"

"Well, you got your robe on and you look like I woke you up. You ain't in there with nobody, are you?" Yolanda looked back toward my room.

I smiled and shook my head. "Yolanda, you are really something, you know that? I was really looking forward to last night. Only you can have so much drama going on you. Shit, you'd think I'd learn my lesson about you, by now."

"What the hell does that mean?"

"It means I wanted you so bad, that I could taste it. Then this Mr. Basketball muthafucka comes in and I got to go." I stood, facing her.

"You know, you didn't have the courtesy to say goodnight to me. I even waited outside thinking you would come to your senses and send Mr. Basketball packing, but hell no. You know Yolanda, that's pretty fucked up. If the situation were reversed..." I just shook my head and lapsing into silence looking at her.

Damn, she looked good, though. Those black jeans were fitting her really well. Her hair was pulled back and her lipstick was wet. I pulled my robe closer around my body. I was naked from the waist down. *'No hard on...no hard on...'* I thought repeatedly to myself.

"I'm sorry, Rome. Claude caught me off guard. I knew you were angry." I shook my head. "Don't shake your head, Rome. Please don't. Let's sit down together, ok?"

"Yolanda, I had a long night and I need some sleep. Me and Billy are going to the Classic and I need some rest." I had to admit that Yolanda's contrite attitude was a turn on.

"Well, I guess I better go so you can get your rest." She said the word 'rest' with her voice laced with disappointment. "Will you call me after the game? I'd like to see you if possible and make it up to you."

"Yolanda, I'll think about it, ok? I tried to sound still peeved at her, but those moist, full lips weren't helping my resolve. "Will you be at home?"

"I don't know. Why don't you page me. When you call, just use our code. You do remember it, don't you?"

"Of course I remember it, Yolanda. Triple zero, right?"

She smiled. "Yeah, that's right. May I have a kiss before I go?"

Aw shit. "Yolanda," I said. I attempted to sound as authoritative as Tanya did yesterday when she threw me out of Yolanda's bedroom.

Yolanda stepped back looking down at me. Her left eye was closed and her head was cocked to the left as well. Her fists were balled and placed firmly on her hips.

"What's wrong with me, Jerome?"

"Wrong?" I stood and leaned against the wall in the foyer.

"Yeah, wrong?" Yolanda's gaze was steady and unwavering. Then she turned and walked into the living room and sat on the couch looking at me. She took a deep breath.

"Jerome, I get so tired of relationship drama." I followed and sat beside her pulling my robe as tight as possible against my body.

Her eyes were moist. Was she gonna cry? I pulled her to me. When I kissed her, I let my passion loose. She responded in kind. Our tongues began their exploration recklessly.

"I want you, Rome. I want you now." I wanted her too.

I took her hand and led her back to my bedroom. Yolanda sat on my bed, with moist lips and moist eyes.

"Take off your robe, Rome," she said quietly. I did as she asked. She stood up and ran her hands up my arms and over my chest. "Still working out I see," she said with a smile.

I looked into her eyes, I began unbuttoning her shirt. I pulled it out of her jeans and finished the unbuttoning job. I opened the shirt and looked at her black bra. It was almost transparent and so sexy. I could only take a deep breath.

I removed the shirt and threw it on the chair in the room. The bra clasped in the front which I undid and slid the bra off her arms. It joined her shirt on the chair. Her nipples were hardening. I ran my hands over them coaxing them, caressing them.

Yo moaned. She held her head back as I kissed her neck sliding my lips to her breasts. I sucked each nipple until it was like a small rock in my mouth. I gently bit and lashed each with my tongue. She tasted so good.

I held Yolanda as she arched her back. Slowly, I lowered her to the bed. She lay back with her eyes closed. I dropped to my knees and removed her shoe boots and socks. I undid her belt and opened her jeans.

Yolanda lifted her butt as I slid off her jeans and tossed them in the direction of the chair. I stood and looked down at her. She opened her eyes and looked back at me.

"God, you are so beautiful, Yolanda," I whispered. "I want to make love to you. Can I?" She nodded her head and reached her arms out to me.

"No, lay back. It's been a long time. I want to enjoy this for a while longer, ok?" She nodded her agreement. "Get more on the bed," I said softly. She did. I crawled up on the bed and began kissing her neck. "Turn over." She did.

Her ass was so magnificent that I could only exhale as I looked at it. It was barely covered by the satiny, black panties she wore. Her cheeks were flawless and round. I ran my hands over that ass and down the backside of her legs. I could only shake my head as I looked at the body beneath me.

I held up her hair and began kissing her on the back of her neck as I straddled her. She involuntarily flinched at each kiss.

"Oh, Rome that feels so good," she mumbled. Her voice was muffled by the sheets.

"I'm glad, baby. You look, feel and smell so good."

"You want me, Rome? Do you?"

"Yes, baby." I kissed down her spine. I took the time to kiss each cheek of that beautiful ass. Then I kissed down her legs. I stood at the foot of the bed. "Turn over, Yo." She did. I lifted her leg and kissed her foot. Then I encircled her toe with my mouth and slowly sucked it. I remembered how hot that made her.

"Oh, Rome. Rome. I want you inside me."

"Not yet, Yo. Not yet." I released her leg. I dropped to my knees and pulled her body to edge of the bed. I grabbed her panties and with a quick motion, I tore them from her body.

"Rome! Rome!" Yo moaned louder.

I began kissing her up the inside of her thighs. I could smell her wet, moist womanhood as she waited.

"Do me, Rome. Do me!" Yo gushed.

"I will baby. Let me taste you, first."

"Yes! Yes!" she said as she squirmed in my grip.

I pulled her closer to me. I put my nose in her now quivering womanhood. Her scent was so sweet. As I remembered, her pubic hair was neatly trimmed and perfectly done. I flicked my tongue inside of her, tasting each juicy morsel of her.

"Yes, Rome, eat me baby! I missed you so much! Oh, yes!"

"I will baby, I will," I responded. "I missed you too. Open up for me." Yo's fingers went to her now dripping womanhood and spread open her lips exposing her quickly hardening clit. Her painted fingernails were long and tapered and looked especially sexy against her chocolate skin and the lips of her womanhood. I took her clit in my mouth and lashed it with my tongue.

"Oh, God, yes! Yo said. Her fingers were holding herself open. "Do me, Rome. Oh, God!"

I replaced her fingers with my own. One of her hands moved to my head. The other grabbed at the sheets on the bed. As I worked her clit, her grunts and sighs were coming faster and faster. If there had been a nuclear explosion, I wouldn't have known about it or cared. She tasted so good. I couldn't get enough.

"Stop, stop!" Yolanda said huskily.

I did as she asked. Once her breathing slowed, I attacked her womanhood with fervor. This time I wouldn't stop, no matter what. For long minutes I sucked and licked. I heard her moans and shrieks and I held her legs even tighter in my arms. Her thighs throbbed and vibrated.

Yolanda's screams shook the bed. Her thighs clamped tightly against my head. I loved her orgasms. They were acts of perfection.

"I…can't…breathe…I…you…Rome…I…OH, GOD!"

As her breathing slowed, I pulled away from her womanhood and began kissing her inner thighs again. "You ok?" I whispered.

"Yes, yes," she whispered several times. "I guess I forgot…uh…never mind. Come here and kiss me."

I crawled up on the bed and lowered my head to kiss her.

She rolled me over and began plastering kisses on me as fast and as furiously as she could. Down my body she went. Her sucking on my nipples was unbelievably good. She licked and bit them. Once I flinched.

"Did I hurt you, Rome?"

"Just a bit."

"Good. That's for not calling me back."

I just shook my head. "Touché, my dear Yo, touché." Yo continued her journey down my body. She whispered as she kissed and sucked on me.

"Your thighs are so hard…you taste so good…I missed you, Rome…I really did." She ran her finger along the length of my dick.

"Oh, yes, and I have truly missed him," she said with a small laugh. "I want you to go sit in that chair." She pointed to the chair where her clothes were deposited.

"Now?"

"Yes, now. Go ahead." As I got up to go to the chair, she slapped me on the ass. "Not bad, Rome. Not bad at all."

"Thank you, Yo," I responded as I rubbed my ass where she hit me. Before I sat, I tossed her clothes on my dresser. I sat and waited for her.

"Open your legs for me," she said huskily. Yo took lipstick out of her purse and put it on. I watched and marveled at how sexy she was. I also wondered where her purse came from. I thought I had seen it on the couch in the living room.

"I'm gonna take care of him," she said pointing at my penis, "as good as you took care of her," she pointed to her vagina.

She took a pillow off my bed and placed it on the floor in front of me. Then she got on her knees with her forearms balanced on my thighs. She looked at me as she lifted my penis and began licking it from the underside. Her tongue lingered at the tip.

"You like that?" I nodded in response. She did it again and again. Each time she lingered a little longer at the tip of my member.

Then without warning, she took the whole thing in her wet, hot mouth. I could only grab the arms of the chair. Oh man. If there was anything better, it was still in heaven.

Each time she went down on me, I was barely able to contain myself. I put my hand in her hair and held her as she went up and down on my rod. Her fingers played gently with my balls. She stopped going down on me and with a lustful look at me, she began licking the head of my dick.

"You like this, Jerome?" she whispered looking at me as her tongue continued its work.

I could only nod my head. I closed my eyes and leaned back in my chair. This was so good. Yo knew every little button, every spot.

I felt like I was spinning. I tried to take deep breaths, but her mouth was doing such an expert job, I gave up. Then she stopped again. Yo used her hand expertly pumping up and down on my rod. Damn. This was just too good. I opened my eyes and looked at Yolanda.

Her eyes were locked on my penis. From time to time she licked her lips. I ran my fingers down her face. She never looked up, but she kissed my fingers as they moved past her lips.

I felt my body jerking. "Yo, I…can't…oh man…"

"Let it go honey," she said soothingly. "I want to see it. Let it go." She dipped her head and tasted me again. "You taste so good. So sweet. I love it when you dribble. Ooooh!" She pumped me harder. "Give it to me, baby. Just relax and give it to me."

I closed my eyes. "Baby…I…I…"

"Give it to me, Rome. Give it to me…"

I exploded. "Oh, baby…Yo…Yo…"

"Yes, baby. Oh yes, Rome. It's so beautiful. Soon, I'll want more." She looked at me and smiled. "You ok?"

"Yes baby. So good. I'm sorry I…"

"Shhhh." Yo smiled as she looked at me. "That's what I wanted. The next time, you'll be inside me. Let me clean you up."

I took a deep breath and nodded. Yo left and returned with a hot, wet, soapy wash cloth. She cleaned me and it felt really good. "You know, Yo. This had to be what I felt like to be a baby and get cleaned by my mother."

"Don't be thinking about your mother while I'm cleaning your dick, mister."

"Good point." Just then the rhythmic screech of my pager filled the room.

"Must be one of your other women calling," Yolanda said sarcastically.

"Must be," I said just as sarcastically. Yolanda squeezed my penis. "Ouch, damn girl, I was just kidding. Would you hand it to me?" Yolanda walked across the room, grabbed the pager off my nightstand and tossed it to me. It was Billy.

"What time is it, Yo?"

"About quarter to three, why?"

"Billy's on his way. Let me up." Yolanda stood and watched as I fell on the bed reaching for the phone on my nightstand. I dialed Billy's pager and put in my number with '911' at the end of it.

"I'm going to take a quick shower," she said.

Just as the water began, the phone rang. It was Billy.

"What's up, Rome?"

"Billy, I'm not even ready. How long will you take to get here? I had an unexpected visitor."

"About fifteen minutes. Unexpected, huh? Who?"

"Yolanda," I whispered.

"Yolanda Walker, huh?" Billy said. Then he exhaled loudly.

"Yep. She's in the shower now."

"So, you ain't going huh?

"Yeah, I'm going. But I won't be ready in fifteen minutes, though. That's all I'm saying."

"Ok. Look, I'll just come over and then we'll leave when you're ready. How's that?"

"That's cool. But can't you just get here about three thirty?"

"Damn, Rome. Ok. Three thirty. But look. I got some plans after the game for BOTH of us. Can you hang or are you tied up with Ms. Thang?"

"During and after the game, I'm all yours, bro. Ok?"

"Cool. See you at three thirty. Later!"

"Peace." Just then, Yolanda came into the room with a bath towel wrapped around her.

"Y'all getting ready to go?"

"Yeah. But look, I heard from Tanya last night about your new job and you'll soon be the head magistrate. Congratulations."

"She can't keep nothing to herself, I swear," Yolanda said with a smile. "But thank you. I am enjoying what I'm doing. At least I like it better than working at the bank."

"Well again congratulations, Yolanda. I gotta say, you do keep moving. That's impressive about you."

"What a compliment! Thanks, Jerome."

"Of course. Now, I know me and Billy will probably be out most of the night. I would like to finish what we started."

"I do, too. Tell you what. Why don't we plan a night sometime soon when we can get together. Call me and let's do that, ok?"

"Ok, but I wish you had waited for me to take a shower with you."

"Then you would have never gotten to that football game, Rome. I guarantee it."

She continued dressing. "Rome, this was wonderful."

"I agree with you. This was really good. I'm glad you came over."

"Are you still mad at me?" she asked. I looked her incredulously.

"I'll take that look to mean 'no.'" Yolanda pushed me toward the bathroom.

"Now, you better get in the shower. I'll wait till you come out, before I leave."

While I got the shower water to the temperature I liked, I found myself briefly thinking about something my brother Robert told me shortly after he met his future wife Jewell.

"Jerome, there are two perfect times to make love to a woman. You know what those times are? "He took a deep breath.

"The very first time and the first time after a long time."

Now I knew what Robert meant.

While I was in the shower, my phone rang.

"You want me to get that?" Yolanda yelled into the bathroom.

"What?" I yelled back over the noise of the shower.

"You want me…oh never mind…" Yo went to the phone. "It's probably Billy anyway," she said to herself. She picked up the receiver. "Hello?"

"Hello? Is this Jerome Mitchell's home?" the soft feminine voice asked.

"Who were you calling?"

"Never mind." And the caller hung up.

"Well, good bye to you, too." Yolanda said to the dead phone and hung up.

"What are you doing? "I asked Yolanda. I stood before her naked and wet from the shower.

"Nothing. I was planning to call Tanya, but I changed my mind. Look, I'm gonna go. Call me later, ok?"

"Ok." We kissed as I wrapped a towel around my waist then Yolanda rushed out the door. Through the partially closed blinds, I watched as Yo got in her car and drove away. The phone rang.

"Hello?"

"Jerome? Jerome Mitchell?"

"Yes. Is this you, Sam?"

"Yeah, it's me. I'm calling from Charleston. Just wanted to say hello. I called earlier, but a woman answered. She was kind of rude so I hung up."

"Oh, sorry about that, Sam." I pursed my lips and shook my head. Yolanda! No wonder she rushed out in such a hurry. I know she knew better than to answer my phone.

"Are you having a good time?" I asked Sam.

"Actually, I am. Look, I was to meet with you on Monday but I wanted to tell you that I won't be back until Monday evening. I've already called Edna at home and she said she would take care of everything."

"You need me to cover for you?"

"No, I'm just going to cancel classes. I don't want to rush back, you know? I've needed a break for so long."

"Ok, well no problem. Call me when you get in and we'll reschedule, ok?"

"Are you sure that's not a problem?"

"No, it's not a problem, Sam. Have fun and I'll see you when you get back."

"Ok. Well, I've got to go. See you on Tuesday."

"Ok, Sam. Tuesday it is. Bye."

Sam hung up, but the slightly familiar woman's voice on Jerome's phone stayed in the back of her mind.

My phone rang again. "Hello?"

"Hey brother man. I'm in the parking lot. Is it alright to come in?"

"Yeah, fool. Come on." I laughed and opened the door while I continued dressing.

"So, what's been going on?" Billy asked as he entered the apartment.

"Billy, you won't believe the night, and day I've had. I'll tell you all about it while we go to the game. I promise you it's a good story."

"A good story? I thought you said there wasn't much to tell."

"I did. But man, how things have changed."

"Damn, I can't wait. But after you tell me that story, I got something special planned for us after the game. You are gonna be real happy, brother. Real happy."

"Sounds good. Let's just get out of here and hang out, for a while." I grabbed my keys and we left the apartment. While he drove, I told Billy the story of my Friday night and early Saturday afternoon.

XVI

As the ball went through the uprights, the crowd noise was almost deafening. With the score 30-27 and six seconds left on the clock, the hometown, CG Woodson Golden Warriors were almost assured a victory over the South Carolina A&M Wolves, breaking a five year losing streak in this annual game.

Practically, everyone in the stadium was on his or her feet. The Woodson University Golden Warriors' band and the A&M band were dueling it out in anticipation of the upcoming kick off. The ball sailed through the October sky, high but short. The Wolves' receiver began running with the ball. As the clock ticked down to 'zero' Wolf teammates made a series of laterals in an attempt to keep the return alive.

Warrior fans wailed as one of the A&M players took a lateral and broke away from the pack. Just as he made a cut to avoid the kicker, he fell and the alert Warrior kicker immediately fell on him. The referees' whistles blew and the game was over.

The Warrior team rushed the field as did many of their fans and alumni, to celebrate the end of a losing streak to the SC Wolves. The Warrior marching band partied in the stands as did the students.

The cheering or groaning fans made a cacophony of noise. Young men and women, presumably students at the two schools yelled at each other, Warrior students danced in jubilation while A&M fans pretended not to notice. With many of the Warrior fans, Billy and I stayed for the trophy presentation and the bedlam that accompanied it, once the trophy was presented to the Head Coach and President of CG Woodson. The Woodson players were jubilant.

I held out my hand to Billy, who reached in his pocket and but a twenty dollar bill in my hand. We watched the massive crowd exit the stadium.

"Man, what a game, " Billy said almost breathless.

"Damn right. Truly a classic. Sorry about your school's loss."

"No problem, bro. We gave as good as we got. And my boys almost pulled out the impossible. I'm just glad you didn't change your mind about going with me." Billy swallowed the last of his soda. "You ready to go?" he asked. I nodded and we headed for the exit.

While walking to the parking lot, we enjoyed watching various sisters also leaving. Every once in a while, we'd stop and talk a little junk to them. Being single was sure nice, today.

Billy and me exchanged numbers with several fine, black women. A couple times we were asked if we knew *'where the party at?'*

Billy's standard answer, "Wherever you and I can be alone together. Even if being alone is in a crowded room." Sisters usually smiled and said, *'Puleez!'* or *'Alright, now!'*

"Billy, you are one smooth talking brother. I'm going to be just like you when I grow up."

"Yeah, right. I think your aspiration is right on time, but sadly," he put his hand on my shoulder, "you'll never match my awesome power with women. Sorry, Son!"

By now we were at the car. "Man, unlock the doors and let me in the car," I told him. As I got in, I shook my head. *'Awesome power? Shiiiiiiii....'*

Traffic crawled as people hollered greetings to one another and as men tried to pick up some of the women walking to their cars.

Billy and I enjoyed the girl watching and from time to time we laughed as we were able to hear some of the lines brothers were using as they called to women who passed by them.

"Yo, sister! C'mere, c'mere! What you gon' do tonight? Why don't you hang with me. I'll do anything you want to do and some things you don't want to do. Heh, heh, heh!"

Me and Billy smiled and shook our heads. "That's a line that won't result in company tonight." Billy said. I gave him 'five' concurring.

Once free of the congestion leaving the stadium, Billy turned to me.

"So, your booty call didn't work out, huh?"

"Naw, man. That sister wanted to talk and just play most of the night. She wasn't serious."

"But why'd you stay so late, Rome?" Billy said laughing.

I laughed with him. "Billy, you know how we are man. Just trying to *'keep hope alive,'* man. I figured if I stayed long enough, she'd get tired of talking, run out of energy and just give it up."

"Never ran out of either one, huh?"

"Never." I shook my head as I looked at Billy. "Man I was so horny last night I was willing to promise that woman almost anything!"

"I know what you mean, man. I've been there myself. Too bad, Rome. But then, there's your girl Yolanda."

"Yeah, Yolanda." I nodded my head and looked out the passenger window. "Where are we headed?" I asked.

"I thought we'd get some juice to go with the gin I got in the trunk and then we're off to Rock Hill."

"What's in Rock Hill?" I asked.

Billy snuck a look at me. "Hey Rome, don't try to change the subject of Yolanda. That fine-ass sister did you right, huh?"

"Damn right, man." We gave each other 'five'. "But she only did me 'right' after I did her 'right' you understand."

"Mr. Jerome Mitchell, or should I say *'Gentleman Jerome'*. You are ever the gentleman," Billy pushed me on the shoulder as he said that.

I leaned back in my seat. "Ah, yes. *'Gentleman Jerome'*. I like the sound of that."

"Yeah, yeah," Billy said. "I hear all that 'Gentleman Jerome' stuff, but you owe me. I called and got you out of conversation and that cuddling she would have wanted, right?"

"And you know this!" We both laughed and gave each other 'five', again. "Now what's going on in Rock Hill?" I asked.

"Jerome, my brother. Prepare yourself." It was clear that Billy was relishing what he was about to tell me. He glanced at me out the side of his eye as he drove, had a big smile on his face and shook his head all at the same time.

"In Rock Hill, there is a house. In this house there are three women. Two are white and one is black. Got that picture, so far?" I nodded slowly. "Good. Now add this to the picture.

"On a scale of one to ten with one being butt ugly and ten being mega bomb, the worst looking one living in this house in Rock Hill is an eight. You still with me?" I nodded, only faster and I began to smile.

"One of them is in Philly for the weekend, modeling. The eight wants me bad, but would only let me come over if I came with a single friend for her roommate."

"And her roommate rates a …?" I asked.

"Let's see, I hate to give tens because that leaves no room for improvement. But in all honesty, I wish I met her first. Rome, she's got to be an eleven."

"Is this the white or black one?"

"One of the white ones. The sister is the one I'll be with." He looked over at me. "Will that be a problem for you?"

"Nope. What about her?"

"Rome, Vernay says that the only men her roommates are really interested in are black guys. Rome, these girls do underwear ads and shit!" Billy hit the steering wheel. "Rome, I'm telling you, this is going to be a great night. You down?"

"I'm definitely down, Billy. You sure they're going to be there?" We had pulled into the 7-11 lot. "You got to call and confirm or something?"

Billy thought for a moment. "That's a good idea, just to be sure all is copasetic."

He motioned with his head at the row of pay phones. I followed his look. Every one of the phones had someone on it.

"Don't worry. Why don't you pull up. While you go in the store I'll stand by the phones and grab the first available one."

"Good idea, Rome. Let's do that!"

Billy parked in front of the pay phones and we got out. He went in the store and I waited for a phone to become available. Shortly, a young sister hung up, looked at me and smiled.

"You finished?" I asked her. She nodded and walked away without another word. Just as I picked up the phone, Billy approached me with cups filled with ice and a bag with a bottle of grapefruit juice in it.

"Cool Rome, you got a phone. Here take this." He handed me a cup of ice and the bag of juice. Reaching in his pocket he took out a slip of paper as he grabbed the phone I held out to him.

"Why don't you make us a drink, while I make this call, Rome?"

I nodded and went to the trunk of his car, which seemed to magically open.

I filled our cups with gin and juice and walked back to the phones to join Billy. He had just connected as I handed him his cup, which he sipped and gave me the 'thumbs up' sign.

"Is this Vernay? Hey girl, this is Billy...Told you I would call...Why not?... Baby, there is no way, I wouldn't call you.

Look, we still on for tonight? Yeah...yeah...no, I'm serious...Allison still down?...yeah?...yeah?...I do...he's right here, wait a second..."

"Rome," Billy put his hand over the receiver. "This is my girl, Vernay. V as in victory-E-R-N-A-Y. She wanted to be sure I was bringing somebody with me. Talk to her." He held out the phone to me.

"Vernay?…yeah my name's Jerome…yep…yep…divorced…uh-huh…Is your roommate there?…good…can I talk to her?" I looked at Billy. He gave me a 'thumbs up'. "Hello?…yeah this is Jerome…

you're Allison, right?…good…thanks and you?…good…yeah, what time?…ten?" I looked at Billy. He nodded and smiled. "Ten is good."

Again, I looked at Billy. Now he gave me two thumbs up. "Yeah, I like your voice too…you want us to bring anything?…Oh, you got everything we need, huh?…Cool. Alright, ten it is." Billy was reaching for the phone. "Can you put Vernay back on for Billy?…yeah, ok…see you then…me too…later."

I handed the phone to Billy and moved to the next available phone to call Yolanda. She wasn't there, so I left a message on her voice mail.

When I hung up, I leaned on the hood of Billy's car, sipping my drink, watching Billy as he continued his conversation with Vernay. He was writing directions on the back of the phone directory.

"Ok, got that…now what's the name of the street with the blinking light, again?…" He wrote furiously. "Ok, I got it…look," he looked at me and smiled "…since you're going to the store anyway, do me a favor…" Billy looked at me and gave me nod.

"What?" I mouthed to him. He put his index finger up and nodded.

"I want you to buy a red light bulb and put it in your outside lamp. That way it'll distinguish your house from all the others on the block and it'll look real hot when we pull up." He paused. "You will?

Good. V, when the clock strikes ten, we'll be parking in front of your door." He paused again.

"Ok, I'll change it back once we get in the house. I will, no problem. Trust me!" He hung up, tore the back cover with the directions off the phone book and looked at me.

"Man, you are crazy!" I laughed as I walked back to the car.

"Crazy like a fox." Billy turned back to the phone and picked up the receiver.

At Cynthia's prodding, Akeba had suggested an evening date with Craig, a professional photographer. Prior to tonight, since meeting at a pool party a couple months ago, their time together consisted of coffee and weekday lunches.

She felt giddy about the date tonight and she had changed outfits three times.

It had been a long time since she had been out on a date on a Saturday night. She stood in front of the mirror wearing the outfit she started with an hour ago, a midthigh, fitted deep blue skirt, which had a slight slit in it, with a matching waist length leather jacket, white silk blouse with a medium plunge and navy heels. Akeba then glanced at the other clothes on the bed.

"Mom, you keep changing clothes. You look good in all of them. I really like that, though," Danisha said.

"Really? I hope so. I want to look just right!" She turned to Dani.

For a moment, Akeba felt a twinge of guilt. Should she be dating? She took a deep breath. The feeling went away.

The doorbell rang. Akeba and Dani looked at each other, frozen. Akeba moved first.

"Girl, go on down. Make sure it's Mr. Witherspoon and invite him in. Tell him I'll be right down."

Dani ran downstairs. She looked through the peephole and verified that it was indeed Mr. Witherspoon, her mom's date. Dani deactivated the security system and opened the door.

"Hello, Miss Danisha. Good to see you again. Is your mom ready?"

Dani smiled. She liked Mr. Witherspoon's deep voice. "Hi, Mr. Witherspoon. Mom said she'll be right down."

He sat and exchanged small talk with Dani until Akeba came downstairs. He stood.

"Wow. Impressive," he said, watching Akeba descend the stairs. He took her arm and the three of them went to his car.

After dropping Dani off at the sitter's house, Spoon and Akeba arrived at their destination, where Witherspoon was slated to take photographs of the fund raising event happening that night. After parking, Spoon got out and opened the trunk to get out his equipment.

Spoon grabbed one of his cameras. "Akeba, let me get a picture of you before we go in. She smiled and stood next to the car. The slight chill in the air felt good to Akeba.Spoon snapped a couple photos.

"How about a little cheesecake?" he asked. Akeba put one hand on her hip and pulled her skirt up a couple inches with the index finger of her other hand.

"Oh, yeah, sweetie. That's good!" Spoon gushed.

Akeba let go of her skirt and put her face in her hands, giggling. "I can't believe I did that!"

"Well, you did baby and you looked so good. You need to consider doing some modeling."

"You think so?"

"Psyche!" Spoon laughed. Akeba swung at him as he danced away from her.

"You are so lucky I don't have anything to throw at you!" They both laughed as they walked into the hall together, Spoon pulling a cart with his photographic equipment on it and Akeba by his side.

"Damn, Billy, where we headed? Seventy-seven is in the other direction." I said.

"We got some time, so I figured we can stop at one of my partner's house."

"Where we headed?"

"There's a part time security guard at the building where I work who I talk to sometimes. In fact, he's the brother whose house Robert dropped me off at. Remember me telling you about that? He lives near here and we can stop there, twist one and bullshit before we head to South Cack-a-lacka."

"Oh yeah," I said nodding. "You went there to buy a sack." Billy nodded.

I continued, "I remember. So, what's up with him?"

"I don't know. He seems cool, but at times, he's got an edge. You know what I mean? It's hard to explain."

"What, like he's crazy or something? That what you mean?"

"Not really. It's like he's mad about something and it's just under the surface.

"Man, I'm a college professor. Don't be taking me to no crazy man's house for smoke."

"Ease up, man. Bernie's cool. But to be sure, let's not piss him off," Billy said laughing. "We'll blow one and split."

I took a long drink from my cup. "Billy, how do you find these edge of night characters?"

Billy just shrugged his shoulders. "Just lucky, I guess. I found you, didn't I?"

"Don't even try it." I pushed him in the shoulder. "You're lucky me and my brothers even let you hang out with us. You little cockroach."

"I got your cockroach," Billy said grabbing his crotch with his right hand. We both laughed. I think the gin and juice were having some effect on me. In addition to the comfort of me and Billy's long-standing friendship.

I shook my head to get back in the moment. "So, how does a part time security guard get money for the weed and pay his bills?"

"I think he works full time somewhere else. I don't know where, but I heard someone say that it's in law enforcement. I don't know. Shit. You planning to be his financial advisor or something, Rome?"

"Naw. Just asking." I turned and looked out the window. The name 'Bernie' seemed to mean something to me. I couldn't place it.

Oh, well. After about fifteen minutes, Billy pulled in front of a house on a small street off Beatties Ford Road.

"This is it, Rome." We got out and went to the door. Once the door opened, I immediately recognized the person at the door. Billy greeted the person.

"Bernie, what's up?"

"What up, Billy?"

"You, baby! Want you to meet my best friend—"

"Jerome," Bernie said interrupting the introduction. "Yeah, we met. Come on in."

"What's up, Bernard?" I said, extending my hand. He took it lightly, dropped it quickly. Then he turned and walked in the house. Me and Billy followed.

"So, Billy what brings you by here. You don't need more shit already?"

"Well, to be honest just a little for me and my friend here. We got some stuff to do tonight and we plan on baying at the moon."

"Where y'all headed? To Club Premier?"

"Nope. We're on our way to South Carolina to get with some ladies there. We got some extra time, so we decided to stop by and check you out. I figured we could blow one with you." Billy slid off his jacket and threw it on a chair.

"That's cool. Let me get my stash."

"Bernard?" I said. He turned to look at me. "Don't you deputies get piss tested?"

Billy looked from me to Bernard, quizzically. "Deputy? I didn't know you're a deputy. Wait a minute, how you two know each other?"

I responded to Billy. "We met at Yolanda's party last night."

Billy smiled. "Oh, you're the Bernard, Rome was talking about who was cooking at the party, huh?" he asked Bernard.

"Yeah, me and my boy."

Ignoring Billy, I continued talking to Bernard. "You two left early, to hook up with somebody, right? How'd it go?"

"It went alright." Bernard sighed. "Look, y'all want to burn one or not?" We both nodded. "Cool." Bernard looked at Billy. "Thought you said on the phone you had some gin?"

"I do, but it's in the car. I'll go get it." Billy got up and ran out.

After the door closed behind Billy, I turned to Bernard. "Look, Bernard, if I said or did something to piss you off last night, let me know."

"Naw, forget about it." After rolling a fat joint, he lit it, took a long pull and passed it to me.

I took the joint and took a hit. After exhaling, I looked at him. "It's just that something—" Just then Billy came in.

"Damn, I forgot my keys." He picked up his jacket and took the keys out the pocket and went back out.

"—Something was in the air between us," I continued after Billy closed the door. "What was that about?" I asked Bernard.

"Just my own shit. How'd it go with you?" he asked through a thick cloud of smoke. He looked at me intently.

"What do you mean?"

Bernard took another pull on the burning joint. He looked at me as he exhaled the smoke. "You know, later with Yolanda?" He began to smile as he looked at me.

I felt a dull thudding in my head. Something was not quite right with that smile. "Nothing happened. We're just old friends that's all."

"It didn't look like it, the way you two greeted each other."

"Yeah, well that's her way, you know?"

"I don't know. She's never greeted me that way and I've known her longer than you. I heard she's dating a hometown NBA star, uh, Boozer."

"Look, I don't know about that. Who she dates is her business."

"Yeah, right." Just then Billy came in with the bottle of gin.

"Y'all started without me, huh?" Pass me the weed, puff, puff, pass" Billy said doing a good imitation of Chris Tucker. We all laughed. Billy took a deep pull on the joint and handed Bernard the bottle at the same time. As he exhaled, he looked at Bernard.

"You know, Rome is right. What about your piss test? You don't need to lose your job."

Bernard got up silently. He left the room and returned with three small bar glasses. He sat and poured gin in each glass and left the bottle on the coffee table, still open.

Bernard shook his head. "I ain't worried about those piss tests. I always beat them, anyway."

"How do you do that?" I asked.

"I got all kinds of tricks, you know?"

"You need to school a brother on your techniques."

"Maybe, one day," Bernard said as he sipped from his glass of gin.

Billy snorted. "Bernie's one of the county's finest. I'll be damned."

"You didn't think I could afford my life on a part time security guard income did you?" Bernard said holding the joint up in front of his face pointing it at Billy, while he spoke through the cloud of blue smoke.

"Your lady friend who was here the other day was nice," Billy said taking the joint from Bernard.

"Melody? Yeah, she's ok. Mostly make-up beautiful, you know what I mean? You look at some of these hot looking bitches, and then without their make-up they look like a hot mess." He chuckled. Me and Billy just looked at each other.

"But yeah, Melody said the same thing about you, that you seemed to be a nice guy."

"Can a woman be any more right than that?" Billy said laughing.

"Don't know, guess you'll have to ask her someday, if she ever comes around. We kind of on the 'outs' right now. She wants more than I even want to give."

We smoked and drank in silence for a while.

"I heard that the sheriff's office has access to a lot of confiscated drugs and money," Billy said.

Bernie drained his glass of gin. He looked pointedly at Billy.

"You saying I'm dirty or something?"

"Naw man, I'm not saying that. I was just bullshittin'. Ease up." Billy looked at me. I shook my head.

"What?" Bernard asked looking at me.

"What, what?" I said with a calmness I didn't feel.

"Why you shaking your head?"

"Damn, man. I'm just wondering why you took that shit so serious. Nobody thinks you're stealing from your job." I reached for one of the glasses and sipped the gin, never taking my eyes off Bernard.

Bernard laughed out loud. "I was just fuckin' with y'all." He looked at the joint in his hand. "Damn, this is out." He passed the joint to me and I lit it, somewhat ill at ease.

Billy's laugh sounded fake to me, but then I was getting high so I couldn't be sure. "I knew that, Bernie," he said. He looked at me. "Pass the joint, chump." I did. Billy took a deep pull and passed it to Bernard.

"Yeah well I have to admit, I've wondered if I could get away with it, you know?" Bernard said as he took another pull off the joint.

"But then, it ain't worth it, you know."

He then grew quiet again and seemed to be in his own world for a moment. Me and Billy looked at one another.

Over Bernard's shoulder, I wasn't sure; but it looked like a gun in a holster was sitting on one of the bookshelves. I shuddered a little; then eased closer to the table on which was the heavy glass ashtray we were using for our ashes. Bernard spoke, shattering the silence.

"Now what about these women in South Carolina?"

"We're just rolling down there, hanging out with these two sexy ladies. If they had a friend, I'd invite you, but you can come and watch if you want to."

"Naw, I don't think so. If you two gonna be in South Carolina, I need to make a call to hook myself up here in the QC." Bernard poured himself more gin then took a deep swallow from his glass as he looked at me.

"Well, good luck, bro." I said.

"Luck ain't got shit to do with it," he said, looking at me, taking another drink.

Billy cleared his throat. "What's up between you guys?"

I looked at Billy. "What are you talking about?"

"Look, y'all can call me crazy, but I can tell there's some kind of tension between you two. Have I missed something?"

Bernard rolled and lit another joint. "I don't know what you're talking about." He looked at me. "Do you?"

I shook my head and took the joint from Bernard. "Naw, I don't either." I took a hit off the joint and passed it to Billy. "You just buggin' again," I said to Billy.

"So, how you two know each other?" Bernard asked looking from Billy to me.

Before responding, I noticed how stained the tips of Bernard's fingers were. He must smoke a lot, I thought.

"Me and Billy grew up in Philly practically as brothers." I looked at Billy.

"Until he came down here to get educated. Once he found a job, he invited me to come down and I been here ever since.

"Yep, that's true, Bernie. Rome's father always wished that I was his son rather than Rome and his two brothers," Billy said laughing.

"You are so full of shit!" I said to Billy.

"Educated? Where?"

"I went to A&M."

"Y'all lost today, huh?"

"Three points."

"An 'L' is an 'L'."

"True. True." Billy puffed the joint. "That's all for me."

"Let us buy a couple off you for later tonight. We'll all have a drink and me and Rome are out."

"Yeah, ok." Bernard quickly rolled three joints. He looked at Billy. "These enough?"

"Yeah. How much?"

"Give me five bucks and let me keep the gin and we're square."

Billy looked at me. "I'm cool with that. I'm driving anyway. You cool with that?"

"Absolutely," I said. I chose to keep my eyes on the muted USC football game on Bernard's small TV.

Billy took the joints and stood up. "Rome, you ready to roll?"

I looked up, "Yeah, I'm ready." I took a five-dollar bill out my wallet and handed it to Bernard.

What you gon' do, Bernie?" Billy asked.

"I'm gonna call a little sweetie for the night. I know she won't be busy." He and Billy shook hands. Bernard ignored my outstretched hand. Shrugging, I followed Billy out of the house to the car.

Once we were off the street, Billy turned to me. "So what's up between you and Bernie?"

"Like I told you, I think he wanted to be with Yolanda and it pissed him off that she was with me. You know what? I'll bet he calls her tonight."

"So? Tonight you gonna get your groove on and you had Yolanda earlier today." He looked out the windshield. "Rome, you ain't getting all emotional about her again, are you?"

"Shit, Billy. Just drive the car."

"Ok, but remember, that's not an answer." We rode in silence for a while, listening to the music coming out of the cassette player.

I turned to Billy. "I don't know what's up with your boy, but he's not quite right, you know?"

"Bernie? He's just got a chip on his shoulder. Not everyone is a social butterfly like you and me, Rome."

"I hear that, Billy, but I sure don't want to be around when Bernard's chip falls off his shoulder. And as a deputy, that brother has a permit to carry a gun."

Billy did a toneless whistle. "Tru' dat, Rome. Tru' dat."

We talked no more and the music from the car radio, filled the space between us while we rode toward South Carolina. Once we entered the city of Rock Hill, we stopped to replace the gin we left at Bernard's. I then read the directions Billy wrote on the phone book cover to our destination.

Eventually we pulled up to the house with the red light burning outside. Billy smiled as he looked at me.

"It's showtime, Rome. You ready?"

"I'm definitely ready, my man."

"Good. Here's a couple doobies for you and a couple for me. Grab the bottle and let's go." He hit my shoulder. "Hey Rome, check out that red light."

We sat in the car looking at the red light, burning in the porch light fixture. "Do I got it going on or what?" Billy asked, with a big smile.

"Yeah, you the man alright." We gave each other 'five', got out of the car and headed up the stairs.

Akeba looked in the mirror and reapplied lipstick. She checked her hair and smoothed her blouse and skirt. She took a deep breath and exited the bathroom back into the restaurant at Caswell's.

As she approached the table, Spoon stood up. "Akeba, I could look at you all evening. I am so glad you suggested a Saturday evening date. I've been wanting to ask, but I didn't want to seem pushy."

Akeba smiled broadly as she sat. "Thank you, Spoon." She scanned the menu then looked at Spoon. "What's good, here?"

"Plenty here is good. You want an entrée or an appetizer?"

"Well, I'm not too hungry. There was a lot of food at the reception. I guess I'd like a salad."

Spoon made a motion in the air and a waitress appeared. He ordered a carafe of white wine. He looked at Akeba. "Is that ok?" Akeba nodded. "You want to order that salad?" Akeba nodded again. The waitress smiled as she looked expectantly at Akeba.

"Just a garden salad, no tomatoes or onions with Ranch dressing," Akeba said. The waitress nodded and looked at Spoon.

Stuffed mushrooms for me, thanks."

Very well. I'll be back with your order, rather quickly," she said and moved hurriedly away.

Spoon cleared his throat.

"I'm not a baby boy and I know you're a new divorcee.

From what I've learned in my life, that sets up a rebound kind of thing, you know?" Akeba chewed slowly on her salad, saying nothing. Spoon continued.

"All I'm saying is that while you go through your post divorce stuff, I'd like to stick around, but I know that that doesn't typically happen. Just commit to me that when you're ready to move on, you'll tell me, first. Will you commit to that?"

Akeba sipped her wine and nodded gently. She was touched by his sincerity. She wanted to reach out and touch him, but she didn't trust herself.

She blamed it on the wine.

XVII

In Yolanda's Mercedes headed toward the nightclub, Premiere's, Yolanda and Tanya talked about a myriad of topics. Eventually, they got around to talking about Claude, the cook out and the time Yolanda spent with Jerome earlier in the day.

"YoYo, I knew you would have sex with the professor if you went over there. Was he what you remembered? Details, details!"

"T, Jerome's in better shape than I remembered. Girl, he rubbed my feet AND sucked my toes, damn! He was making me crazy.

Then he went downtown." Yolanda fanned herself with her hand. "Girl, I'm pulling over. I got to get out of this car and …Ooooh!"

Tanya laughed. "Well, alright now! So, what did he say about Claude coming over?"

Yolanda looked at her friend. "T, he was real upset. I know he had a right to be, but it wasn't my fault. For a while there, I thought we were gonna do our *'I got to go'* thing." Yolanda shook her head as she drove. She glanced at Tanya. "You know he and I have a history of just walking away from each other."

Tanya nodded. "Yeah, I know, but the two of you seem to always find each other again, somehow."

Tanya looked out the window then back at her friend's profile.

"Can I say something and you won't get mad?"

At that moment, Yolanda slowed to a stop at a light. She looked over at Tanya. "Go ahead, T. Speak your mind."

Tanya sighed deeply. "Ok. Do you think you two got some kind of obsessive thing going here? You two do seem to find a way to be together. Am I making any sense?" Tanya looked out the windshield.

"Light, YoYo."

"Huh? Oh. Thanks." Yolanda took off, staring straight ahead.

"So, what do you think?" Tanya asked.

"Wouldn't we be hurting folks if we were obsessed with each other, though?" Yolanda asked her friend.

"Well, let's see. Jerome's wife caught you two in her house. That hurt her, broke up their marriage and had some impact on their kid."

Yolanda nodded. "Yeah, you're right," she said quietly. She again glanced at Tanya. "You could be right about this obsessive thing, but like I told Jerome, I'm tired of relationship drama."

"I hear you, YoYo. I think most of us get tired of that shit sooner or later."

"Guess I'm in the later category, huh?" Yolanda said shaking her head.

Tanya shook her head, briefly closed her eyes, then opened them to focus on her friend.

"You know what? Who cares, YoYo. We're together tonight and I'm really glad about that." She turned up the radio. Music filled the cabin.

"Me too, T." Yolanda pulled into the parking lot. "And here we are. You know, we haven't done this in a while. And we look so good!"

"Don't we now! And the brothers will be out, tonight. It's going to be a good night."

"That's for sure, T. Club Premier will be packed. And we are gonna strut our stuff tonight." As they walked toward the door, two men in nice suits approached them.

"Girl, let the games begin," Tanya whispered to Yolanda.

"Yes, let the games begin," Yolanda whispered back.

"What up, B?"

"Yo, Rick. Guess who was just here?"

"Who?"

"Guess, man!"

"B, I'm not playing guessing games on the phone. Look, it's Saturday night and I need to get to a club, somewhere. So, who was there?"

"That guy, Jerome from Yolanda's party, last night."

"What? What was he doing at your house?"

"He came with a brother I know from my part time job."

"Oh, everything cool?"

"Yeah. Think I'm going to call Yolanda tonight, though."

"Man, screw that. There's gonna be some serious partying at Club Premier tonight. With the game in town, everybody's out tonight. Most of them will be in Club Premier uptown. That's where I'm going. That's why I called you. You down?"

Bernard thought for a moment. "Yeah, I'll meet you there. What time?"

"Fuck meeting me there, B. I'm getting ready right now. I'm gonna be at your place in an hour and a half, at the most. Can you be ready by the time I get there?"

"I think I can manage that, Rick."

"Good. Can we ride in that new truck? I really want to hear that sound system you been bragging about."

"No problem. In fact, I'd rather go in my ride. I know Yolanda is gonna dig it. I certainly thought about that when I bought it. I'll see you when you get here. Later." Bernard hung up.

After pondering for a moment, he picked up the phone and dialed Yolanda's house. Her answering machine came on. At the beep, Bernard said,

"Hey, Yolanda. This is Bernard. Just calling to see what's up for tonight. I'm on my way to Club Premier. If you can, come on down. I'd like to party with you for a while. Peace!"

He hung up the phone somewhat disappointed about not having the opportunity to speak with her directly.

"You did, what?" Rick asked looking at Bernard. He hit the brakes and stopped quickly at the light.

The driver behind them blew the horn and waved his hand out the window. Bernard turned to look at the driver in the car behind them.

"You know something? You are one crazy white boy driving like that and you're driving my new truck. That dude could've hit us in the ass."

"B, forget him. Man, what you did was wrong! Why you playa hatin'?"

"Rick, I ain't playa hatin', ok?" Bernard was getting angry. "Last night was supposed to be my night. It pissed me off how he acted with Yolanda, so I decided to mess with him a little." He looked up at the light. "It's green, let's go."

Rick shook his head and slowly took off. "B, if you're going to mess with the man, burn his food, drink his liquor or hide the stuff. You spill wine on him…you send him to a whack barber, you know? You don't call a girl's ex-boyfriend."

"Man, nothing happened. I don't know why you buggin' so tough."

"I'm buggin' because you done lost your mind. By the way, how did you get Boozer's number? I know it just ain't in the phone book."

"What difference does that make?" Bernard looked out the passenger window.

"You're right. Besides, I don't want to know. Look, I know you want to be with Yolanda, but damn, man. That shit ain't right. Calling Boozer just ain't cool. I just hope they don't find out you did that."

"Screw them! Damn! Drive the truck. I need a good party."

"You need something, B. But I'll say no more about it. Let's just dig on this music and get to Club Premier."

"Yeah. I agree. Let's just get to Club Premier." Bernard lapsed into silence and he looked straight ahead. A part of him felt a little guilty, yet he believed that Yolanda should have made sure Jerome was more considerate of his feelings.

"She should have kissed me like that," he said to himself as he pictured Yolanda and Jerome's kiss as she entered the house and saw Jerome there.

"What you say, B?" Rick asked glancing at Bernard in the passenger seat. When Bernard didn't answer, Rick shook his head softly and focused on driving.

With his eyes closed, Bernard found himself imagining himself in Jerome's place, kissing Yolanda. He settled in his seat and bobbed his head to the music.

XVIII

After some convincing by Craig, Akeba agreed to go to Club Premiere with him. Spoon said they were going to meet a client there who was also his friend. While she was apprehensive about it, once in the club she had to admit that the music in Club Premier sounded good.

She could feel the bass chords coming through the carpet into her shoes and up her legs. She glanced over at Spoon.

He looked so handsome. She liked his profile and the way he scanned the crowd. She knew he was looking for Al and she too glanced around.

She nervously expected to see Jerome or Billy in the club. She saw neither, but the club was crowded. She felt a touch on her arm. It was Spoon.

"I see them, Akeba."

"Who?"

"My friend Al and his group at their table."

"Oh," Akeba said sheepishly. "I told you I had too much wine to drink."

All of a sudden, Spoon pulled Akeba to him and kissed her. The kiss electrified her. She put her hand on his chest and looked up at him.

"What was that for?" she sputtered.

"No reason. I just felt the urge to kiss you. You are just so sweet. I thank you for allowing me to indulge myself."

He took her hand and walked her toward the table. Her heart thudded in her chest as he touched her. She could feel his strong fingers as they intertwined with hers. She dutifully followed him through the crowd. As they approached the table, Al stood as did another male at the table whom Akeba immediately recognized.

Al extended his right hand toward Spoon as he and Akeba approached.

"Craig, Akeba! So glad you showed up. Let me introduce everyone." He pointed toward a pretty black woman on his right. "This is my wife, Pamela." Pamela smiled. "Next to her is Pamela's sister, Carlita and her date, Todd." They shook hands all around.

While shaking his hand, Akeba asked, "Todd, how are you?"

"Fine, Akeba. And you?" Carlita looked from Todd to Akeba and back again.

"You two know each other?" she asked.

Todd turned to Carlita. "We work together at the bank in the same department." Akeba nodded and smiled at Carlita as she extended her hand.

"Good to meet you, Carlita. That is such a pretty name. Is it a family name?"

Carlita smiled. She extended her hand as well. "Yes, it is. My great grandmother is Spanish and that was her name. Thanks for asking."

Al beamed. "What a small world. You know, they say that most people are only separated by six other people. Interesting, huh?"

"You got a point there Al," Spoon said. The band launched into an old Commodore song. Spoon began snapping his fingers. "I like this. Come on Akeba, let's dance." Akeba got up and followed Spoon. Spoon turned to Al.

"Order us some white wine, ok?" Al nodded as he began grooving to the beat.

Akeba followed Spoon as he plowed through the crowd, making space on the crowded dance floor. They danced song after song. At times, they were forced together by the crowd. She loved the way his body felt. She enjoyed watching how he moved. So smoothly. So confidently.

When he touched her, Akeba trembled. After another couple songs, the band announced they were about to take a break. Before leaving the stage, they sang a ballad by Atlantic Starr. Spoon took Akeba in his arms and slowly pulled her to him. She could feel his heat through his now damp shirt.

She could smell his cologne mixed with his perspiration. She leaned her head against him.

At one point, she could sense he was looking down at her. She looked up at him. His face was shiny from the perspiration.

"You're hot!" she said.

He smiled at her and pulled her to him. "No, I'm not. But you certainly are." He bent his head and kissed her again. Akeba responded. Throughout the dance, they kissed several times. She pressed against him, feeling his arousal and enjoying it. By the time the dance was over, Akeba knew she had a call to make.

"That is her, I told you!" Yolanda said after swallowing her drink. Tanya looked at Akeba as she danced with the tall, dark skinned brother, then she looked back at Yolanda.

"And so?"

"And so, I don't want her to see me."

"Yolanda, it's been a long time. And as you can see," Tanya motioned toward the dance floor where Akeba was kissing her dance partner, "she hasn't spent a lot of time worrying about it or you."

"Yeah, ok, T. If you say so." Yolanda motioned to the waitress and ordered a couple more Pina Coladas. "Guess you got a point there. Do you know him?"

"No, and to be honest YoYo, I don't care. And you don't need to know either. We're out here to have a good time. But if you are going to sit here and freak out about seeing the professor's ex-wife, then we need to leave."

Yolanda reached out and touched Tanya's arm. "No, I'm not going to do that, T. Seeing her just rocked me for a moment, you know?" Tanya nodded and patted Yolanda's hand.

"Yeah, I do. Just relax, ok?"

Yolanda smiled and sat back. She looked toward the door. She tapped Tanya's arm.

"Well, well look who's coming in." Tanya turned and looked in the direction of the door. They both watched as Bernard and Rick entered the club and looked around. Bernard noticed Tanya and Yolanda and he waved.

He then tapped Rick on the arm and they walked toward the table Tanya and Yolanda occupied. When they got to the table, Bernard spoke first.

"Two beautiful ladies sitting with all this good music playing?" He looked directly at Yolanda. "Damn, Yolanda, you look so good. Will you join me on the dance floor?"

"Uh, hello Bernard." Tanya waved at him. "There is someone else sitting here, you know."

"I'm sorry, Tanya. Hi," Bernard said with his eyes still on Yolanda.

Rick sat and slid his chair closer to Tanya. "Forget him, Tanya. I'm the one who wants to talk to you. We planned all this in the car." He took her hands in his. "So, what up girlfriend?"

"Come dance with me, Yolanda," Bernard said snapping his fingers to the beat.

"I'm not sure I want to dance, Bernard," Yolanda whispered.

"You need to shake your thang, girl," Tanya said. Then in Yolanda's ear, she said, "let it go, gurl. Let it go."

Yolanda nodded, then reluctantly got up to dance with Bernard, still somewhat nervous about having seen Akeba.

Tanya laughed and pulled her hands from Rick's grasp.

"Rick, you got to be the coolest white boy I ever met."

"Me? White?" Rick shook his head and looked at his hand as he turned it over and over. "I ain't white, T. I'm just light skin-ded." They both laughed. The waitress appeared.

"Ok, light-bright. You going to order a drink?" Tanya asked looking at the waitress, smiling.

Rick looked at the waitress. "How about a couple Hennessey's on the rocks?"

"No problem," the waitress responded. She then looked at Tanya.

Tanya shook her head, looking at Rick. "No, I just got another one. I'm fine."

"Ok, just the two cognacs and put a cherry in one of them, ok?"

"Ok. Two Hennessey's and one with a cherry in it." She smiled and moved to the next table.

Rick and Tanya turned their attention back to each other.

As Bernard and Yolanda passed Al's table, Al shook his head as he watched Yolanda walk by. He looked at Todd and Spoon.

"I'm sure glad the ladies are gone. Damn, look at the body on that sister."

The other men at the table nodded their agreement. Al continued watching Yolanda while she danced. Over his shoulder, he said "Now that's a brother who'll roll over and smile all night long."

"What does that mean?" It was Pamela. The ladies had returned. Spoon started laughing.

"Yeah, Al. What does that mean?" Spoon said still laughing.

"What does what mean?" Al asked sheepishly. He looked at Spoon and Todd as if to say, "Why didn't you say something?" Pamela glared at Al for a moment then began to smile.

"Come on and dance with me and you better focus on me the way Craig did when he danced with Akeba." Al got up.

"Absolutely, Mrs. Graydon. Let's show these amateurs how it's done." Carlita and Todd got up and followed Al and Pamela to the dance floor. Akeba slid her chair around and sat closer to Spoon.

"Finally, we're alone," Spoon said quietly. "I am really enjoying myself, Akeba. Thanks for being with me, tonight. Is Danisha alright?"

"She's fine and I'm enjoying myself as well, Spoon. You are a good dancer."

"I try. I try. Did you and your ex dance a lot together?"

"Spoon, don't think I'm trying to be mean, but I don't want to talk about him. Let's just focus on us, tonight. Ok?"

Spoon put his arm around her shoulder and hugged her gently. "Agreed." They turned toward the dance floor and watched everyone partying.

Akeba saw Yolanda. For a moment, she felt a surge of anger. Then she turned to look at Spoon. She relaxed a little. "I refuse to let that bitch screw up my night," she thought to herself.

She was glad she had called Dot and told Danisha she could spend the night. Akeba was determined to make this night last as long as possible.

Yolanda and Bernard were walking to Yolanda's car after leaving Premiere's. Tanya and Rick were a few steps behind.

"Yolanda, I'm glad you were able to meet me here like I asked," Bernard said smiling.

"Well, actually, me and Tanya were planning to come here, anyway, but it was certainly nice to see you and Rick again, so soon after the cookout.

"And me and T are glad you two walked us to the car. There are a lot of nuts out here, tonight."

But I gotta tell you," she took a deep breath and lowered her voice before continuing, "you got a little silly in there. You weren't my date and at times you got a little off center with some of the guys who came to talk to me."

"I know. I get stupid sometimes when it comes to you. Last night, I was really hoping you and I would get the time to really know each other better."

"But I told you in my office that I was expecting someone. And I told you that I really didn't want you to read anything into your helping me out. I like you, but not in that way. Let's keep working on our friendship, you know? I don't like feeling awkward around anyone."

"I certainly didn't mean to make you feel awkward. I just wanted you to know that I wanted to be with you, that's all. And tonight, some of those guys were looking at you like you were just meat hanging on a hook. Brothers need to learn to be more respectful."

"Oh, and you were looking at my mind, huh?"

"Come on, Yolanda. You know what I mean." They had reached Yolanda's car.

"No, I don't know what you mean. Why don't you tell me?"

"Come on, Yolanda. Stop teasing me," Bernard said. He felt panicky. *'A friendship?' 'Awkward?'* he thought to himself. At that point, Rick and Tanya caught up with them at Yolanda's car. Rick had his arm around Tanya's shoulders.

"Man, I tell you. I can't believe it's one-thirty in the morning already. The club was on fire tonight and this woman feels good on my arm Not to mention how good that dress looks on you."

Rick turned to the black Mercedes and slid his hand across the hood. "How long have you owned this?" he asked Tanya.

"Not mine. This beauty is Yolanda's," she said pointing.

"Yes, this is my baby, my guilty pleasure," Yolanda said. "I've wanted one for a while and the opportunity presented itself, so I went for it. Glad you like it."

"I do. I do. You and B got new rides huh? Y'all got it going on!"

"Yeah. I got a new Ram truck," Bernard said a little too loudly.

"And it's got the crazy sound system in it!" Rick added. "But on another note, it just so happens that Bernard and I have free time for breakfast right now and if you are willing, I am buying. Then, Tanya, off to ourselves, you can share with me the naughty fantasies you had of me tonight. And if you ask me nicely, I'll do my best to make your fantasies come true!"

"Look, white negro…don't even try going there! Just sitting in a restaurant with you at two in the morning will be making one of your fantasies come true!" All four of them laughed. Tanya turned to Yolanda.

"What do you think, you want to get breakfast?"

Yolanda thought about it. She didn't want to encourage any more feelings in Bernard, but she was hungry.

"Ok, let's do it." She looked at Bernard.

"In fact, we'll buy since you guys cooked last night. So go get your car and we'll follow you."

Bernard looked at Yolanda. "You'll buy? Right on! But, why don't we all go together? Yolanda I'd love for you to ride in my new truck."

"I don't think so," Yolanda responded. "I got to go to Indian Trail tonight and after breakfast, I'm going straight home!"

"Yolanda, you don't have to go to Indian Trail tonight. You can stay with me, in Charlotte," Bernard said seriously.

"Bernard…" Yolanda said with a sigh. "Look, go get your truck and we'll follow you, ok? That way we'll all get to see it."

"Yeah and hurry up, it's getting chilly out here!" Tanya added. "Girl, let me in the car." She turned to Rick. "See you at breakfast, Mr. Lightskinded." Rick laughed and pulled on Bernard's arm.

"Come on, let's go!" Bernard took another long look at Yolanda as she got in her car and then he followed Rick as they walked quickly to Bernard's truck.

As they got in Bernard's truck, Bernard just sighed. "Man, she gave me the kiss of death."

"B, what the hell are you talking about?"

"Man, she said she wanted to 'work on our friendship'. Ain't that a bitch?"

Rick pulled out and drove to the spot they left Yolanda and Tanya.

"Look B, you got to chill a little. You are taking this thing too far, you know?" Bernard didn't respond. He just looked out of the passenger window.

"B, maybe we shouldn't go to breakfast with them. You sound out of it. B?"

"Naw, I'm cool." He pointed. "There they go. Flash the lights." Rick did as requested.

Yolanda flashed her lights in return and pulled out to follow Rick and Bernard. "Ok, man, they're right behind us. Don't lose them," Bernard said.

Rick nodded. "So, B. Where we going?"

"Go to that place on Central. They got good food in there."

"Cool." Rick did most of the talking. He talked about the women he met and the numbers he collected. Bernard only grunted in response most of the time. He was lost in thought about Yolanda and his feelings for her.

"How could she not see that I am one person who really cares for her?" Bernard thought to himself. He'd convince her. He would let her know what changes he'd go through just to prove his feelings for her.

As Rick drove, Bernard mulled over how he could do just that.

XIX

"Crazy about you, huh?" Tanya said looking at Yolanda's profile as Yolanda drove.

"I told you a long time ago, Bernard felt like that. He probably thought that the cookout was his moment to win you."

"In fact, he kind of said that, T."

"Watch that boy, YoYo. Something ain't quite right with him and his feelings for you. And look at that truck. That is a testosterone machine if I ever saw one."

"You know men and their toys."

"Ok, if you say so."

"T, you need to concern yourself with Deputy Manzetti. He was on you, tough. Any possibility for him?"

"Not now, I do want to spend some time with this new thing with Glenn, but maybe I'll let Manzetti be my down low dick when times get hard. Shoot, you know they say those white boys can really go downtown RIGHT!" They both laughed again and gave each other five.

"T, you are crazy. But back to Bernard, I told him I only want to be his friend. I told him the same thing before he cooked for the party. I wasn't being mean was I? I was trying to be up front with him the whole time."

"Yolanda Walker worried about being mean toward a man? I know we're in the last days now! But seriously, it was good you told him. That way he won't misunderstand, but you know men.

"If they can misunderstand…They Will…" They both said the last part together.

Following Bernard and Rick, they soon turned into the parking lot of a restaurant. They parked a few spaces away from Rick and Bernard's red truck. As they got out of the car, they saw that Rick and Bernard were standing by the truck waiting for them. Bernard pulled a bottle from his pants pocket, twisted off the top and took a quick swallow. He replaced the top and slid the bottle back in his pants pocket. Yolanda and Tanya walked up to them. Rick smiled.

"You ladies ready for some good eating?"

"I am," Yolanda said. "All that dancing made me hungry."

"I could eat something too," Tanya said.

"Prepare yourselves. The food in here is really good, right B?" Rick said, looking at Bernard.

"It's alright," Bernard responded. He took another swallow from the bottle in his pocket.

"Is that the breakfast of champions, Bernard?" Tanya asked with a strained smile.

"At least you recognize a champion when you see one," Bernard said looking from Tanya to Yolanda.

"Yeah, well anyway, let's go in. I'm hungry," Yolanda said.

The four of them approached the door of the busy restaurant. It was full and there was a line waiting to be seated.

"Damn, T, everybody and his mama are in here. Have you eaten here before?"

"Actually, I have and the food is really good for a late night bistro. It's always crowded in here after the clubs close. Don't let the cars fool you. They usually seat pretty quick," Tanya responded.

"That's right, Yolanda. Listen to your girl," Rick said squeezing Tanya's arm. Yolanda just looked around the crowded room. Even the stools at the counter were full.

Tanya was right, they weren't in the restaurant long before they were seated. The waiter appeared with a tray of glasses of water. Bernard ordered a glass of Coke. They chit-chatted as they waited to order.

When the Coke was delivered, Bernard looked around and pulled out the bottle he had been drinking from. He drank a quarter of the Coke and filled up the remainder of the glass with the whiskey. He offered the bottle to the other three, all refused.

"Hey B, you better take it easy, man. You been drinking pretty hard tonight," Rick said.

"It's not the alcohol, my dear Richard. It's the intoxicating beauty of Lady Yolanda," Bernard responded. He turned to Yolanda, "Guess what? That guy who came to your party last night was at my house before me and Rick hooked up with you two at the club."

"What guy, Bernard?"

"The one you kissed when we got back from the store. You know who I'm talking about, don't you?"

"Jerome? That who you mean?"

"Precisely." Bernard took another swallow of his homemade cocktail. There was an uncomfortable silence. The waiter returned. They ordered their meals and the ladies got up.

"Excuse us. We are going to the ladies room," Tanya said.

"You won't need any help, will you Tanya?" Rick asked.

Tanya laughed. "I don't think so, but I'll holler if your services are required." She and Yolanda left the table.

Rick moved across the table to Yolanda's seat. He looked at Bernard. "B, I know you know what you are doing, but I think you need to chill on this line of conversation. You know?"

Bernard swallowed the last of the drink and ordered another Coke. When it was brought to the table, Bernard drank some of the soda then filled the glass with more liquor. Rick grabbed the glass and moved it.

"I think you've had enough of this too, B."

"Manzetti, if you touch my glass again, I won't be responsible for what I'll do," Bernard said with a noticeable growl in his voice.

He reached for the glass and took a healthy swallow. Afterwards, he looked at Rick.

"You know what pisses me off the most, man? Do you?" Rick shook his head, mournfully.

"What pisses me off the most is that bitches like them think they the only pussy in the city. *'Working on our friendship'*. Fuck that. I cooked for that woman, you know? Man…"

Rick held up his hand. "Chill on that bitch stuff, man. Yolanda and Tanya ain't no bitches. You just got your feelings hurt. Don't worry about it. You ain't the first and you ain't the last, either." Bernard picked up his glass and drank again. Rick pointed at Bernard's glass. "And you need to leave that shit alone."

"Alright, alright. No more bitches, Rick, but damn. Be her friend? That chump Jerome ain't just her friend. That Boozer, ain't her friend. What's wrong with me?"

Rick looked toward the ladies room. "I don't know how to answer that question, but chill. They're coming back. You ok?"

Bernard nodded.

"You sure? You ain't going to do nothing stupid, are you?" Bernard shook his head. "Cool." Rick stood as the ladies approached. Bernard shakily followed his lead.

"Glad you're back ladies!" Rick said. "We've missed you." He looked at Bernard. "Didn't we, B?"

Bernard picked up his glass and took a swallow. He nodded and looked at Yolanda. "We sure did." He sat sloppily. Rick returned to his seat next to Bernard across from Tanya. The waitress appeared with their orders.

Yolanda looked at Bernard and turned up her lip. She then looked at Rick. "Your boy is drunk. Forgive me, but I don't like to eat with drunk people.

I don't mean to be rude, but I'm not really hungry anymore." She looked at Tanya. "You can stay if you'd like. I'm ready to go." As she got up, she looked at Bernard who was looking at her legs.

She took a twenty dollar bill out her purse and laid it on the table. Tanya also got up to leave.

Rick stood up. "Come on, Yolanda. He's alright. Stay a while. We've had a good time. Enjoy your breakfast." He turned to Tanya. "T, tell your girl to stay!"

Bernard spoke while still looking at Yolanda's legs. "No, go on Miss *'I got it going on'*." He reached out and ran his hand up Yolanda's leg from the knee to just inside the hem of her skirt. She slapped his hand away.

"Bernard, I know you're drunk, now. At least I hope its liquor and not just an extraordinary amount of stupid. No man touches me unless I allow him to touch me. Now stop staring at my legs and look up at me."

Bernard struggled to his feet. "I'll do better than that, Miss Thang!"

"B, sit down, man. Cool it!" Rick hissed at him.

"Bernard, YoYo, sit down! Don't make a scene in here!" Tanya added through clenched teeth. For long moments, they both ignored the pleas from Tanya and Rick as they measured each other.

"YoYo, come on girl. Sit down. Come on," Tanya said quietly.

Rick pulled on Bernard's arm. "You too, B. Sit down man." Yolanda and Bernard sat warily eyeing each other across the table. The food had long since been forgotten. Other diners were watching intently.

Eventually, the other diners seemed to lose interest in them and their table conversations continued. Bernard broke the silence.

"Yolanda, I shouldn't have touched you like that. I'm sorry, but…"

"See, everything's cool again. Let's eat!" Rick said quickly.

"Not yet," Yolanda said looking at Bernard. "You said *'but'*, go ahead and finish what you were going to say."

"What I was going to say was that we practically grew up together, in Cherry. I've cared about you for a long time. I really wanted to talk with you last night, but you just acted like I was hired help. That hurt."

"Bernard, that was not my intent. And I told you in my office—" her voice faltered.

"I don't care what you told me. You spend a lot of time trying to impress men. How many times have you flirted with me? Now I'm not saying you're a tease, but you got to admit, you dress and walk like you trying to get somebody hot. You then play this *'I wasn't trying to turn you on'* shit. And you've been that way a long time."

"Is that it?"

Bernard didn't respond, just sipped his drink.

"Hello?" Yolanda said snapping her fingers at Bernard.

"Ok, you're obviously pretty drunk and you're mad. That's not a good combination, so I'm gonna go," Yolanda said. She looked at Rick.

"Rick, I'm sorry, but this just ain't good, you know?" Then she turned to Tanya. "I'm sorry honey, you ready to go?"

Tanya looked from Bernard to Rick, then at Yolanda. "Yeah, I guess so." She stood.

Rick also stood again. "Aw, come on, ladies…"

"Fuck that. Let them go, Rick." Bernard growled looking up at Yolanda and Tanya. "You know something? We could be real good together, but no, you waste your time with bastards who only want your packaging. I guess that was kind of hard though when both your lackeys were there at the same time, huh?"

"Bernard, what are you talking about?" Yolanda asked with a deep sigh.

Rick interceded. "You're right, Yolanda. Maybe, y'all better go. B's not doing too well. We'll take care of the check." He handed Yolanda her money back.

"Screw your white ass. Ain't nothing wrong with me," Bernard said to Rick. He looked up at Yolanda. "How did you decide who to fuck, or did you do a threesome last night after the party?"

"Aw B. Cool out!" Rick moaned.

"No, Rick. Let him talk." Yolanda looked back at Bernard. "Go ahead. Say what you got to say, with your drunk ass."

"I bet you was all fucked up when your NBA player showed up, huh?" Bernard smiled and looked around the room. Again, diners focused their attention on their table.

"Yeah, everybody. Check out one of the pro basketball sex machines." He turned back to Yolanda whose face was contorted with rage and embarrassment.

"Now all these hungry people know about you dating a fucking NBA player. You must really think you all that. Those pro players got women like you in every town. And most of them look better than you!"

"You drunk bastard! You called him didn't you? Didn't you?" Yolanda's voice was loud and shrill. "You went through my private stuff and got his number! I don't…"

She picked up a glass and splashed the contents on him. Then she pushed plates and everything in his lap. Before anyone could react, she slapped him so hard her hand stung.

"You sorry, punk! I'm gonna kick your ass!"

Bernard jumped up. A man from another table and Rick grabbed him and held him. The police officers stationed by the door rushed to the scene. Tanya grabbed Yolanda, pulling her away from Bernard and the table.

The restaurant was really buzzing now. The noise of dishes and glasses hitting the floor garnered a lot of attention from the other diners. The crack of Yolanda's hand against Bernard's face caused even more diners to jerk their heads toward the table. Those waiting for tables and those already seated, gawked at the scene unfolding in front of them.

"I can't believe you would do that!" Yolanda screamed at Bernard. While looking at Bernard, she calmed her voice.

"Let me go, Tanya. I'm alright." Tanya began to release her. Yolanda used the opportunity to rush Bernard again. She was intercepted by a police officer that held her around the waist. There were a few catcalls and whistles as Yolanda's skirt was hiked up inadvertently by the police officer who grabbed her. Tanya reached over and pulled her friend's skirt down. The officer spoke to Yolanda.

"Lady, you have to calm down or I'll take you to jail! Calm down!" he ordered. Yolanda nodded.

Bernard struggled to free himself against the guys who were holding him. "Yeah, you better calm down, bitch! You hit me and you know you gonna pay for that!"

"Bernard, you come near me after tonight, and I swear, I'll…"

Tanya put her hand over Yolanda's mouth. "YoYo, stop!"

Rick spoke. "B, you got to calm down, man."

"Calm down? Calm down? Look at me! Look at my clothes! Calm down?" He looked at Yolanda. "No, I didn't call your basketball player, but I know who did. But hitting me? You fucked up now woman!"

The other police officer put his hand on Bernard's chest. "That's enough from you, as well. You'd better calm down, or I'll take you to jail. Listen to your friend."

Bernard took a deep breath. He looked at Rick.

"And I don't know why you're so calm. Acting like you didn't know shit!" Rick turned and looked at Tanya and Yolanda. They both glared at him.

"Hey ladies, I didn't…" Tanya put her hand up in his face. Rick looked down and shook his head. How could B say that? It had turned out to be a really fucked up night. The other police officer spoke.

"Sir, you'll have to sit and be quiet," he said to Bernard. Bernard sat, still glaring at Yolanda. The officer then looked at each person at the table.

"Look, anyone want to press charges, here?" He looked all around at the principals. No one said anything.

"Officer, can we leave?" Tanya asked quietly.

"You can leave after I get your names and addresses, just in case." Yolanda and Tanya handed him their business cards.

He looked at them. "Oh, you're just downtown, huh?" They both nodded. "Ok, you can go." He looked at Bernard.

"You stay seated until the ladies leave, then you can leave as well after I get some information from you."

People moved out of their way as Yolanda and Tanya left the restaurant. At the car, Yolanda asked Tanya to drive. Once in the car, Yolanda began to cry in earnest. Tanya put her arm around her. "You want to stay at my place, tonight?" Yolanda nodded.

"All I ask is that you don't get pissed off at me, Ms. Tyson!" Yolanda smiled through her tears.

"At least I didn't head butt him!" They both laughed weakly.

While Tanya drove to her house, Yolanda looked out her window shaking her head from time to time.

"I'm sorry I embarrassed you like that, T. I was so pissed off at him, I just lost it. I can't believe I embarrassed myself like that! I did just what that bastard wanted!"

When Yolanda and Tanya arrived at Tanya's house, Yolanda ran to the bathroom, then joined Tanya who was in the kitchen.

"Well, at least we know what actually happened regarding that phantom phone call to Claude, YoYo. But damn, I can't believe it, either. I would have never figured Rick and Bernard for those kind of guys. I mean I know Bernard is crazy about you, but damn!" Tanya went through a couple cabinets pulling out items.

"You want some hot chocolate?" Yolanda nodded.

"Thanks, but I'm also hungry as hell. You got any eggs and bread for toast?" They both laughed heartily at the irony of that comment. The release felt good.

Tanya nodded. "Yeah, I got some stuff we can fix, then we'll get some sleep!" She heated cups of water for hot chocolate and got out four eggs and the bacon. "What a crazy night this turned out to be!" she said

Yolanda agreed, "Yeah, crazy." She rubbed the hand she hit Bernard with. "T, you got something I can put on my hand? It hurts."

Rick pulled up to Bernard's house, parked and turned off the engine. He and Bernard said nothing to each other the entire ride home. Rick took the keys out of the ignition and tossed them on Bernard's lap.

"I'm out. Later, man." They both exited the red pickup truck. Rick strode to his car.

"Hey Rick. You ain't coming in the house?" Bernard asked.

Rick turned to look at him. He shook his head as he walked back to the truck. Once there he stood on the driver side talking to Bernard who was standing on the passenger side.

"Hell, no. You put my name in your bullshit, B. You know I didn't know you called Boozer until today. That was really fucked up."

"Look Rick, I didn't call him. I had one of our honey's call him. She was all freaked out that she was calling a pro athlete. So, it's not like I actually called him, but I did arrange it." Bernard maintained his gaze at Rick.

"Look, B. Whatever, man. However you did it, it was wrong and you know it too. You can't be that far gone not to know that. Then you put my name in it. Fuck, man."

Rick walked around the front of the truck toward Bernard. Bernard walked to meet him and suddenly, they were standing nose-to-nose. Bernard balled his fists at his side, just in case Rick swung at him.

"How could you do that? I'm your friend, man." Rick asked searching Bernard's face. Rick shook his head and turned to walk away.

"Your friend," Rick said again into the air as he walked to his aging Mustang. He got in, started it and took off, without another word.

Bernard walked in the house still stinging from Rick's words and the look on his friend's face. He stripped off his stained clothes and threw them in a plastic garbage bag, which he set near the door. He hoped the cleaners could get the stains out. He looked in the mirror in the bathroom noticing a cut on his cheek. He guessed it might have been from one of Yolanda's rings. Now he was angry.

"That bitch cut me! She's fucked. That's all there is to it. She's fucked!" he said out loud. "And fuck you too, Rick!" he spat out.

After a quick shower, he got out his stash, rolled a joint and lit it. He searched until he found the gin left by Jerome and Billy. He filled a large glass with the remainder of the gin, got a couple ice cubes and tossed them in the glass as well.

Bernard ran his finger over his cheek and looked at the dried blood on his fingers. Replaying the scene of Yolanda slapping him in the restaurant, he bit his bottom lip and walked to his dark living room. He sat in the dark sipping, smoking and thinking.

XX

In Rock Hill, Allison and I sat on the couch talking. Billy and Vernay had gone to Vernay's room about midnight. Prior to that, the four of us had gotten acquainted by playing a few animated hands of *Spades*. Allison and Vernay had beaten us fairly quickly. But then, me and Billy's minds weren't on the card game.

"We need some music and the moment would be complete," I said to Allison as I stroked her hair.

"Go ahead and pick out what you want. I trust your musical judgment."

I walked across the room to check out her CD's. I picked out five and handed them over my shoulder to Allison. She took them and put them in the player and pressed play. Miles Davis was the first musician to play. His haunting trumpet sounded so mellow.

Eventually, we fell asleep; her head on my shoulder, my head resting on her head. That's the way Billy and Vernay found us. Our heads together, my arm around Allison's shoulder. Billy shoved me, gently.

"Rome, you ready? Wake up!"

I began to stir. "What time is it?"

"It's four o'clock. Time to go."

Allison stirred. "Why don't you guys just stay?"

"Maybe, next time," Billy said. I nodded in agreement as I extricated myself from Allison.

"Hope we can come back sometime," I said to Allison.

Allison kissed me and gave me a hug. "Of course you can. Thanks for being the guy you are."

"No problem. That's what I'm really good at."

"Jerome, the next time, I really want to show you just how much I enjoyed the time we had together, ok?"

She reached up and put her arms around my neck. Then she kissed me with fervor. I returned her kiss with the same energy until I felt Billy pulling on my arm.

"Come on, man. Should've kissed her earlier. It's time to go," Billy said laughing.

Once on the highway, Billy set the cruise control and turned to look at me.

"So, was I right?" he asked.

"Man, you were so right. How did you meet them?"

"I met Vernay at the Afro-American Cultural Center at a wedding a few months ago. Nobody was even trying to talk to her. So I did."

"Anyway, over time, I got to meet her roommates. I've been scheming for me and you ever since. Now you owe me for two things, huh?"

I shook my head. "Billy Truesdale. You are one sweet, sweetback muthafucka."

"And you know this Rome. You know this."

We lapsed into silence. I must have fallen asleep. The next thing I knew, Billy was telling me we were at my apartment. I gathered myself to get out of the warm car and get into my place.

Once in the apartment, I collapsed on the bed. My clock said 5:05 am. I didn't even bother to take my clothes

The insistent ringing of my phone forced me to wake up. I reached for the receiver.

"Hullo?"

"Good morning, daddy!"

"Dani. Good morning. What's up?"

"Nothing. Just wanted to say 'good morning'. You still sleep?"

"Yeah, honey. At least I was until you called. Where's your mother?"

"I guess still at home. I'm over at Miss Dot's house with Chloe. Mom went out last night and let me stay overnight here. You going to church, today?"

"I don't know, sweetie. What time is it?"

"A little after nine o'clock."

"Well, honey, I guess I'm not going. Church begins at eleven. By the time I got ready, it would serve no purpose. I'd be so late it wouldn't matter." I sat up. "Did you want to go?"

"Daddy, I have to. My choir sings today."

"Damn!" I said under my breath. "Did you call your mother?" I was so tired.

"No, I didn't. Not yet. But I'll call now. You want me to? I thought about not calling her. She hardly ever goes anywhere, so I thought about just letting her sleep."

"What a thoughtful child," I thought to myself. "Wish she'd let me sleep." I thought for a moment. Akeba is the day to day parent. Ok, maybe this will win me some brownie points.

"Ok, Dani. Do you have your church clothes with you?"

"No, I don't. Mom said she was going to pick me up last night, but she called and said I could spend the night. Can you pick me up and take me to church?"

"Ok, honey. I'll pick you up and take you home to get your stuff. Get ready and I'll be there." I dragged myself out of bed, took a quick shower and put on some clothes.

Kids!

Spoon rolled over and put his arm around Akeba. She nestled in his arm and pushed against him.

The phone rang.

"Let it ring girl," Spoon pleaded.

"Ok," Akeba said sleepily, but she glanced at the clock. It was nine-fifteen.

"Oh, shit! It's probably Dani." She reached for the phone. "Hello?" She tried mightily to control her breathing.

"Mom? Hi. Dad's on his way to get me and bring me home. My choir sings today and dad's going to take me to the church. You have a good time?"

"Damn. Yes, honey I did have a good time. It's sweet of you to ask." Akeba pushed Spoon and motioned for him to get up.

"When did you talk to your father?"

"This morning. He's on his way to pick me up. I decided to let you stay sleep, but I thought I should let you know daddy's coming with me."

"Well I appreciate your call, Dani. Ok. I'll get your choir outfit out. So let me go. See you in a few minutes."

Akeba hung up. She turned to Spoon. "Baby, you got to go. Dani's on her way with her father. I 'm not ready for Dani to see me and you early in the morning, yet." Spoon didn't move.

"Craig, did you hear me?"

"Yeah, I heard you. You know, this ain't about Dani at all. This is about your ex." He rolled onto his stomach and looked away from her.

"He's got to get used to the idea that just because he didn't want you, doesn't mean you have to waste on the vine."

He sat up and ran his hand up and down her leg. "You know what they say. One man's trash is another man's treasure."

"Hold up, Spoon. I'm nobody's trash," Akeba said frostily, sitting up.

"Right now, I need you to get out of here. No disrespect intended." She pushed him.

"Ok, ok." He said nothing else. He got dressed and headed to the bathroom. Akeba stripped the sheets off the bed and hustled to the washer. She started the washer and threw the sheets and pillowcases in. Only then did she stop and think. "What am I doing?" She laughed a little. "I'm a grown, divorced woman and I'm acting like I'm sneaking around."

Spoon came out with his jacket on his arm. He looked at Akeba coldly.

"I'm out. Thanks for a lovely evening."

"Craig…" she said quickly. He was already gone. Akeba watched from the front room as he got in the car.

He slammed the door, started the car and peeled off. Moments later, Jerome's car pulled into the driveway.

I watched as a blue car passed my car quickly, going in the opposite direction. I couldn't see the driver, but it appeared the car had come from Akeba's driveway. I glanced at Dani. Her eyes were focused on her lap. I had a feeling she recognized the car, but I dared not ask. I took a deep breath and let the impulse pass.

I pulled into the driveway. "Dani, go get your stuff and I'll wait here."

"Ok, daddy." She got out. Akeba opened and stood at the front door. She waved to me as she hugged Dani, then motioned for me to come in.

I still wasn't sure I could trust myself not to ask about that blue car that just passed me, so I leaned my head out the window.

"Are you sure?" I yelled to her.

"Yes. Come on in." With some hesitation, I decided to go in the house. Akeba met me at the door, "I'm sorry Dani got you up. You look just as tired as I feel."

I nodded. "Bad day for her to sing, huh?"

Akeba nodded and went upstairs. "I'll check on her. Thanks for going, Jerome. I don't feel like it."

"I understand. As long as it gets me some brownie points, Akeba." I put on my best smile.

"Noted, Dr. Jerome. Consider yourself *'brownie pointed'*."

I leaned back as I sat on the couch. I glanced around the house; the house that used to be our family home. I had to admit that I liked the way Akeba re-decorated the rooms I could see.

I sat up and thought about the blue car. I was surprised at my feelings of jealousy, as I imagined the driver of the blue car. Akeba's voice directed at Dani woke me from my thoughtful silence.

"Come on, girl. You're already late. Your father's waiting."

"I'm coming, mom, dad."

"Ok, honey. Just move a little faster," I said out loud to her. I watched as Akeba came down stairs. "She about ready?"

"Yeah. I'm sorry, Jerome. I stayed out too late last night and I forgot she had to sing today. You think she'll be mad if I don't go?"

"I don't think so, but what the hell. I'll be there. You got plenty of time to see her sing. Late night, huh?"

"Yeah. You too?" I nodded.

"Hanging with Billy. You know how nuts he can be."

"Yeah. How is he?"

"He's ok." I took a deep breath. "So, what did you do?"

"Just went to Club Premier. I know that's you and Billy's spot. Thought I'd run into you there, but I guess not."

I shook my head. "You went to Club Premiere's? On a Saturday night? That's different."

"Well, I was on a date and—"

"You don't owe me any kind of explanation, Akeba."

"Not my intent. Sorry. I had a good time. Been a while since I've been out. You have a good time with Billy?"

"Yeah, we did." This conversation felt surreal, like a bad *Lifetime* script. I wondered if Akeba felt the same. Dani came bounding down the steps. Boy was I glad to see her.

"You ready, girl?" I asked.

"Yep."

"Yes, Daddy" Akeba corrected.

"Yes, Daddy." She turned to Akeba. "You not coming, mom?"

"Not today, honey. You better get going. It's almost eleven o'clock." Dani kissed her mother and took my hand and we left the house.

"Get some rest, Akeba," I said as I left the house with Dani. Akeba nodded and closed the door behind us.

"Dani, you were really good! I'm glad I got to hear you sing."

"Thanks, daddy. I'm glad you came, too. I always sing better when you or mom are there. Could you hear me?" She hugged me.

"I sure did. Loud and clear. You really knew those songs."

We got in the car and headed back to the house. We rode in silence for a while.

"Daddy, can I tell you something?" Dani asked, breaking the silence in the car. I nodded.

"Of course."

"You won't get mad?"

"Of course not. What is it?"

"It's about mom," she said quietly.

I cleared my throat. "Honey, unless mom is sick or something, you don't need to tell me anything. What your mother does, is her business. It has to stay that way, unless you're being hurt or she's sick. You know what I mean?"

"I do, daddy."

"Dani, I know this is a crazy situation, but you'll be ok. In fact, we'll all be ok, eventually. I don't want you to begin the habit of telling me stuff about your mom. If she wants me to know something about her, she'll tell me." I reached out and squeezed her arm. "Ok?"

"Ok, daddy." She turned and looked at me. "Can you stay for Sunday dinner?"

I shook my head. "No, Dani. I got a lot of work to do. So, I'm gonna drop you off and get home."

"Ok, daddy. Boy, you and mom sure stay out late." She laughed and punched me on the shoulder.

"Watch out girl. I'm too old to be hit like that. I bruise easily." I rubbed my shoulder.

"Daddy, don't even try it," Dani said with a giggle. I joined her in her laughter.

See, I told you I like the times like these with my daughter. Smiling, I drove back to the house to drop Dani off.

Akeba came out to meet us. With her black wind suit on and matching head band, she looked really chic. Little did I know about the storm that was brewing.

"Hey guys!" Akeba hugged Dani. "Go on in and change your clothes. Don't throw your church clothes on floor either!"

"Alright mom." Dani ran toward the house. She stopped and turned.

"Bye, daddy, thanks for taking me!" I waved and smiled. Dani ran in the house.

Akeba folded her arms across her chest. "Thank you, Jerome. I know this got kind of sprung on you at the last minute. I'm glad you were able to do this for her." Akeba folded her arms closer around her body and seemed uncomfortable. "Wow, it got chilly out here, didn't it?"

I nodded in agreement. Something was up, but I didn't know what. Akeba had that look on her face that indicated that something was wrong.

"What's up, Akeba?" She looked around for a moment before speaking.

"Can we get in the car? I'm cold," she asked.

"Sure." I opened the door for her and then got in myself. "What's going on, Akeba?"

She looked at me, sharply. "What do you mean?"

"Well you got that look that you want to say something. What is it?"

Akeba took a deep breath and seem to melt into the seat in the car.

"Look, Cynthia's coming over this afternoon. Can you take Dani home with you so we can have some 'girl time'?"

I know I probably should have just agreed, but I was really tired and I had gotten up to take Dani to church without bothering Akeba.

"Akeba, I'm really tired. And I've got an early class in the morning."

"Jerome, I haven't asked you to do this in a long time. Can't you just do this for me…for Dani? You'd think I was asking you to give birth. She's your daughter, too. Damn." Her look at me was steady.

I was honestly confused. What was all this about? "Akeba—"

"Look, never mind." Akeba got out of the car, slammed the door and headed toward the house. I got out as well.

"Akeba, this isn't called for. What the hell is wrong with you?" She continued to walk to the house. "Akeba!" I yelled. "I'm talking to you!"

Akeba stopped in her tracks and wheeled around.

"Yes, master?"

I said nothing. *What the hell is going on? Shit, I just wanted to get some sleep.* Akeba marched toward me. Her words hissed out at me through clinched teeth.

"You know something? You're just selfish."

I just looked at her. *What in the world did I do?*

"And don't try to look so innocent," she continued. "Dammit. All I asked, was for you to keep your daughter for the day." Akeba's voice was rising dangerously fast.

Oh man, screw this. I need to get out of here. I rubbed my forehead.

"Akeba, tell Dani to come on. What time you want me to bring her back?"

"Thank you! Now was that so hard?" Akeba asked as she stood in my face. I wanted to say 'hell, yeah!' but I stayed quiet and got back in my car.

Akeba watched my face. Then she spoke, "I'll pick her up from your place about eight. I'll call you when I'm on my way." Then without waiting for a reply, Akeba turned and marched back to the house.

Moments later, Dani came out with her bookbag and a big smile. I leaned out of the window of the car to call to Dani.

"Come on honey, we got to go!"

Dani ran toward me and jumped in the back seat. She waved to her mother out of the window. I tooted the horn, for Dani's sake, and began to back out of the driveway. Before I got to the street, that same blue car drove slowly by. Then it picked up speed and pulled away.

"*Screw this, I'm out of here*," I said to myself. I backed into the street and drove to my apartment.

"What the hell is he doing?" Akeba asked herself as she watched Craig's blue Camry drive by. *Men! After last night, he thinks he owns me? Oh, hell no! We need to get this straight!* Akeba went into the house and turned on the radio then dialed Spoon's number.

The phone seemed to ring forever. Finally, the answering machine clicked on. There was soft jazz and then Spoon's baritone voice.

'Hope you're enjoying the sounds of Gerald Albright. When you hear the tone, leave a message and I'll get back to you.' There was a soft tone and Akeba spoke quickly.

"This is Akeba. I saw you ride by a little earlier, so did my child and her father. What's that about? Call me." She hung up.

Me and Dani arrived at my apartment after leaving Akeba. I was exhausted and still a little miffed at Akeba about her attitude earlier.

As Dani got out of the car she asked, "Daddy, can I call Chloe?"

"Sure, honey. Stay on the phone as long as you like. I don't want to talk to anyone. Unless your mother or your grandparents call, I'm unavailable.

"Ok? That includes your uncles as well. I'm just tired and I don't want to talk to anyone. I just want to sit in my chair and look at football until I fall asleep."

"So if Mr. Truesdale calls, you don't want to talk to him either?"

"Right. That especially includes Mr. Truesdale. Got it?"

"Got it, daddy. I'm gonna go to my room and call Chloe. Sleep good daddy."

"I plan to, sugar." I settled down and covered myself with a quilt. I was ready to finally relax for the weekend. My daughter had some movies we rented on the way home.

There's a VCR and TV in the room she sleeps in and I had plenty of snacks for her. I agreed to order pizza for dinner. There was a game on, but I barely focused on it. Damn, I was tired.

While Dani was on the phone, the call waiting clicked. "Wait, Chloe somebody's on the other line." She clicked over. "Hello?"

"Is Jerome Mitchell there?" a female voice asked.

"My father is sleep and he doesn't want to be disturbed. Can I take a message?" I heard Dani say that and I smiled. She was such a good daughter.

"Oh, ok. Yes. Tell him Ms. Walker called. Will you tell him to call me back?"

"Yes, I will. Does he have your number?"

"Yes he does."

"Ok, bye." Dani clicked back to Chloe.

"Just some lady for my dad. So tell me what Rashawn said to you…"

XXI

Answering machine again! Bernard slammed down the phone. "Where is everybody?" he wondered to himself.

This was the third time he had called Yolanda. Moments before, he had tried to reach Rick for the second time. There, too he got Rick's answering machine.

He got up and poured himself a glass of gin. He sat on the couch and rolled himself a large joint, which he lit and began to smoke. Bernard turned on the TV and flipped through the channels.

"Shit, nothing I want to see," he said. He went to his video cabinet and got out his favorite Jackie Chan movie and popped it in the VCR.

He sipped and smoked as he watched Jackie Chan fight his way through a seemingly avalanche of men determined to kill him.

"Kick their ass Jackie," Bernard said out loud. "Yeah, you don't take shit from nobody!" A lady who was caring for Jackie Chan after a particularly difficult fight triggered a memory of a person he hadn't seen in a while. He turned down the TV and picked up the phone. On the second ring, the phone on the other end was answered by a voice he recognized.

"Hello?"

"Hey Gina. What's happening? This is Bernard."

"How are you, Bernard."

"Just sitting here smoking a fat one and thinking about you. What are you doing?"

"Just enjoying my Sunday. Been a long time."

"Yeah, it has. Too long. Look why don't we get together, blow one together like the old days and do whatever, you know?"

"I'm sorry, Bernard. I gave that stuff up months ago. Not only that, I'm involved with someone, now."

"Really? Shit, I'm having some bad luck, today!"

Gina said nothing.

"Gina, you still there?"

"Yeah, I am. But I really got to go. Right now I want to concentrate on this new thing, you know?"

"Yeah, right, later."

Bernard hung up quickly not bothering to say goodbye. He took a deep pull on his joint and after exhaling, he took a big swallow from his glass. He thought he and Gina had had a pretty good relationship. They smoked a lot and had great sex. She had gotten pregnant, but he convinced her to abort. Shit. Now she's with someone else, huh? "I'll bet he don't do her like I did her," he said to himself.

He puffed on the joint as he pictured Gina's long black hair and her full lips. He leaned his head back. "I wonder if I should've held onto her?" he asked himself quietly.

After a few minutes, he roused himself and grabbed the phone. He quickly dialed a familiar number.

"Hello?" The soft voice answered.

"Melody, this is Bernard. What's going on?"

"What do you want, man?"

"Look, I apologize for the way I talked to you."

"That's not good enough, Bernard. You are a mean person. You are mean to people who even don't deserve your being mean to. You drink too much and smoke too much shit—"

"Are you finished?" Bernard interrupted.

"No, not really. But go ahead. Why you calling me? Your 'future' not available?"

"Mel, come on. I—"

The phone was dead in his hand. Melody had hung up.

"Fuck you," Bernard said to the phone as he slammed the phone down.

"Fuck all you bitches who think you too good."

Bernard finished smoking the joint he had lit earlier and rolled another one. He sat in his chair, thinking.

The doorbell rang and it startled me. Still groggy, I looked toward the door. The bell rang again and Dani ran toward the door. "I'll get it, sleepyhead!"

"Make sure you look out the peephole." I sat up attempting to wake myself up.

"Dad, its Chloe and her mom." Dani opened the door. "Hey, Chloe!"

"Hi, Dani. Hi, Mr. Mitchell."

"Hi, Chloe. Come on in. Hi, Dot."

"Hi, Jerome. Hi, Dani."

"Hi, Mrs. Meriweather." Chloe and Dani walked quickly to Dani's room.

"Have a seat, Dot." I pointed at the couch.

"I'm not staying, Jerome. I just wanted to get Chloe over here. I talked to Akeba and she said she would be happy to give Chloe a ride home when she picks up Dani. Looks like you're still sleepy."

"I am. I've been out all weekend and I ain't no spring chicken any more. I need some rest, if I plan to go to work tomorrow. I'll get the girls pizza and watch some football, or have football watch me.

"I know what you mean, Jerome." Dot put ten dollars on the coffee table and after checking on the girls, she left. I put a twenty dollar bill on the table next to Dot's and slid a coaster over the bills.

"Dani, Chloe?" They both came out to me.

"I ordered a large pepperoni for you. I'm going to my room to watch the game. Here's thirty dollars. The pizza man is bringing breadsticks and Pepsi as well. When he comes, pay him and make sure you save me at least two slices, Ok?" The girls nodded.

"I want you to stay in the living room, at least until the pizza man gets here. Wake me up before you open the door and let him in. Is that clear?" Both girls nodded

Both girls nodded and sat in front of the TV. I got up, went to my room and partially closed the door. I turned on the radio in my room to listen to the NFL broadcast.

Moments later, I was sleep again.

"Daddy, wake up!" I awoke with Dani pushing on my shoulder. "Come on daddy, wake up!"

"What, honey? What's wrong?"

"Nothing. Mom is here to get me and Chloe."

"Really? What time is it?"

"Eight-fifteen. Come on daddy, get up!"

"Ok, ok, I'm up. Where is your mother?"

"In the living room. Come on, she's waiting for you. She said she wants to talk to you." Then Dani ran out the room, shutting the door behind her. I heard her yell to her mother, "He's coming, mom!"

I got up and went to my bathroom. I vaguely remembered getting up to welcome the pizza man. I ran the brush through my hair and across my infant beard that was itching a little. I gargled with mouthwash and went out to see Akeba.

"Hi, Jerome. Dani says you slept most of the day."

"I did. I told you I was tired. So, what's up?"

Akeba looked at Dani and Chloe. "Y'all go get your stuff and put it in the car and wait for me. I'll be right there."

Dani hugged me. "Bye, daddy. Thanks for the pizza!"

"Yeah, Mr. Mitchell. Thanks for the pizza!" echoed Chloe. They grabbed their bookbags and headed out to the car. Akeba turned to me.

"Rome, I so owe you an apology for my behavior earlier. I do appreciate your taking Dani to church and I had no right to act like that with you. I'm sorry."

"That's ok. I bet you had other things on your mind." *Like that blue car cruising by the house,'* I thought to myself. We hugged briefly and Akeba left. As she walked toward the car, she yelled over her shoulder.

"Thanks for keeping them today."

"My pleasure. That's double the 'brownie points'."

"Noted and recorded, Mr. Mitchell," Akeba said over her shoulder as she walked to her car.

I went back into the apartment, glanced at my answering machine. There were no messages, so I grabbed a slice of the pizza the girls left me, a beer and sat in my chair. I flipped on the TV to watch the night game between the Saints and the Falcons and relaxed sipping on a cold beer, eating cold pizza reflecting on Akeba's apology.

I wondered how I would redeem those 'brownie points.'

Just as Akeba and Dani walked in the house, the phone rang which Dani answered.

"Hello?"

"Hello, Danisha. This is Mr. Witherspoon. Is your mom home?"

"Hi, Mr. Spoon." Dani turned to look at her mother who nodded at her. "Yes she is. Hold on."

"Thank you, ma'am," Spoon responded and waited. He didn't have to wait long.

"Hello, Craig." Akeba waved Dani upstairs with her hand. After a long look at her mother, Dani trudged up the stairs.

"Hi, Akeba. Look, let me just launch into my speech, ok?"

"Sure. Go ahead."

"Akeba, I was wrong. Walking out in a huff like that this morning and then riding by your house were stupid things to do. I want to be with you, but I know that if I do stupid stuff like that, that opportunity will go away." He paused. Akeba said nothing.

"I really want to make it up to you. That is if you'll let me." He paused again, hoping that Akeba would respond.

"You still there?" Spoon asked quietly.

"Yes. I'm just thinking." She paused again. "How would you make this up to me?" she asked.

"Well, do you like lasagna?"

"Actually, I do. Why?"

"I bake a mean vegetable or meat lasagna. You and Dani, dinner at my place complete with salad and red Kool Aid for her and Moscato for us. What do you think?"

"Let me get this straight. Your way of making up with me is cooking for me and my daughter?"

"Better than Chef Boy Ar Dee!" He laughed.

"Oh really? We are fans of both types of lasagna."

"Well, then. Tell you what. Why don't you and Dani come over on Thursday and let me prepare my world famous meat lasagna."

"Ok, Craig. I'll think about it. Can I get back to you with my decision, tomorrow?"

"You got it. Thanks for hearing me out on this."

"Have a good evening, ok? I'll call you tomorrow after work."

"Works for me, good night, Akeba."

After an evening spent drinking and smoking pot, Bernard found himself ruminating about the night at Club Premier with Rick and Yolanda as well as the events after they left the club.

Yolanda, Bernard thought. She likes to play games with people. He began to wish that he had been attracted to Tanya instead of Yolanda. Tanya always seemed more real. More down to earth. She wasn't as fine as Yolanda, but she seemed to be more genuine. He liked Tanya.

"I should have just kicked it with you, Tanya," Bernard said out loud. "Yolanda don't know how lucky she is to have a friend like you," he murmured to himself. He pictured Tanya's body in the green dress she had on at Club Premier. The dress clung to her body. He wished he had touched the material. It looked so soft and sexy.

"I should've kicked it with you, Tanya," he said again. He shook his head. Yolanda was such a trophy, though. A trophy he had allowed himself to want more than almost anything else in his life.

Yolanda. He had to let her know that she didn't have any more power over him. He would, too. She'll know.

Bernard got up and got a pitcher of water from the refrigerator, which he turned up, almost emptying the container. He went to the bathroom and grabbed a few aspirin, which he swallowed quickly. He fell in bed and lay awake staring at the ceiling.

XXII

Yolanda picked up the phone and dialed a familiar number. After the beep, she left a message on voice mail.

"Hi, Jerome. It's me. I wanted to tell you about Bernard. I've solved the riddle of the call to Claude. Page me or call my office when you get the opportunity. You have the number."

She hung up and drummed her fingers on the desk for a moment, turned to her computer and began to do her work. About twenty minutes later, there was a soft knock on the door.

"Ahem…Ms. Walker, can I come in?"

Yolanda looked up, slightly startled by the voice she knew so well.

"Come in, Claude." She didn't smile.

He walked in and closed the door softly behind him. He was carrying a large flower box.

"I bought these for you and I wanted to deliver them myself." He laid the box on her desk and stood back, watching Yolanda intently.

"What are these for?"

"Just open them, Puff." She did. There was a large mix of roses and carnations. Yolanda looked up.

"Claude—," Yolanda began. "An apology?"

He nodded. "For Friday night. I heard a lady's voice on my voice mail asking me to come over, so I did. She said she was a friend of yours and that you had talked about missing me.

But, like you said, you don't do business like that. I guess I was looking for a reason and the call was it."

Yolanda considered telling him about Bernard, but decided against it.

Claude continued. "Look, Puff. I'm crazy about you. I know I get a little over the top, sometimes, but you know it's you I want to be with, don't you?"

"Claude, I don't know…" as she shook her head.

"Puff, don't say anything, yet. Let me finish. Sometimes, I'm not paying attention to how I come off. I don't know if being a professional athlete contributes to this sense of entitlement.

"Look, we've both had a lot of relationship noise in our lives. Speaking for myself, I'm tired of it." He stopped and looked at Yolanda.

She nodded slowly. "Go on."

"I care deeply about you and I've been picturing my life beyond basketball." He walked toward her, leaned over her desk and took her hands in his. "In all my pictures, you are there."

Yolanda took a deep breath. What was he saying?

"I really needed to say that to you, Puff."

"That's sweet, Claude. And the flowers are beautiful. It's just—" Claude put his finger to her lips, silencing her.

"Say no more. I just came by to tell you that and to apologize for Friday."

Yolanda took a deep breath. She was confused about the meaning of his words.

Claude spoke. "Look, will you agree to get together later in the week and have a deeper discussion." She nodded watching his face intently.

"Good," Claude said as he released her hands and stood. Yolanda stood with him.

Then, without warning he reached across the desk, pulled her face to him and kissed her deeply. Without another word, he turned and walked out.

Yolanda sat numbly at her desk. She took a deep breath, stared at the flowers, then the door.

"Yo, Fox!"

Bernard turned around when he heard the voice calling him. It was his supervisor, Sergeant Copeland.

"Good morning, sarge." Bernard nodded tightly. He didn't like the look on the sergeant's face.

Sergeant Copeland moved closer to him and lowered his voice as he looked Bernard in the eyes. "Look, you need to report to the clinic for a mandatory county drug test."

"Damn, sarge. I just had a test a few weeks ago. They trying to catch me or something?"

Sergeant Copeland shook his head. "Fox, you know how these things go. Just go over there and do what you got to do." He started to move past Bernard, but Bernard grabbed his arm.

"Look, sarge. I'm not refusing, but I know what's behind all this. Or rather, should I say, 'who' is behind all this."

"Fox, you need to let go of me and get to the clinic as ordered." Bernard dropped his hand. "This ain't personal, so do what you got to do and make it quick. We're shorthanded today." Sergeant Copeland strode away from Bernard.

Bernard felt lightheaded. He was certain this was somehow Yolanda's doing. He knew she and the nurse in the clinic are friends and she must have gotten the nurse to move his name up to the top of the random list.

Bernard headed to the clinic, but first he wanted to make a call. He went to the payphone in the lobby of the building and dialed a number he knew well.

"Magistrate's office. Ms. Walker speaking. How can I help you?"

"Well, hello, Ms. Walker. Congratulations."

"Who's speaking?"

"Cut the shit, Yolanda. You know who this is. Again, congratulations."

"Bernard? What are you talking about?"

"Congratulations on getting me to take a drug test. You really found a way to get back at me."

"I still don't know what you're talking about."

"Look, Yolanda. I know you and that nurse in the clinic are friends. And since I pissed you off, you called her and asked her to move me up to the top of the random list for a piss test. But I got news for you. I always beat those tests and I'll beat this one too."

"Then why are we having this conversation? Man, you are really buggin'. Look, I got to go." She lowered her voice and clenched her teeth.

"But before I go, let me say this. You are really fucked up. You know that? Don't call me anymore. You hear me? I'll repeat what I told you. Don't call me again."

She dropped the phone in the cradle. Tanya was right. That boy really needed some help.

The phone rang again. Yolanda hesitated before answering. She hoped it wasn't Bernard. It wasn't. She breathed a sigh of relief.

I sat in my University office with the door partially closed. It was four thirty and I was tired. It had been a long, but good Monday.

I leaned back in my chair and enjoyed the solitude.

I looked through my cassette case. I really wanted to hear some relaxing music. I reached in my mini refrigerator and pulled out a bottle of Evian. I sipped and leaned back listening to Hiroshima.

After a couple swallows of Evian, I decided to play my messages and see who called. The messages were mostly business and one from Yolanda. I dialed her pager and put in my number.

I leaned back enjoying the cool water, reflecting on my day. After a while the phone rang.

"Jerome Mitchell speaking, may I help you?"

"Well, hello Jerome Mitchell. Are you busy?"

"Hello, Ms. Walker. What's up?"

"What's up? I called you yesterday. You didn't get my message?"

"Sorry, Yo. You must have talked with my daughter, huh?"

"Yep, I did. You got a minute?"

"Yeah, actually I do. What's up?"

"Let me tell you what's been happening." Yolanda related the story of Saturday night. She spoke fast and as she got closer to the slap of Bernard, she sounded more and more angry. Eventually, she stopped talking.

"Wow, Yo. What a night!"

"Tell me about it. That man had the nerve to have someone call Claude. Can you believe it? I should have just kicked his fat ass."

"Yo, it sounds like you did the job, yourself."

"See, and you thought the drama about the call was my fault, didn't you?"

"Well, to be honest, I did. But I'm glad you found out the truth."

"Well, there's more."

"More?"

"Yep. Today, he called accusing me of getting him drug tested."

"Can you do that?"

"Hell no. I can't do that. I guess Bernard thinks I have that kind of influence. He and everybody who works here knows I'm a friend of the nurse who does the testing, but she and I don't talk about drug test stuff."

"Damn, Yo. That's what you get for being so fine and making brothers worship you."

"Cut the comedy, Jerome. I'm serious. This boy's starting to get on my nerves. Hold on a minute, ok?"

"Sure." I waited. I could hear her talking in a muffled way to someone. I couldn't tell if the other voice was male or female. Yolanda came back on the phone.

"Jerome, Tanya is here. She says hello."

"Tell her I said hello as well."

"Jerome, can I call you back? There's one other thing I wanted to talk with you about."

"No, I'm really swamped. Why don't you call me tonight at home, Ok?"

"Ok. Thanks for listening. I really appreciate it."

"No problem, Yo. Talk to you, soon." I hung up and shook my head. Drama. Drama all the time.

'Thanks for listening. I really appreciate it,' Tanya said with a laugh as she mocked Yolanda's phone voice.

"Really girl, you sound like a school girl when you talk to the professor. Did he send those?" she pointed to the flowers.

"Don't be jealous, T." They both laughed and Tanya sat down.

"So, what's up, YoYo?"

"Gurl, I've had a high and low of a day."

Tanya sat up. "Go ahead, keep talking."

"Well, the flowers are from Claude. He hand delivered them to apologize for just showing up on Friday night."

"You tell him about Bernard?"

"I thought about it but changed my mind. I didn't need him to get macho and do something crazy. But guess what?"

"What?"

"I think Claude is going to propose to me."

"What?!"

"T, I'm serious. He came in here all mushy. He talked about wanting to end the 'relationship noise' in his life and he said he always sees me in his life even after basketball."

"Oh my God! But what about the professor?"

"I don't know, T. It's time I put on my big girl panties and made big girl decisions. Me and Claude are going to get together later this week and talk. And you know I'll fill you in."

"Your low point?" Tanya asked.

"Bernard called me today because he got to take a county drug test. He swears that I set it up."

"What?"

"He thinks I arranged it somehow, because he knows that Shirley is a friend of mine. The brother is buggin'."

Tanya shook her head. "Yeah, he is. But why didn't you say something to Claude when he was here? He probably would have wanted to know what actually happened with that mysterious phone call.

"Yeah, I know. But he gets so protective and he might do something stupid. And I don't want that. Claude's career is important to him and I don't want Bernard's bullshit to interfere with that."

"Wow, YoYo. Listen to you! You're talking like you've already made a 'Claude' decision."

"Well…" Yolanda said as she fingered the flowers on her desk.

"Aren't these lovely, T?"

"Yeah, sweetie. They are." She pulled a carnation from the box and sniffed it. "I need to talk about something else, if that's ok."

"Sure. What is it?"

"Thursday, I got to put my car in the shop. But also on Thursday I have a meeting in Gastonia with the hospital people there."

"You talking about that job in the legal department you're interested in?"

"Yep. It's not an interview, but an information session. My teacher at the college told me about it and suggested I go." Tanya took a deep breath and slowly exhaled. "I need to borrow your car."

"Not a problem. You've done it for me. What about your car?"

"Well, they are going to pick my car up from work. I know one of guys that drives a tow truck for them. He's gonna come by the job and pick up my car and tow it in. I'll leave my car at the shop Wednesday night. After the meeting, on Thursday, I'll come back here and if you can, I want you to take me to my car on Thursday after work."

"No problem. But be careful, Tanya. You drive too fast for me."

"Yes, mom. I'll be careful. Thanks, YoYo."

"We're sisters T. What reason can I give you for not helping?" They hugged and smiled at each other.

"Look, T. I hate to rush you but I got to get to my Yoga class. Call me tonight if you get the chance."

"Think you can squeeze me in with the Professor?"

"Alright, T. I told you to stop being jealous."

"Me, jealous? Just because you have two men who would do almost anything for you and they're intelligent, good looking and single?

What in the world do I have to be jealous about? I'm out, girl." She hugged Yolanda and strode out of the office.

Yolanda had a fleeting thought about Bernard. Her stomach tightened. She took a deep cleansing breath, grabbed her bag and left the office.

After talking with Yolanda, Bernard hung up the phone and went to the clinic. He felt a sense of dread. Bernard had had trouble before with the drug test. He had been in some treatment group; but of course it didn't work for him. So, he knew that if he failed this test, he would be suspended and possibly fired. Now he was really angry at Yolanda. He said a silent prayer as he waited for the nurse.

The door opened and the nurse walked in. She was dressed in street clothes and Bernard could smell the faint aroma of antiseptic as she moved around the office.

Bernard looked at the nurse's name-tag as she sat to fill out papers and prepare the sample cup.

"So, Nurse Shirley Foster. Do you think this is fair?"

"What do you mean Mr. Fox?"

"I'm sure you remember me from a few weeks ago. Now here I am again. Is this what you would consider, random?"

"I don't have anything to do with who is sent to me. I just collect the samples for the lab."

"Well, maybe not Nurse Shirley Foster. But there are people in my unit who have never been tested. Now here I am being tested for the second time in three or four weeks. How is that random?"

"Well, actually, what you're saying sounds even more random. I guess it would be like jury duty. I've been called for jury duty, five or six times, some of my neighbors have never been called for duty." She looked at Bernard.

Bernard locked eyes with her. "What an interesting story." He moved to the edge of his seat. "But let me ask you something, ok?"

"Sure," Shirley responded. She coolly sat back

"You know Yolanda Walker? She works in the magistrate's office."

"Actually, I do. She's a friend of mine. Why?"

"What input did she have on my name coming up, again?"

"Mr. Fox, what are you suggesting?" Nurse Foster stood up and looked at him.

"I'm not suggesting anything. I'm just asking if Miss Walker had any influence on my name coming up again, so soon."

"Look, Mr. Fox. I don't think I like what you're suggesting, so if you want to refuse to take the test, just say so. I have a form for that here."

Bernard thought for a moment. Maybe he could convince the powers that be, that he was being unfairly singled out for excessive testing for no apparent reason. Then he could take the test again when he wasn't so toxic.

He looked at Nurse Foster. She was holding out a paper to him.

"What is this?"

"The 'refusal to accept testing' form. Just sign it and you're out of here."

"Look, you and I both know that refusing testing is grounds for suspension or termination. I'm not signing that paper."

"Your choice." She handed him two cups with lids. Then you know what to do. I'll be waiting." She sat.

Bernard took the cups and moved to the restroom. When he returned, Nurse Foster explained the procedure to him again as she tested the samples for temperature. Once satisfied she sealed them and tagged them. She turned to look at Bernard.

"Ok, you're done. Thank you and have a good day. We'll only be in touch if we get a positive."

Bernard grunted and got out of his seat. He left the office without another word and went to the pay phone down the hall.

He dialed Yolanda's office number. Her voice mail came on. At the tone Bernard left a message.

"Yolanda. I just finished my drug test. The nurse denies it, but I know you had something to do with my being called.

"I tell you if I lose my job, you have to lose something." He slammed the phone down, went to his truck and returned to work.

Back at work, Bernard ran into Rick who was coming in late to cover for another deputy who was ill.

"Hey Rick. I was wrong the other night putting your name in my shit. I apologize. I just got back from a drug test and I know that Yolanda had something to do with it."

"Damn, B." Rick lowered his voice and moved closer to Bernard. "You know you been hitting the stuff pretty hard, this weekend. You think you beat the test again?"

"I don't know, Rick. I don't know. Right now, I'm worried about my job. Look, I got to get back to work. Later, man."

"Yeah, later B." Rick walked away shaking his head. He always knew that one day, Bernard's using was going to catch up with him. He was a little worried about Yolanda, though. Bernard seemed fixed on making her his problem.

Rick made a mental note to call her. He never got around to it.

XXIII

The workout felt good on this chilly Tuesday morning. I took off my sweats and stood in the mirror. It's been a week since my divorce was finalized. My mustache and beard was really growing in well. I was excited about my new look. But it did itch a little. I shaved carefully and got ready for the shower. The jazz on the radio sounded good and I was ready for a good day.

I chose to wear a white, long-sleeved, dress Nautica with black slacks and loafers. I put on a black vest sweater and checked myself out. I was ready to go.

After arriving on campus, I checked my mail and sneaked a peek at Sam's box. I missed seeing her. Her box was still full. Oh, well. I went to my office, turned on my computer and checked my e-mail.

There was nothing of any real interest there, nor was there anything requiring my immediate attention. I wrote a brief 'welcome back' note to Sam and sent it. Then I headed to class.

From that moment on, my day was a whirlwind. Class, student consultations, class, committee meeting, class and so on. I didn't have the time to think about Sam again until I returned to my office late in the afternoon.

When I checked my e-mail, Sam had responded. She wrote that she was back and her day was more than full. She hoped to catch up with me today or at least tomorrow. I had plenty to do. I began writing my midterm examinations. I was hard at it, when I heard a faint knock on my door.

"Yes?" I said not even turning around.

"My, my. Aren't we hard at work earning the big bucks?"

I smiled at my computer monitor. I knew that voice. I turned around.

"Come on in, stranger. Glad you decided to grace the school with your presence." Sam came in and sat down. She had a big, handled shopping bag at her feet. She really looked good.

"Sam, looks like you got some sun while you were in South Carolina."

"Tanning salon. Uh, my friend has a salon membership and I used that while he worked. You like it?"

I nodded slowly. I liked it a whole lot. "Yeah, looks good on you. If you ain't careful, you might be mistaken for a redbone."

"Redbone?" Sam looked quizzically at me.

I gave a short laugh. "Don't worry about it. It's a black people term."

"Don't tease me, Jerome."

"And why not?"

"Because I said so and if you continue to tease me, I won't give you your present."

I looked at the bag at Sam's feet. "Is something in there for me?" She reached in the bag and brought out a big book and with both hands handed it to me. I took it and smiled. It was a book on antebellum artwork, artifacts and history.

"Wow, Sam. This is beautiful!" I said as I turned the glossy pages. "This must have cost an arm and a leg."

"An arm and both legs," Sam said with a smile. "Do you like it?" I nodded as I continued to thumb through the pages.

"Good. I'm so glad. Jerome, I know how much you like African-American artwork, so when I saw this, I knew it had your name all over it."

"Sam, I love it." I turned to the inside front cover and noticed it was inscribed.

'To Dr. Jerome Mitchell. Your heritage is as rich as you are. All the best, Sam.'

I looked at her.

"Dr. Jerome Mitchell, huh?"

She nodded. "Just a little something to keep you motivated. Whenever someone sees this book and reads the inscription, they'll say that they didn't know you were a 'doctor'. If you aren't you'll have to tell them that you're working on it. If you are, then what a bragging point, huh?"

I nodded. Then I got up and went around my desk to hug her. She felt so good in my arms. Her scent filled my nose.

"You're welcome, Jerome. Very."

At that moment I was acutely aware we were still holding each other. I released her quickly.

"What you got going for the afternoon?" I asked walking behind my desk.

"I'm supposed to meet with our glorious leader, later."

"You better hurry up and finish with me then. You know he's got a wicked crush on you, don't you?"

"Oh, Jerome that's not true and you know it."

"I don't know anything of the kind, Samantha Carlton. Everyone's seen his face when he looks at you."

"Henry's just not my type, you know?"

"And what is your type, Sam?" Sam looked intently at me.

Her tanned face was smooth and attractive. Her eyes focused on mine without wavering.

"I'll keep my own counsel about what my type is, Mitchell."

"Oh, come on Sam. That's not an answer."

"Yes, it is an answer. Or at least all the answer you're gonna get right now." She smiled as she looked at me.

"Sam, you're being coy. Now how does that sit with such a strong, liberated woman such as yourself," I said wagging my finger at her.

"And Jerome, you're getting all up in my business. How does that sit with such an independent, role model such as yourself," she responded wagging her finger back at me.

"Where did you learn to talk like a sister, Sam. *'All up in my business.'* You go, girl with your tanned, urban self." We both laughed. Sam turned to leave.

"I hope you enjoy the book, Jerome and thanks for the hug." Just before she left, she turned to me. "By the way, I know a redbone is.

That's what some black people call a light skinned black woman. So there!"

"Sam, you never cease to amaze me. Get out, so I can finish writing my mid-terms."

"Bye, Mitchell," and she walked out.

"Bye, Dr. Carlton," I responded as the door closed. With a smile, I looked at the inscription in the book and turned back to my computer. I had to get my work done.

Damn, Sam really looked good.

Bernard's Tuesday afternoon shift was almost over when Bernard got the message to report to Sergeant Copeland's office, immediately when his shift ended. The feeling of hope he had earlier, dissipated. He suddenly felt heavy and tired. He was sure this summons meant that the test results were in. If they were negative, he wouldn't have to go to the sarge's office. But then, it could be anything. Anything at all.

He took a deep breath to compose himself and walked to the office. He felt like a child going to the principal's office. As he walked, he knew why he was going there.

No amount of telling himself that it was something else was easing his mind. He had finally gotten caught. He was facing suspension and most likely termination.

"Goddamn Yolanda Walker!" he said to himself. "She better hope this ain't what I think it is."

The secretary barely looked up at him. "Go on in, Deputy Fox. He's expecting you." Bernard's insides quivered. That did not sound so good.

"Come in, Fox. Have a seat." Bernard went in and sat down across from the desk.

"You wanted to see me?"

"Yes and I guess I need to get right to it," Sergeant Copeland said. You tested positive for cocaine and marijuana."

Bernard jumped up out of his seat. "That's bullshit, sir. I haven't done any cocaine!"

The sergeant said nothing as he looked at Bernard. Bernard slowly sat down. As he sat, he realized what he just said. The marijuana alone was enough to get him suspended.

"Fox, you know county rules, especially for law enforcement. I have to suspend you, with pay, pending a test on the second sample you gave, right?" Bernard nodded weakly.

"Now, you know sometimes these tests get all messed up. If the second sample comes back clear, all is well. If not, given your history you will be immediately terminated. You do understand that, right?"

"How soon will you know?"

"I'll know by late tomorrow afternoon or early Thursday morning. I'll call you as soon as I get the results. I won't tell you on the phone. I'll ask you to come in and then we'll talk. I'm sorry, Deputy, but you know the rules. And if you're terminated, then you have to know you did this to yourself. Anything else you want to ask?"

"No sir," Bernard said quietly.

Sergeant Copeland stood. "Alright then. As of now, you're suspended. You need to leave the premises immediately, after you change out of your uniform. Then, stop by here and leave your keys, badge, and gun with the clerk. Is that understood?" Bernard nodded, looking down.

The sergeant continued, "I'll be in touch. I'm sorry, Fox. I am. But there is nothing more or different I can do at this point."

Bernard felt his anger growing inside of him. He could barely breathe. His head began to pound. He felt lightheaded. He got up stiffly and walked out saying nothing. He wanted a drink.

He went straight to *Cody's*, his favorite bar, after checking out of work. It was one-thirty in the morning before he decided to go home.

Bernard snatched the phone off its base and called Yolanda's office number. After the voice mail message, he just said 'Congratulations' and left the phone off the hook until the voice mail system cut him off. He then got an idea. He continuously called Yolanda's voice mail at work and said Yolanda's name or sat just breathing into the receiver until the system cut him off.

Once the voice mail system informed him that Yolanda's mailbox was full, he went into his room and lay on his bed fully dressed. He turned on the TV, tuned to a mindless variety show with the sound muted. He was lost in his thoughts about his job and what he believed Yolanda had done to ruin him.

XXIV

When the phone rang, I knew it wasn't good. Don't ask me how I knew, but I knew. I answered on the first ring. It was Yolanda and she sounded rather panicky.

"Hey, Yolanda. What's wrong?"

"Jerome, I am so glad you are home. I really need to talk to you. You got some time?"

I turned off the TV and sat up.

"What's going on, Yolanda. You sound pretty upset." I shook my head.

"I'm sorry. I didn't want to sound like that, but I needed to talk or at least hear myself talk. I don't know. I told you about Bernard, the fight and the drug test, right?" I waited for her to continue.

"I'm worried that if Bernard fails that drug test, he'll blame me somehow. I know that sounds ridiculous, but I wouldn't put it past him. He's druggin' and it's gonna be my fault somehow."

"Yolanda, what are you afraid of happening?"

"I don't know. Sometimes I think he'll try to get me, somehow. You think?"

"Yo, you've known him longer than me. What do you think?"

"I don't know. I asked Tanya the same thing. She said that he's more bullshit than action." I took a long sip of beer as I listened. Yolanda was clearly scared of this silly brother.

"Yolanda, can't you tell the sheriff department of your concern? Won't they do something to, uh, protect you from his bullshit?

"Jerome, I work in the magistrate's office. You know how many restraining orders we issue?" She didn't wait for a response. "Probably a hundred a week. Most of them are violated the same day."

"Maybe so, but you need to report any threats. You need to develop a paper trail to protect yourself, don't you think?"

"That's just it. He hasn't really communicated any real threat. Well, maybe I should say, *'yet'*."

Yolanda seemed so vulnerable, so needy. I felt my heart go soft. I reassured her that I would do whatever I could to help her. I also pointed out she had Tanya and even Claude if need be. None of us would desert her.

'Be careful Rome,' I said to myself. I recommended she call her attorney in the morning. If she didn't have one, I would give her the number to mine.

"Thanks, Jerome. You are so comforting. I'm gonna go now and I'll keep you updated, ok?"

"Sure. Good night, Yolanda. Sweet dreams." I hung up and stared off into space for a while. I remembered the gun on the shelf at Bernard's house. I shivered.

"And you chose to call the Professor and not Claude, huh? How did you come to that decision?" Tanya asked Yolanda.

"I don't know why I called him instead of Claude. O lord, am I losing it or what?

"We're ending, T. I know it. I feel it," she pointed to her heart, "and I know it," she pointed at her head,but I'm just not ready for that to happen, you know?"

Tanya exhaled slowly.

"I got your message about your voice mail at work," Tanya said.

"I know it was Bernard. I just know it," Yolanda said

"What are you gonna do?"

"What can I do? I don't have any proof that it was him, but filling up my voice mail is pretty harmless, if that's all he can think of to do. You agree?"

"That's true. If that's the worst, then yes, that is pretty harmless stuff. What did your professor say?"

"He suggested I contact an attorney for legal advice on what my options are."

"Makes sense." Tanya ran her fingers through her hair.

"Yolanda, Bernard is getting weirder by the day."

"Well, that's true."

"Did you call an attorney?"

"Yeah, I called mine, but he's out of town, this week. I left a message for him to call me when he checks in for his messages.

"You know, uh, Claude probably has a myriad of attorneys who would be more than glad to handle this situation."

"I thought about that, T. And I will use that as an option if nothing else works.

"Well don't take too long to make your mind, sweetie." Tanya twirled the phone cord in with her finger.

"I hate to change the subject, but I wanted to remind you about using your car tomorrow. I'll be leaving about twelve thirty and plan to be back about three or three thirty. Thanks, sweetie."

"No problem."

"YoYo, look, I got to go. Catch you later."

"Bye, T." Yolanda hung up. She wondered if she should have told Jerome about Claude, and the flowers he gave her. She liked Jerome's supportive style, but she admittedly felt safer with Claude's *take charge* style.

Bernard sat in his truck watching the café where Yolanda usually ate lunch. *'Please don't call me anymore,* huh?' he laughed to himself as he rubbed the small scar on his face. "You like to scratch people, huh? Well, you don't know what I'm capable of, if I lose my job," he said out loud. It was half past noon and he knew she would be headed toward the café soon.

Sure enough, moments later, he spied Yolanda walking toward the café. He waited until she went in and sat down and settled, before he strolled over to the restaurant. He stood outside the glass window staring at her.

"I am not going to allow him to intimidate me!" Yolanda said to herself when she noticed Bernard looking at her through the window. She decided against going out to confront him.

When Yolanda looked up again, Bernard had disappeared. She was startled when a moment later he stood at her shoulder.

"Hey Yolanda. What's up?"

"Nothing. Why?"

"Just wondering. Been a lot of shit lately." Bernard ran his fingers over his facial scar as he pulled out a chair and sat.

"You see what you did, don't you?" He asked pointing at his face.

"I didn't mean to hurt you, Bernard."

"Bullshit. Bullshit. And you need to know that my clothes from the other night are ruined. Thanks to you."

"Look, send me a bill and I'll pay for them." She rooted around in her purse and pulled out her checkbook. "I can write you a check right now. Give me a number."

"The hell with your money, Yolanda. Maybe I'll just get what I'm owed another way."

"Are you threatening me?"

Bernard said nothing. He simply stared at her with a half smile on his face.

"Right now, I need to eat and you're disturbing my alone time. Is there anything else you needed to say to me? Because, I surely don't want your company." She took a large gulp of water.

"Just admit that you were the one who got me tested, yesterday. I flunked, by the way and they are checking the second sample. If that's dirty, I'm probably terminated. You know that, right? So, you go right ahead and order your lunch. I think I'll sit here anyway and keep you company. You got a problem with that, tough."

"Bernard, this has gotten way out of hand. I had nothing to do with you getting a drug test. And I know that was you on my voice mail, wasn't it?"

"Maybe, maybe not. You come clean, then maybe I will."

Yolanda stood up. "I'm not going through this with you again, Bernard. I didn't have anything to do with your drug test and you can't scare me. So don't even try it."

Bernard looked up at her and clinched his teeth. "Sit down and don't raise your voice. I ain't playing with you, Yolanda. If I lose my job, you will be sorry," he hissed at her.

For a moment, Yolanda felt a wave of fear pass through her. She regained her composure. "I'm not sitting down and," she raised her voice, "if you are threatening me, let me tell you that I will do what I got to do to protect myself. I am a county magistrate and I know what harassment is." A few diners looked over at them.

Bernard felt a sickening feeling of déjà vu wash over him. He got up without a word and walked out.

The glass in the door creaked from the force of his push. Yolanda watched him as he walked across the street and got into his red pickup truck. He pulled off spinning his tires and leaving a trail of blue smoke. Yolanda took a deep breath. A waitress stood by her.

"Are you ok, Miss Walker?"

Yolanda nodded slowly. "Yeah, thanks Carrie. Can I have another glass of water?"

"No lemon, just a few cubes of ice," Carrie said.

"You got it. Thanks, Carrie."

"Sure, honey. Men can be such assholes." She rushed off and returned with a glass of ice water. "You want your regular salad to go?"

"No, Carrie. All of a sudden, I'm not hungry." Yolanda drained the glass of water, left five dollars on the table and hurriedly returned to her office. Carrie watched her go with a worried look on her face.

Once in her office, Yolanda sat silently for a moment. "The hell with this," she said out loud and forcefully. She dialed a number she knew well. After a voice mail message, she left a message of her own.

"Claude, call me when you get the opportunity. I think I really need your assistance with a situation I've got."

XXV

When I got home Wednesday night, Billy was already in the parking lot. He rushed out of his car as soon as he saw me.

"Rome, I'm on my way, man. I am on my way."

"Damn, Billy. You're on your way to the funny farm if you don't slow down and tell me what you're talking about.

"Rome, check this out. Stoker, my manager, hooked me up. I'm going being tasked to work a big job tomorrow. Man this is the break I've been working for."

I walked to the door with Billy trailing me like a like a child. His words coming so fast, it was difficult to keep up. I opened the door and Billy rushed in, before me. I followed, shaking my head.

"Billy, what are you so juiced up about?"

Billy breathlessly told me about his promotion and opportunity to represent his company on a huge project in Gastonia.

"Rome, this is big, really big." He grabbed a two beers from my refrigerator and tossed one to me. After popping the beers, we touched cans in a toast.

"Well, congratulations, man. When do you go?"

"Tomorrow afternoon. You know, tomorrow will be the greatest Thursday of my life, so far." He drained his beer, grabbed another one and opened it, all in the same motion.

"So, you want to give me details of this big job?"

"It'll get boring to you, but let it suffice, it's the bomb opportunity."

"Well, go kick some ass, Billy. Hell, let's go celebrate. Tell you what, I'll buy dinner. Where you want to go?"

"I don't care, man. It's Wednesday night. You know they got karaoke at the Ramada and dollar drafts. Let's go there this evening and tie one on. What do you say?"

"It's your night, Billy. I'm cool with that! Let me change into something a little more comfortable and I'll be ready to go."

"Cool, Rome. Look, I'm sorry I kind of jumped you this evening."

"Man, we've been lifelong friends. There is absolutely no apology necessary. I'm just happy to share in your good news."

"Thanks, Rome. Get changed and let's go!"

I did and we spent the evening celebrating my best friend's good fortune. He was as happy as I had ever seen him. Billy was large and in charge. And I was excited just to be with him.

Early Thursday morning, Bernard's phone rang loudly. He reached for it clumsily, knocking it to the floor. Silently cursing, he reached over the side of his bed feeling around on the floor for the receiver. Finding it, he dragged it from the floor to his ear.

"Hullo?" he asked groggily.

"Mr. Fox?"

"Yeah, who is this?"

"I'm Sergeant Copeland's secretary."

Bernard sat up in bed. His head began to pound. He rubbed his eyes to wake himself up.

"Yes, this is Officer Fox. What can I do for you?"

"I'm calling to set up time for you to meet with Sergeant Copeland. He has time to see you at eleven and expects you to be in his office. That won't be a problem for you, will it?"

Bernard glanced at his clock. It was nine-thirty. "No, I'll be there, but what's this about?"

"You'll have to talk with Sergeant Copeland about that. He's not here right now. But you will be here promptly at eleven?"

"Yeah, yeah. I said I would, didn't I?" Bernard paused. He didn't need to alienate this woman. "I'm sorry. I was sleep when you called."

"No problem Mr. Fox. See you at eleven." She hung up.

Bernard stared at the phone in his hand. Why did the sarge's secretary keep calling him 'Mr. Fox', instead of 'Officer Fox.'

"This is it, Bernie. It's over," he said to himself. He got up and showered. He decided to go to the office in a shirt, tie and suit. As he dressed, he felt panic rising in him. He didn't want to lose his job. He enjoyed being a deputy.

He sat on the bed, and noticed that his knees and hands were shaking. He reached for a cigarette and lit it, then stubbed it out on the floor.

"What am I supposed to do, now? Sarge is going to fire me, I just know it. I know it!"

Bernard sprang up and began pacing. "How does a brother like me get a break?" His pacing became faster. "I can't believe this is happening to me. Me! Like I'm the only person that drinks and uses a little weed every now and then in the department."

He began to rehearse his speech to the Sergeant. "Sarge, come on. I know I got a problem, but I can go to rehab. Don't fire me. Suspend me, send me to treatment, put me on probation, but don't fire me."

He pictured Sergeant Webster Copeland's round dark face. He could see the sarge take off his glasses and clean them as he does when he talks.

"I'm sorry Fox," Bernard could imagine the sarge saying as he returns his glasses to his face. "You knew the rules and the consequences. I'm sorry, I really am."

"Fuck it!" Bernard said out loud. "It may not even be that. I'm just getting myself all worked up over probably nothing."

Standing quietly he thought for a moment then got his stash of marijuana. At his kitchen table, he rolled two huge joints.

"These are to celebrate, or calm down," he said to himself. For a moment, he looked at the joints on the table and considered leaving them home. With a vigorous head shake, he swept the joints off the table into his hand and went outside to his new red Dodge Ram truck.

Once there, Bernard opened the glove compartment and took out a bank deposit envelope. He sealed the joints in the envelope and slammed the compartment door.

Bernard looked at himself in the rearview mirror. His eyes were clear. He noticed that he had neglected to shave. Under his seat was a small leather bag. In it was a cordless shaver and a half used container of after-shave, which he decided to use quickly before he left his parking space. With an old newspaper held under his chin he hastily shaved and slapped on some aftershave. Checking himself again in the mirror, he nodded.

"It'll have to do," he said to himself. With that, he started his truck and pulled out into traffic to get to Sergeant Copeland's office, downtown.

While driving, he found himself thinking about Yolanda. He considered stopping to give her a call, but decided against it. "If I'm fired, there'll be time to tell her," he said to himself. "All of this is probably her fault, anyway. The bitch."

Once he arrived at the Law Enforcement Center, he went straight to Sergeant Copeland's office. Everyone there seemed so busy, Bernard wasn't sure he wanted to interrupt them. Bernard went to one of the desks where a petite black woman was typing furiously on her computer. The name plate on her desk said *Julie Rogers.*

"Uh, Miss Rogers." The lady looked up at him. "I'm Officer Fox. I have an eleven o'clock appointment with Sergeant Copeland?"

"Oh, yes. I spoke with you earlier today. If you'll have a seat, I'll let him know you're here."

Bernard sat and watched as Miss Rogers walked down the hall and disappear around a corner. Bernard looked around. The office looked so clean. There were at least five desks that he could see. Four of the desks were occupied by women, typing or talking on the phone.

As usual, each of them looked like they had coordinated their outfits. Each had on a white blouse and from where Bernard sat, it appeared that a couple of them were wearing dark, or khaki knee length skirts.

The empty desk was clean and neat. The phone sat quietly, but the computer screen was on. When Bernard looked around, Miss Rogers had returned. Bernard noticed that she had on a white blouse and a khaki, knee length skirt. On her feet were black soft shoes. They almost looked like sneakers.

"He'll be right with you," Miss Rogers said brightly. "You want coffee or anything?"

"No, thanks. I'm fine," Bernard replied. Miss Rogers nodded and returned to her desk. Once there, she busied herself with some work on her computer.

Bernard watched the ladies work. His stomach was tight and he felt a slight headache beginning. Suddenly, Sergeant Copeland was calling to him from the hall Miss Rogers had walked.

"Fox. Come with me," Sergeant Copeland said motioning toward him.

They walked in silence. Sergeant Copeland led the way and Bernard followed. After rounding the corner, they passed two doors. The second door had Sergeant Copeland's name on it, but they walked right by it.

"We're not going to your office?" Bernard asked stopping and looking at the door.

"No, we're going to a conference room."

"A conference room? What's this all about, Sergeant?"

"Fox, we'll talk when we get to the conference room. Just follow me, ok?"

Sergeant Copeland led the way and around another corner he stopped at an oak colored double door.

He pushed open one of the doors and stepped back. With his arm outstretched, he indicated that Bernard was to go in. He did. The sergeant followed and closed the door. In the room were several people and a stenographer. Bernard looked at the sergeant.

"What's going on?"

Sergeant Copeland took a deep breath. He pointed to each person as he said their name. "This is Jim Madison from the deputy association, Kathy St. Clair from the EAP office, and Mark Greenlee from County Human Resources. Have a seat Fox."

Bernard felt like someone had punched him in the face. He sat absently in the chair the sarge had indicated. He licked his lips and tried to swallow as he faced the persons in the room. He couldn't swallow. He felt like a lump as large as the entire city had just taken residence in his throat.

Sergeant Copeland began to speak. "Fox as you know, you were asked to take arandom drug test. The first sample failed so we did a check on the second sample. That too came up dirty. Therefore, given your past opportunities to correct your usage issues you are being terminated per the policy. I'm sorry, Fox."

Mark Greenlee reached in a file folder in front of him and slid some papers across the table to Bernard. He cleared his throat.

"The first paper is the actual policy for your review, which as you can see you signed. The second is a termination letter with reasons for the action taken against you. We need you to sign this and of course you'll get a copy."

"I'm not signing shit!" Bernard exclaimed as he looked at Mark. He then looked at the association person.

"Come on, Jim. Is this all? You ain't gonna say nothing? Come on, I pay my dues. I can be suspended, put on probation or something. Come on Jim, say something!"

"Calm down, Bernard," Jim said quietly. You know the rules. Getting angry isn't going to help anything. There's not much I can do. I tried to do what I could, but we all know the rules and the consequences. That's why we're asked to sign that form."

"Then why are you here?" Bernard asked.

"I'm here to be sure you're treated right, during this process."

"Treated right? Treated right?" Bernard stood up. "How am I being treated right? I'm being fired, Jim. Fired. Does that sound like I'm being treated right? Is any of this getting through to you?"

"Sit down Fox," Sergeant Copeland said patiently. "Sign the termination paper and let's not make this anymore unpleasant than it already is." Bernard just stared at him. Sergeant Copeland stood up.

"I said, sit down."

"Sergeant, uh, Deputy Fox. Please sit down. This is getting really tense," Kathy said softly. Both men sat down slowly. "Mr. Fox, I can work with you if you'd like to talk about your thoughts and feelings about this situation."

"My thoughts and feelings?" He looked at Kathy. "I'm losing my job, my source of income. I'm losing a job I really like. And mostly because of a person who called and arranged for me to be tested because she was pissed off at me. Those are my thoughts and feelings. And as for that paper, I refuse to sign, so go ahead and write that."

"That's your choice Fox," Sergeant Copeland said authoritatively. He slid the locker keys across the table. "We need your uniform and any other departmental property signed out to you." Bernard stared at the people looking at him. His jaw twitched violently.

"Fox…" Sergeant rubbed his forehead.

"Bernard. Go clean out your locker and bring the keys back later," Jim said calmly.

"No, I won't. Clean out my locker yourself and throw the shit out, I don't care. I don't believe you would do this to me. I don't. Because of a woman who complains. I can't believe it.

"Fox, what are you talking about?" Sergeant Copeland asked.

"Sarge, do me a favor, will you? Stop calling me 'Fox'. My name is Bernard or Bernie, but this 'Fox' shit is getting on my nerves. Besides, you know what I'm talking about." Bernard looked at each person in the room.

"You're doing this because of Yolanda Walker, right?" Bernard continued.

"Bernard, who is Yolanda Walker?" Kathy asked.

"It doesn't matter who she is," Sergeant Copeland snapped. "No one did drugs for you. You did that to yourself. No one outside of the department made any complaint about you. Your drug test was random as always. But you got to take responsibility for your own actions." The sergeant sat back and seemed to calm somewhat.

"Why don't you make an appointment with Ms. St. Clair, here. We'll pay for it for a few sessions." Kathy nodded in agreement.

"No, I pass. Thanks, sarge." He looked at Kathy. "Nothing personal. I know what I got to do to deal with this." He looked at the stenographer. "I know she's here just in case you're afraid I'll sue the department. Well, I might and I might not. I'll have to think about it.

"Well, don't try to work through this all alone, Mr. Fox," Kathy St. Clair said with a slight nod. "I am more than willing to work with you."

Bernard looked at Kathy St. Clair. "You think I'm crazy? Do you?" She said nothing. Bernard turned to Sergeant Copeland. "Is that all?" The sarge nodded curtly.

Bernard stood, tossed a sarcastic salute at Sergeant Copeland and turned to walk out. Two officers accompanied him to the parking lot. They said nothing to Bernard as they escorted him out of the building.

As he left the building, Bernard's grief turned to anger. He went to his truck. Once there, he opened the glove compartment and took out the envelope that contained the joints he rolled. He ripped open the envelope and poured the contents on the seat beside him.

After Bernard exited the official parking lot, he lit one of the joints and took a deep drag. Putting the burning joint in the ashtray, he reached under the passenger seat for a liquor bottle he kept stashed there. Taking a furtive look around, he took a deep swallow.

The clock in his Ram indicated that it was eleven forty. He didn't realize so little time had elapsed.

"I'm gonna get that bitch for fucking with me like that," he growled to himself.

Looking around, he noticed a pay phone on the corner and decided to call Yolanda, but just as he slowed at the corner, he saw a car that looked like Yolanda's Mercedes drive by him going in the opposite direction. He hurriedly made a U-turn to get behind the vehicle. He looked at the license plate. It was her car.

"I'll be damned. There she is, now." He took another pull from his joint and another swallow from the bottle. He decided to follow her.

Yolanda's phone rang. "Magistrate's office, Ms. Walker speaking," she said into the phone.

"Hey Puff. What's up? I got your message. Sorry I didn't get back to you, yesterday."

"Oh, hi Claude. I'm glad you called. Have you got a few minutes?"

"I'm home and I've got as many minutes as you need. Is something wrong?"

"Well, kind of. I've solved the mystery of the phantom phone call to you on Friday night. Well, actually he didn't call, but he had someone call you. He wanted to be with me and since I chose not to be with him, he had you called just to mess with me."

'*Damn you, Bernard,*' she thought to herself. "Claude, you still there?"

"Yeah baby. I'm here." He took a deep breath.

"Why would this Bernard think he was gonna lose his job? And why would he blame you? Why did he think you even wanted to be with him?"

Yolanda related the story of her interaction with Bernard. She left out few details. Afterwards, she said a silent apology to Jerome for involving him in this. She openly apologized to Claude for keeping him in the dark.

"Puff, I'm hoping to be your husband, someday. I don't want to lose you because of my stupidity or another person's obsessions."

"Claude, what are you saying?" Yolanda was now sure she could hear her blood racing through her body.

"I'm saying that I know I love you and I have loved you for a long time. I should have manned up a long time ago and told you how I felt. But more than anything, I want to help you right now. This brother needs to have his ticket punched."

Yolanda was still in shock. She had never heard Claude talk like this before. He sounded so sincere, so sure of what he said. The shock of his words pushed her into silence.

Claude intruded on her thoughts. "Puff, you still there?"

"Yes, I am. Did you say you love me?"

"You heard me correctly. Yolanda."

"Thank you for using my name, Claude."

"Yolanda, I've always loved your name. I just got used to calling you 'Puff'.

But telling you what I told you, makes Puff sound so childish. I know you're not a child and I don't want you to feel like one around me."

"Claude, I appreciate that," Yolanda said holding her hand against her chest. She sunk into her office chair, shaking her head. She couldn't focus or think straight. With some effort, she tried to remember what she called Claude about in the first place.

"Claude, about Bernard—"

"Look, say no more. I'll call my attorney right now and see what legal options we have available to us and then I'll call you back this afternoon. If that bastard calls you, I want to know about it, ok?"

"Ok, Claude," Yolanda said softly. She clearly heard him use the word 'we' as if they were in this together. Again, she found it difficult to focus on the issue of Bernard.

"Look, Yolanda. We'll get this shit handled today. We won't go into tomorrow with this over our head, I promise.

Besides, tomorrow is Friday and no one needs to have bad shit on them on a Friday. If you want, I'll come up and hang around with you."

"Claude, I appreciate it, but I don't want you hanging around my office. I still got a job to do, you know. Please, just call your attorney and get back to me. Right now I want to think about everything else you said."

"Ok, Yolanda. You do that and I'll call you back later. Love ya, baby!"

"Ok, Claude. Bye." Yolanda hung up mechanically and sat shaking her head. "What in the world?" she whispered to herself.

Finally, I had time to relax in my office. I turned on my computer to check my e-mail. One particular piece of mail caught my attention. The subject was my daughter, Danisha Mitchell. I didn't recognize the address: *onthebeat@aol.com…* The message read:

"Dear Mr. Mitchell…hope I didn't unduly alarm you

by using your daughter's name, but I didn't want you

to delete this before you read it…Real quickly, I would

like you to accompany me to the Holiday Ball on Dec.1ˢᵗ.

It's an annual charity event for abused/neglected children…

Please call me at the school for more details…

I hope to hear from you in the next couple days

You have my number…

Cheers,

Ms. Lahti Pearl

I had heard of this ball before, but I had never attended. I pulled out my business card file to locate Ms. Pearl's card then dialed her number.

"Pearl's School of Dance, may I help you?"

"Yes, this is Jerome Mitchell. Is Ms. Lahti Pearl available?"

"I'll check. You said your name is Mr. Mitchell, right?"

"That's correct."

"Ok, just a second."

While on hold, broadway show music played. I was really getting into the music when Ms. Pearl's voice came on the line.

"Mr. Mitchell?"

"Yes, Ms. Pearl, but please call me, Jerome."

"Fair enough, if you'll call me Lahti."

"Ok, Lahti. I got your email. I must say I am flattered."

"Forgive me my boldness, but I thought you might be interested, uh, Jerome."

'Forgive me my boldness,' dawg I liked that. "Consider yourself, forgiven. Want to tell me more?"

"Sure, it's the first weekend of December, Friday the first at the Convention Center. The dress is formal and the tickets are two hundred and fifty dollars each."

I inhaled silently at the price of the tickets. No wonder I had never gone.

"I don't need you to pay my way, but I would like your company, that is, if you're interested."

I only thought about it for a moment. "Absolutely, I am interested and I'm in. But there is one condition."

"What is that, Jerome?"

"The condition is that you'll let me take you out before the Ball. I don't want us to begin to know each other that night. Will you agree to that condition?"

Lahti paused. "I think I can agree to that. In fact, I like your idea immensely."

'Immensely,' I really liked Lahti's vocabulary. "Then it's a deal. Where do I send the check?"

"Just write the check out to me and send it to my studio. I'll handle everything from there," she replied.

I stared at the phone for a few minutes after I hung up. "Damn, Ms. Lahti Pearl."

I wrote a check to Ms. Lahti Pearl, filled out an envelope and inserted the check. I decided to mail it on the way home. I then turned back to my computer to answer my remaining email.

XXVI

Out on the interstate, Bernard continued to smoke as he followed the black Mercedes. Yolanda's face kept filling his mind as he drove. Sometimes, she was smiling, other times she was frowning at him, wagging her finger in his face. It seemed that she was taunting him, daring him. Bernard spat out his window.

"All you had to do was give me a chance," he said out loud. "I only wanted a chance to prove how much I cared about you. But no, you want to just *'work on a friendship,'* huh. Well, let's be friends!" He put the bottle to his lips and turned it up.

Discovering the bottle was empty, Bernard threw it across the cab of the truck, out the passenger side window. He reached in the glove compartment and grabbed a smaller bottle of bourbon he kept there. He opened it, took a sip and then placed it between his legs.

"Queen Yolanda. You don't even know I'm following you," Bernard said to himself with a mean grin. The black Mercedes was heading south on I-85 with Bernard's red Ram truck closely behind.

Tanya looked through the cassettes in Yolanda's car. "Damn, girl all you got is love songs. I got to get you some music," Tanya said out loud.

She slid in the best of the oldies love cassettes and turned up the volume. The Chi-lites singing, *'Have you seen her'* filled the cabin. She looked in her rear view mirror. The truck that had been behind her was still following her. It appeared to be right on her.

"Shit. What is that asshole doing?" Tanya slowed down. The truck also slowed, refusing to pass her up. She speeded up and the truck did the same. Finally, the truck pulled out beside her. The truck looked vaguely familiar, but she couldn't place it. She considered rolling down her window and giving the driver the finger, but she changed her mind.

"Don't know what kind of crazies are out here, nowadays," Tanya said to herself. She looked over to see if she could see the driver, but the tinted windows made it difficult to see inside.

Bernard smiled and rode beside her for a few feet then pulled passed her and got in her lane in front of her. Once he was in front of her, he slowed. In his mind stirred the idea that the driver of the Mercedes didn't look like Yolanda, but it was, he was sure.

"Who else would be driving your baby? Your guilty pleasure?" he said out loud.

"What the hell is he doing?" Tanya said out loud. She tried to make out his license plate as she picked up the car phone. All of a sudden, the truck pulled away.

"You better have, you asshole!" she said out loud. She put up her middle finger in the windshield. Then she reset her cruise control. The Spinners were singing and Tanya sang with them. *"One of a kind, love affair is..."*

She must have been going about seventy when she passed the red truck again. "You want to see how much power this Mercedes has, baby?" she said out loud as she passed the truck.

The truck pulled in behind her again, matching her speed. For a moment, Tanya felt a little shiver. This was getting weird. Who is this?

She looked in the mirror and the truck was really picking up speed and gaining on her bumper.

"What the…" Tanya slowed down, but the truck didn't. It hit her in the rear with a force that stopped the cassette player. "Oh my God!" Tanya screamed. The truck hit her again. Tanya reached for the car phone, but it had fallen to the floor. Tanya struggled with the steering wheel, desperately trying to keep the powerful Mercedes on the road.

Bernard pulled up beside her and lowered the passenger side window. He screamed at the black car as the driver window on the Mercedes inched down.

"Bitch!" he yelled.

Tanya looked across at the truck. She recognized Bernard and yelled his name. Bernard drained the small bottle of bourbon he was drinking and threw it at the black, swerving automobile. The bottle thudded against the door. "Call me names, huh?" Bernard said in a drunken fury. He slowed and pulled in behind the Mercedes.

Bernard felt a rush of power when he hit the black car in front of him. Watching her car go somewhat out of control brought a smile to his face.

"Fuck with my life, huh?" He sped up and rammed the back of the car again. Green liquid poured out of the bottom of the Ram truck. Shards of the truck's headlights and the black car's taillights littered the road. The Mercedes spun wildly across the road.

"Oh, shit!" he said out loud. "Scared now, ain't you, Miss High and Mighty?" He patted the dash board of his truck as he watched who he thought was Yolanda struggling to get control of the black Mercedes.

The Cameron Mitchell Bridge was coming up. Cars were hitting brakes, horns were being blown and a few crashes were occurring as the Mercedes careened across the highway.

Tanya groped around the floor board for the phone as she tried to control the car. Tears were clouding her vision. Fear was clouding her thoughts. She screamed Bernard's name. She tried to signal him out her window. She screamed, "Help me!" just as the red truck rammed her again. She could feel the metal of the car crumpling. Through the windshield that had a crack in it, she could see other drivers doing their best to get out of her way as the black car fish-tailed across the highway.

Tanya fought her panic as she struggled to get control of the car. Eventually, the car straightened out and she put her foot on the brake trying to slow down.

Only then did she notice the bridge in front of her and the red truck approaching quickly from the rear, belching smoke.

She screamed just as the truck hit her again. Her head slammed against the steering wheel and her foot involuntarily pushed down the accelerator.

The Mercedes hit the bridge forcefully, knocking out a portion of the retainer rail. The car teetered and then slowly slid off the shoulder toward the river. Bernard slowed as he looked back at the Mercedes. It looked like it was going to go into the river.

Momentarily, his alcohol soaked brain pictured the face in the driver's window of the black car. The driver wasn't Yolanda. Tanya? Could it have been Tanya? He kept looking back, shaking his head to clear the cobwebs and slow the rage he felt.

He didn't want to hurt Tanya. He wanted to teach Yolanda a lesson. But he didn't want to harm Tanya at all. He was confused as Tanya's face came clearly into focus.

"Tanya!" he said out loud.

Bernard looked up at the last second. It was too late to avoid running into a stopped tractor-trailer. He slammed on his brakes, but it wasn't soon enough. He hit the trailer and the force caused the airbag to deploy. The tractor-trailer was carrying steel rods that began to roll off the truck. One rod headed for the windshield of Bernard's truck. He never saw it coming nor did he feel the force of the car that slammed into the rear of his pickup truck.

Here at the end of his life, Bernard's last thought was of Tanya's terrified face framed by the driver's window of the black Mercedes.

"Awwww man. I hate 85. Honest to God, I hate 85!" Billy said out loud as he sat in a long line of traffic. "What the hell is going on?" He rolled down his window and blew his horn at a trucker sitting next to him. "You know what's up ahead?"

"Yeah. I hear it's a pretty bad accident up there. Down at the bridge. Looks like we're gonna be sitting here for a while."

"Thanks, man!" Billy reached for the car phone that was in every company car. "Damn! Not on this Thursday. Damn!"

He dialed his office and asked for Mr. Stoker. He was in a meeting. Billy left a message about the traffic situation and a request for a call back. The secretary said she'd have Mr. Stoker call as soon as possible.

He then called Jerome. Jerome wasn't in his office so he left a message.

"Rome, it's me Billy. I'm on I-85 stuck in a nasty traffic jam. See what you can find out and call me. Peace."

As Billy moved slowly through the maze of cones set out by the police and fire departments. There was a worker with a vest on directing traffic, which crawled through a single snake-like lane. As he passed by, Billy looked over at the tangled mess of cars, trucks and the black car barely on the highway. It looked like it was hanging by a thread. News trucks with their spires of wire were everywhere. Billy could see reporters holding microphones and speaking in front of mobile cameras on the shoulder of the highway; but at a distance from the action. Ambulances, fire trucks and police vehicles were all over. Their flashing lights formed a macabre rainbow across the highway.

The man with the vest on held his arms out in front him with his hands open stopping the traffic. Billy was right next to him.

"Hey friend. What the hell happened?"

"This is real bad, man. Real bad. Looks like we got two dead, a badly injured woman and more than a few folks with some minor injuries. A lot of vehicle damage and that black car over there," he pointed to the car over by the bridge, "is just moments from sliding down into the river. There was a woman in there. I think they got her out, though. She's banged up really bad."

"Damn, man. That's some bad shit." Billy looked over at the car. It was vaguely familiar to him, but he couldn't be sure. It was banged up pretty badly. "What kind of car was that?"

"I don't know. Looks like it was a nice one, though. Just a pile of twisted metal, now. "He turned to look at the traffic.

"You got to get moving."

Billy pulled off following the slow traffic as it slithered past the scene of twisted metal, broken glass and flashing colored lights.

After talking with Claude, Yolanda felt a strong twinge.

"I probably should have said something about Claude to Jerome," she thought to herself. She decided that she would call Jerome after work once she got home. She wasn't sure what direction their conversation would go, but she didn't want to keep him in the dark about the possible changes in her relationship with Claude. She had too much respect for Jerome to let that happen.

She glanced at the clock. It was nearing four and Tanya hadn't returned. Yolanda dialed her car phone, but the phone rang until a mechanical voice came on notifying Yolanda that there was no one available to answer the phone at this time.

By four-thirty, Yolanda was getting really worried. Just then one of her co-workers burst in her office.

"Yolanda! Yolanda!"

"What is it, Pat?"

"You've been in an accident!"

"What?"

"I know it's crazy, but the news is saying you've been in a car wreck. Come on girl, some of us are in the break room watching the tube. Come on." Pat left in a rush. She headed in the direction of the break room.

The color drained out of Yolanda's face. Her hands and knees were shaking. She couldn't move. All she could see was Tanya's face. "Oh God, no. No." She willed herself to get up. Once up, she ran to the break room, tears streaming down her face. As she entered the room, the people who were there turned to look at her.

Sure enough, Yolanda heard a reporter mention her name as the possible driver of the black Mercedes, now twisted metal, being towed away.

She sat heavily in the nearest chair. Several of her co-workers surrounded her, trying to comfort her. Pat spoke first.

"See, that's why I don't like looking at the news. If they had bothered to check, they would have known that that couldn't have been your car because you're here."

A male co-worker spoke up. "News people only want to sensationalize stuff. They don't check a damn thing! Why would they put her picture up there? I thought the news always tried to get in touch with next of kin before identifying somebody." He pointed at the TV screen.

"It's my car," Yolanda said softly as she began to cry.

"I sometimes keep my insurance information in my car attached to the visor. Tanya was driving my car. Her car is in the shop," Yolanda said. Her tears dropped in her lap. She put her head on Pat's shoulder and cried. Someone turned up the TV.

"…and according to witnesses, the red truck you see behind me was ramming the black car that almost slid into the river…"

Yolanda looked up. She watched the mangled red truck being pulled away. She remembered following that red truck to breakfast after partying at Club Premier. She remembered seeing that red truck pull off in anger when its driver left her in the restaurant just a couple days ago. She jumped up.

"Bernard, you bastard!"

"…he was pronounced dead at the scene by…"

Yolanda sat again. This couldn't be happening. She put her head in her hands.

"Where are they taking Tanya?" she asked, her voice muffled by her fingers and the sobs wracking her body.

"They took her to Gaston Memorial," Pat said through her tears.

"I need to go there to be with her." Yolanda's sobs were deep and sorrowful. "It was me he was after. It was me. This is all my fault."

"Honey, don't be ridiculous, you had nothing to do with this. Why would someone be after you?" Pat asked Yolanda. Yolanda said nothing.

"Yolanda, it really doesn't matter," Christine Selleca said. Yolanda turned to face her supervisor.

"We'll find a way to get you to GMH as quickly as possible. I know how close you and Tanya are." Yolanda nodded and held on to Pat.

"Thanks, Christine."

Christine Selleca had been as good as her word. Thirty minutes later, Yolanda was in a deputy sheriff's car headed toward Gaston Memorial. The deputy had his lights on as he sped toward Gastonia. Yolanda sat in the back seat numb with disbelief and wracked with guilt.

She replayed her conversations with Bernard over and over again. She replayed her actions and reactions and asked herself how this could have happened.

Then she worried about Tanya. Would she die? Would she be disfigured, paralyzed, a vegetable. She leaned forward to speak to the driver.

"Please pull over, I'm going to be sick, please!"

He did. She quickly opened the door and vomited. Her grief was overwhelming. The deputy got out and stood beside the back door of the car, shielding her from traffic.

When she had finished, he went to his trunk and pulled out a small black bag. "I have some personal items in here. There's some mouthwash and tissues in there as well."

He turned his back as Yolanda rinsed her mouth and spat. Without looking at her, he asked if she were ok to keep going.

"Yes, thank you, Deputy…"

"Redding. Otis Redding. I know what you're thinking. We need to get moving.

"You ready?"

"Yes, I am, Deputy Redding. I appreciate your kindness."

"Under the circumstances, I'm glad I can help. I'm sorry for your friend. I hope she'll be alright."

Yolanda nodded. "Thank you, Deputy Redding."

Yolanda sat back and tried to prepare herself to see Tanya.

"Tanya, Tanya," she said to herself as she began to cry again.

XXVII

Once at the hospital, Deputy Redding barely opened the door for Yolanda before she burst out of the patrol car headed into the Emergency Room. The automatic glass double doors seemed to be slow opening and Yolanda pushed on them. They opened and Yolanda rushed in toward the desk just beyond the doors. Deputy Redding watched her go in and once she got to the '*Check In*' desk, he returned to his car and drove off to find a parking spot among the several sheriff and police cars parked in the ER lot.

There were a few people standing at the desk when Yolanda arrived. She tried to wait patiently for her turn, but her concern for Tanya was overwhelming. She noticed a woman off to herself at the end of the desk reading some papers. Yolanda walked over to her.

"Excuse me, may I ask you something?"

"I'm sorry," the lady responded. "I'm just going to have to ask you to wait your turn, we're quite busy tonight."

"Yes, I understand that," Yolanda said as patiently as she could, "but my best, uh, my sister was in the car accident on eighty-five this afternoon and I was told she was brought here." The lady looked up at her. Yolanda continued.

"Me and my sister are really close and she was using my car, please let me see her."

"I'm sorry. I didn't realize. What is her name?"

"Tanya Willis. And thank you for helping me. What is your name?"

"Oh, I should have on my name tag." The lady reached in her pocket and pulled out her name tag, showing it to Yolanda, then clipping it on her jacket. "I'm Sonja Boyette."

"Thank you, Miss Boyette," Yolanda said. "But could you check on my sister, Tanya?"

"And your name is?"

"I'm Yolanda Walker. Will you please check on my sister?"

"Have a seat Miss Walker and I'll do that for you." Without another word, Sonja sat and worked on her computer. Yolanda moved away from the desk and waited. She was too nervous to sit..

She moved back to her bench alternating between sitting and pacing. Otis stood by discreetly, protectively.

"Miss Walker?"

Yolanda looked up when she heard the familiar voice, thirty minutes after she arrived. She saw Sonja motioning for her to again to come to the desk. Once there, Sonja talked with Yolanda in a hushed tone.

"Your sister is still in surgery. It might be a while before she comes out. Apparently, she suffered some major physical trauma, but I don't have any further details. I talked with a nurse who told me that Dr. Kevin Lee is doing the surgery. He is really good and he'll be out to talk with you, as soon as he is finished with her."

"Thanks, again. So, I should just wait for the doctor?"

"Yes. I'll come get you the moment I hear something or the minute the doctor wants to talk to you. Try your best to relax, ok?"

"Ok. I'll try. But you don't have any idea how much longer, do you?"

"I'm sorry. I don't, but I'll come get you right away." Sonja looked at her watch. "Look, I'm here until midnight, so I'll be here for the entire evening. Don't worry."

Yolanda sat on the padded bench against the wall directly across from the desk. She put her jacket over her shoulders and tried to relax. She told herself that if Tanya was in surgery, she was going to be alright. "They wouldn't spend all this time on someone who was going to die," Yolanda thought.

The automatic glass doors slid open and Rick Manzetti rushed in. He looked around, saw Yolanda and hurriedly walked over to her. Yolanda rose to meet him as he approached. Deputy Redding also walked toward Rick.

"You, Manzetti?" he asked.

"Yeah, that's me," Rick responded. "Hey Yolanda. I'm so sorry about all of this." He and Yolanda hugged. Rick then shook hands with Deputy Redding. "Can we walk over there and talk?" Rick asked Deputy Redding.

"Yeah, sure." They walked away from Yolanda.

"What happened?" Rick asked.

"I've only got some sketchy information. But I'll tell you what I do know." He looked Rick in the eye.

"It seems that the driver of a red truck was intentionally ramming a black Mercedes. The driver of the truck died in a collision with a tractor-trailer. The driver of the car, Ms. Walker's friend was seriously injured. She's in surgery now and we're still not sure if she'll make it. The driver of the truck hasn't yet been positively identified, but they do know he was drinking and a strong odor of marijuana in the cab of the truck."

Deputy Redding reached in his pocket and handed Rick a piece of paper. "This is the license number of the truck. Recognize it?"

Rick nodded. "Yeah," he answered looking over at Yolanda. "But I don't know what would have caused him to blank like that," he shook his head sadly. His eyes filled with tears.

Rick quickly swiped at his eyes. He took a deep breath. "So, what happens now?"

"State Troopers will want to talk with you, and Ms. Walker."

Rick nodded slowly and returned to sit with Yolanda.

"This really turned out to be a fucked up day," Rick said to Yolanda.

"I agree. Mostly a tragic day. Do you know if Bernard has any family still living here?”

"Not that I know of. His mother lives with his sister in Louisiana. And as far as I know, B didn't get along with his sister.

“I don't even have her number. Maybe, I'll be able to get in the house and find the number. I'll just…" Rick's tears spilled over. Yolanda put her arm around him to comfort him.

"I know he was your friend and no matter what, friendship is friendship. I'm sorry for your loss, Rick. I really am."

After a moment, Rick sat up. He looked at Yolanda. "Anything about Tanya, yet?"

"Soon, I'm sure." She put her head in her hand, shaking it gently. She looked toward the desk and noticed Sonja pointing at her. There was a slightly built Asian man standing with her. He was wearing a surgical outfit. Yolanda hit Rick on the leg as she stood up. The doctor approached her.

"Miss Walker?" His face was impenetrable. Yolanda could not tell if this was going to be good news or bad news. Her stomach turned. For a moment she felt as if she was going to be sick, again. She grabbed Rick's arm and held him tightly.

He cleared his throat and held out his hand to her. “I’m Dr. Kevin Lee. I’m the lead surgeon working on your sister.” Yolanda took his hand and shook it firmly.

"This is my…" she turned and looked at Rick.

"Friend," Rick said looking at her then the doctor. "How is Tanya?" Rick asked anxiously.

“Well, as you can imagine, the patient, uh, Tanya, uh Miss…” he consulted a metal chart in his hand

“Willis,” Yolanda said wiping her eyes.

“Yes, Miss Willis had some significant injuries, but we’re working to repair most of the major damage. She will need time and a couple more visits to surgery, but we are hopeful. Right now, she is heavily sedated. I would suggest that you get some…”

“Yolanda! Yolanda!”

They all turned and looked down the hall. Claude Boozer and another man jogged toward them, waving their arms. When he reached them, he hugged Yolanda. He glanced at Rick, nodded and looked at the doctor.

“Are you the doctor on this case?” Claude asked. Dr. Lee nodded politely. “Look, doc. Money is no issue.

Whatever Miss Willis needs, you are to see she gets it. How soon will she be able to be transferred to a hospital in Charlotte?”

“And you are?”

“I’m Claude Boozer. I’m a friend of Ms. Willis…” he put his arm around Yolanda’s shoulder, “and Ms. Walker here. And as I said, money is no object. She is to have the very best.”

“Mr. Boozer, we will give her the very best care we can. As for transferring her,” Dr. Lee shook his head “it will be a couple weeks before we can do that. I’m sorry.”

He turned to Yolanda. “As I was saying, Ms. Willis had some broken ribs, a punctured lung," he consulted the chart in his hand.

"She also had a concussion, a broken wrist, a fractured leg and a host of internal injuries. She is still listed as critical, but we think that the next twenty-four hours will tell us more. She is heavily sedated and she'll need a lot of rest.

“In fact, I'm sure all of you need some rest. I suggest that you come back in the morning, there's nothing more that can be done tonight.”

Yolanda wiped her eyes. "Thank you, Doctor, thank you so much. Can I just peek in on her? I won't bother her, I just want to see my sister." Claude and Rick looked at each other then at Yolanda.

Dr. Lee was silent for a moment. "Ok, but only you and only for a minute. I'll send a nurse out to get you once we get her situated."

"Thank you, doc," Claude said shaking Dr. Lee's hand.

"Sure. She's got a way to go, but she's a fighter." He turned and walked away. He stopped at the desk and talked with Sonja for a few minutes. Sonja looked at Yolanda and her friends as Dr. Lee spoke to her, and nodded.

"Yolanda, this is one of my teammates, Chad Ranier. Chad this is my girl…"

"Lady," Yolanda said looking at Claude.

"Yeah, my Lady," Claude said smiling. "Chad, this is my Lady, Yolanda Walker."

"Pleased to meet you, Yolanda" Chad said holding out his hand. He looked at Claude. "You were right, man. She is fine."

Yolanda looked at Chad then at Claude. "What did he mean by that?"

"Come on, Yolanda," Claude said taking her arm. They moved a few feet away from Rick and Chad.

"I'm proud of you and so I told my teammate that you are absolutely beautiful. You certainly aren't going to be mad about that. You deserve to be admired."

"You know, Claude? I actually believe that part of the problem of my life is that I enjoyed being admired too much. I want to be accepted for who I am not just for what I look like." She pulled away from Claude and walked back to Chad.

"Thank you for the compliment, but I'm not in the mood for that kind of shit today. I don't mean to be rude, but I hope you understand."

Chad nodded. "I didn't mean to offend you."

"I've offended myself, long before you came along," Yolanda said. Tears spilled from her eyes as she walked away. Claude, Kevin, Deputy Redding and Rick watched her walk away. She moved to the desk where she picked up the phone and began dialing.

"Damn, what was that all about?" Claude asked to the air.

"She's really hurting man. She feels responsible for what happened to her friend," Deputy Redding said.

Claude nodded. "Yeah, you're probably right."

"Hey Booz, I didn't mean anything by what I said," Chad said softly.

"I know, I know. Don't worry about it."

Deputy Redding looked at the two of them. "Y'all play basketball, right? Both men nodded. "I thought you two looked familiar," he added.

"Well, I'm gonna go back to Charlotte," Deputy Redding said.

"Chad, why don't you ride back with the deputy, that is if it's alright," Claude said.

Both men looked at Deputy Redding. "Yeah, that's fine," he said. Chad shook hands with each of them and followed Deputy Redding toward the door. Deputy Redding waved his hand at Yolanda who waved back, weakly.

"Thank you!" she mouthed. Deputy Redding nodded and walked out the door, followed by Chad.

The answering machine beeped and Yolanda left a message for Jerome. "Hey. It's me, Yolanda. Tanya was driving my car to a meeting in Gastonia and she was in that wreck on I-85. She was hurt really bad and she's having a lot of surgery. I'm waiting to see her." She took a deep breath.

"Bernard was in the wreck too. From what I understood, he was ramming my car and then he hit a tractor-trailer and was killed. I 'm sorry to tell you like this, but I wanted you to know what was going on.

"The doctor said Tanya will probably be alright if she makes it through the next twenty-four hours." Yolanda began crying again. She tried to continue leaving a message for Jerome, but it became difficult to talk. She hung up the phone and collapsed on a padded bench nearby.

"Who'd you call, Yolanda?" Claude asked as he sat next to her.

"Jerome Mitchell. He was the guy at the house when you came by last week."

"The big guy?"

"No, the other one."

"Oh. Yeah, I remember."

"He and Tanya are friends and I know she would want me to tell him what was going on."

"That's cool, I understand." He looked straight ahead. Yolanda sat with her head propped back against the wall. "Can I ask you something, baby?" Claude asked softly.

"Sure," she said without moving her head or opening her eyes.

"Do you love me enough to marry me?"

She looked at Claude, before responding.

"Claude Boozer, I've loved you for a long time, but you were clear about your desire to remain free. I knew waiting for you wasn't going to be healthy for me and I wasn't prepared to wait forever, for you.

"Not only that, I don't want to merely be somebody's trophy. You're a professional athlete and I know how important images are to you guys. I want someone in my life that is in my life for all of me, not just a part of me. You know what I mean?"

"I do. I really do. We've been apart for a couple months and I've missed you terribly. I think about you all the time and I do want to be a part of your life, if you'll have me."

"Are you proposing marriage? Here? With all that is happening, you're proposing marriage?" Claude nodded, looking deeply into her eyes. "Well, do it right, then," Yolanda said. Her eyes searched his face for any clue of a joke.

"Right?"

"Yep, right."

"What is right?"

"On your knee, looking me in my eyes. Telling me you love me and that you'll be my prince for as long as I'll have you."

Without hesitation, Claude Boozer dropped to one knee in front of a seated Yolanda, took both her hands in his.

"Yolanda Walker. Will you allow me to be your prince? To love, honor and cherish you? Will you be my wife?"

Tears of joy, grief, worry and love ran down Yolanda's face. "Yes," she said softly.

Claude stood pulling Yolanda up, wiped her tears from her face and under the florescent lights of the Gaston Memorial Hospital Emergency Room, they kissed.

Rick watched the kiss, then dropped his head in his hands.

Sonja smiled, dabbed at her eyes with a tissue and silently clapped her hands.

"Say what?" I listened to Yolanda's message again. It was her car, but it was Tanya driving. "Oh shit!" I said out loud. Damn! I dialed Billy's car phone. There was no answer. I then dialed Billy's pager. Five minutes later, my phone rang.

"Billy?"

"Rome. Can you call me back on the hotel phone?"

"Yeah. What's the number?"

"It's seven oh four, eight three three, five-thousand. I'm in room two thirty-seven."

"Cool. Call you right back, bro," I said. Moments later, I was on the phone with Billy again.

"Did you find anything out about the accident on eighty-five?" he asked.

"Yeah man, I did." I took a deep breath. "Yolanda left me a message that the car was hers, but her friend Tanya was driving. Tanya is messed up pretty bad."

"Damn, man. I saw the car. Is she going to live?"

"I pray so. Yolanda said the doc just spoke to her and she said he sounded pretty positive about that, if the next twenty-four hours are good."

"Damn. What about Yolanda? How's she holding up?"

"She didn't sound good on my voice mail. She and Tanya are like sisters. And she's feeling kind of guilty about the way everything turned out."

"Guilty? Why? Oh, because Tanya was driving her car, huh?"

"Wait till you hear the rest of this."

"There's more?"

"Yep. According to Yolanda's message, her car was being rammed by a pick up truck according to witnesses. And that ain't all, either.

You ready for this? She said the truck was being driven by your boy Bernard, the security guard. He died out there."

"What? Bernie? What? Are you serious? Bernie?"

"Yup. That's what Yolanda said in her message."

"He was trying to kill her?"

"I guess. I don't know. All this stuff is crazy. Damn!"

"So, are you going to the hospital?"

"I don't think so. Yolanda also said that her basketball player is there and on the case, so I don't think there's any reason to go down there. I do know Tanya, but I'll wait till tomorrow to check on her and see how she's doing."

"You ok? I mean, how do you feel about that?"

"What?"

"About Yolanda not needing you at the hospital. I mean she used to call you for everything, it seemed. You ok with Mr. Basketball being there with her?"

"Yeah, actually, I think I am. It's time, you know?"

"Ok, bro. You know to call me if you want to talk, ok? I'll be back in Charlotte in a couple days. We can get together."

"That sounds good, man. Thanks for your friendship, Billy. I mean it."

"I know you do. You know I got unconditional love for you too, Rome. I'm sorry that that craziness surrounded a person you knew. As for Bernie, that is just too fucked up. I'll let you go. Peace."

"Peace." I hung up the phone and sat in my chair. The room was quiet and I sat there picturing Tanya being rammed by Bernard's truck. How scared she must have been. I shook my head.

"Not being able to let people go, can really cause some bullshit for everybody," I thought to myself. "Damn, Bernard. What were you thinking?" I asked out loud.

I picked up the soapstone sculpture off my coffee table. As I rubbed my hands over the soft, smooth surface, I found myself thinking about me and Yolanda.

My marriage was a testimony to the foolishness of not letting go. My desire to hold onto something regardless of the price had cost me dearly. And now, Bernard had paid the ultimate price for his obsession.

I closed my eyes and said a prayer for Tanya. Whatever was His will would happen, but I hoped His will was for Tanya to live and recover fully from her injuries.

"Miss Walker?"

A nurse motioned for them to come to her, which Yolanda and Claude did. Rick followed behind them. The nurse identified herself as Tina Durrell.

"Miss Willis is in ICU, but Dr. Lee said you can see her for a few minutes," Nurse Durrell said to Yolanda. "I'll take all of you to ICU, but the two gentlemen will have to stay in the waiting area." The three of them nodded. "Ok, follow me."

They followed Tina to ICU. Claude and Rick sat in the waiting area and she indicated that Yolanda was to follow her into Tanya's room.

"She may or may not be able to hear you, but you can try to communicate with her. Remember, you only have a couple minutes, so make them count," Nurse Durrell said as she left the room.

Yolanda sat in chair close to the bed. She looked at the tubes and the monitor in the room. Tanya's face was covered on one side by a white bandage. Yolanda the red coloring on the layers of the gauze covering Tanya's face. Most of Tanya's hair was cut off. Her right arm was in a cast up to her shoulder and her legs were in casts and elevated in slings. Yolanda wanted to cry at the sight of her friend. After taking a deep breath, she leaned close to Tanya's ear.

"Honey, it's me, Yolanda. I'm here. The doctor said you're gonna be fine. I'll be with you every step of the way as you recover." Her voice began breaking.

"T, Claude is here and so is Rick, your favorite white boy. Me and Claude are gonna get married, but it won't happen until you are ready to be my maid of honor and walk down the aisle with me."

The tears then began to flow in earnest. "I'm so sorry, honey. Tanya, don't leave me. I can't make it if you're not around to yell at me. T…T…" Yolanda gently caressed Tanya's fingers. She caught her breath as she thought she felt Tanya squeeze back. Just then, Nurse Durrell came in.

"I'm sorry, it's time to go. Come back tomorrow. Maybe, she'll wake up. No one can know what that could happen and I know she'll be glad to see you when she does."

Yolanda nodded. She looked at Tanya. "I gotta go, honey. I'll be back every day until you're back home with me. I love you." She kissed Tanya's forehead and followed Nurse Durrell out to the waiting area.

Akeba woke up with a smile on her face. It was Friday and Dani had left for school while she took the day off. Last evening, she and Dani had dinner and a movie at Craig's. She got up and went to the door to get the morning paper, then made coffee and grabbed a roll she brought back from Craig's last evening. She ran back to bed, getting all covered up again.

Akeba looked at the color picture on the front page about the accident on I-85, yesterday, then tossed the paper to the floor. "Damn, that looked pretty bad. I hope everyone turned out to be ok," she said to herself, "but I don't want to read about any bad news, this morning."

Akeba stretched mightily and luxuriated in the memory of the night before. She burrowed in the bed, covered her head with the sheets and the comforter.

XXVIII

Six Weeks Later

I picked up the ringing phone. "Jerome Mitchell speaking. May I help you?"

"Are we still on for lunch?"

"Absolutely, Yo. Where are you?"

"I just dropped Tanya off at her Physical Therapy. I can be at Caswell's in thirty minutes. Is that ok?"

"She's in PT already? That Tanya ain't wasting no time. It's only been a few weeks since the, uh, accident and she's making that type of progress? Now, that is a blessing."

"God is really good. And He has really blessed Tanya. See you in thirty minutes."

"Yes, ma'am. Thirty minutes, it is."

When I got to the restaurant, Yolanda was already there seated at a table. She smiled, then stood as I approached her.

"Hello Yo," I said. I hugged her and she hugged me back. She smelled so good. She looked tired, though. "Good to see you, Yo. Been a while, huh?"

"Yeah, it has, Rome. With everything going on with Tanya, I've just been running all the time."

"Well, you wear it well," I said looking at her intently.

"I don't feel like I have, but that's kind of you, Rome." She studied her menu for a moment, then looked up. "How was your Turkey Day?"

"Not bad, actually. I got to spend most of the day with Dani. Billy came over and we had a good dinner, watching football. How about you?"

"Claude had dinner catered in. There was just no way I could have prepared anything with everything going on with Tanya. But it was quiet. Tanya slept most of the day. The next day was a therapy day, so she needed her rest."

"Well, that's good." We settled into silence, covered by our examination of the menus.

"I know what I want, how about you?" Yolanda asked, looking at the menu.

I glanced at the menu. "Yeah, I need a salad. I promised myself that I would try to eat more salads during the day."

The atmosphere felt real formal. I wondered if it were me or Yolanda, or both of us. Our waiter appeared with glasses of ice-water with lemon and warm rolls. Yolanda and I ordered grilled chicken salads with Ranch dressing. The waiter smiled, took our menus and walked away.

Yolanda played with her hair and looked around the restaurant as if she had never been here before. I watched her for a moment then I got lost in the music coming through the speakers. The waiter re-appeared with our salads and more water. Yolanda bowed her head and I joined her in a word of prayer, then we began to eat.

After a while I decided to break the silence. "You know, this is the place Tanya's friend works as a chef. I don't remember his name," I snapped my fingers as I tried to recall his name.

"His name was Glenn, something," Yo said nodding. "I heard that he's cheffing somewhere else now, though. Can you believe my cookout was just a few weeks ago?"

I nodded. "Yeah. What a night that was and since then, shit has been really crazy." I chewed on a yeast roll. "I was certainly surprised to hear from you, last week inviting me to lunch."

"Well I thought we needed to catch up with each other and I wanted to update you on Tanya's condition."

"I do appreciate the invitation, though."

"I'm just glad you agreed to meet me."

I shook my head. "So, what's up with you?"

"Well, I took a leave of absence from my job the week before Thanksgiving, so I could care for Tanya, better. The hospital gave her a trial discharge home. Trying to work and take care of Tanya was wearing me down. So, I decided to quit my job to care for Tanya.

I nodded, saying nothing. I watched her as I chewed on another roll.

Yolanda continued, "I'm staying at Tanya's house here in the city. Her doctor thought Tanya would improve faster if she were in familiar surroundings. She is still having trouble with her memory."

"What does the doctor say about that?"

"That it'll come back on its own. That's why it was important that she be kept in her best known environment for a while." I nodded. We ate in silence for a while before Yolanda began talking again.

"I've decided to go to Carter G. for a degree in social work."

"Really?"

"Well, since the, uh, accident, I have learned so much. I now know what I want to do with my life, professionally. I have applied to Carter G. for the spring semester. I've got a few credits and they will take those, so I guess I'll pick up a few more. If they won't let me start in the spring, I'll take courses at Meck Tech then transfer what will transfer to Carter G. What about you?"

"Things are going well at school. I'm taking another course for my doctorate. But you going back to school for social work? Wow, Yo. That's really good." I played with my salad for a moment as I thought about a tactful way to introduce the next subject I wanted to talk about. I took a deep breath and went for it.

"Yo, you said that you know what you want to do with your life, professionally. What about personally." I looked at her.

Yolanda played with a piece of lettuce on her plate then dropped her fork. She pushed her plate away and returned my look. "I'm gonna marry Claude. I probably should have told you before, but I just couldn't."

"Ok."

"That's it? 'Ok?'" she said looking at me. I shrugged, but said nothing. In order to have something to do, I stabbed a piece of lettuce and forced it into my mouth.

"Rome, I know I've told you things about Claude that weren't very complimentary and I shouldn't have. You and I have had a crazy love affair for almost nine years, but I want more. You know what I mean?"

I did. But knowing was not making this any easier to listen to.

"Rome, Claude's not been so cocky and arrogant. In fact, he's been more human, more sensitive. And his patience with me regarding Tanya has just warmed my heart.

Tanya is the most important person in the world to me, right now." She looked deeply in my eyes. "Am I making any sense?" I nodded slowly.

"I will always love you, I know it," Yolanda continued. You have always been so steady, so sure. But it's time I became my own steadiness, you know?"

"Actually, I do. I've felt that way for a while. In the past, I've used you as a reason not to face myself and now that I have begun to do that, I'm glad. I'm not real happy about what I see most of the time, but I am getting better and stronger every day." My heart was pounding in my chest. I was sure Yolanda could hear it.

"Thank you, Rome for being gracious about this. It's time I shed my flaky image and grew up. Tanya's courage is inspiring." Yolanda drank some water, gently dabbed at her lips with the cloth napkin, leaving a faint red stain on it from her lipstick.

"Have you met someone?" she asked.

"Well, I've recently begun to date someone."

"Anyone I know?"

"I don't think so. She's a dance teacher and we've gone out a couple times. I am enjoying her company."

"No drama, huh?"

"No, no drama. At least, not yet." We both chuckled.

"Did she make Thanksgiving dinner for you?"

"Yep. Sister can cook, too. You know the adage, 'the way to a man's heart'…"

"Is through his stomach," Yolanda said with a tight smile. "Is she getting to your heart?" I shrugged and took a sip of water.

The waiter appeared, cleaned off the table and topped our water glasses. "Would you like the check?" he asked generally. Yolanda nodded. "Ok, I'll be right back," the waiter said, cheerily.

"Is she, Rome?"

"A little," I replied returning the look Yolanda gave me.

"Well, that's good, Rome. I'm happy for you, really."

"Thank you, Yolanda. I'm happy for you, as well

The waiter brought the check and put it on the table. "I'll take that when you're ready. No rush." We both nodded. The waiter then walked away.

"Thank you, Yo. I'm happy for you, as well."

Did we both mean that? I didn't know about Yolanda, but I knew I didn't mean it. The thought of Yolanda committing her life to Claude, stung more than I thought it would. I wondered if my news stung for her.

"I know I'll get an invitation to the big event, right?"

"You know that. And it'll be an even more special event, because I won't plan my wedding day until Tanya can stand with me." Her eyes filled with tears. "Rome, she's trying so hard and sometimes she gets so discouraged. But me and Claude are trying to keep her spirits up."

I reached out and patted Yolanda's hand. "I'd love to come see Tanya. The last time I saw her, she was still in the hospital."

"I know she'd love to see you."

"What about the legal shit surrounding the, uh, accident?"

Yolanda sighed. "Well, from what I understand, Bernard's insurance company is supposed to pay all the medical bills and replace my car, but they are really dragging their feet.

Claude's attorneys say that all this takes time and I have to frequently remind myself to be patient. Bernard's insurance company is also on the hook for the other injuries and damage that happened on eighty-five that day as a result of his actions."

A toneless whistle escaped my lips as I thought about the potential costs the insurance company was facing.

"Any idea how much money you're talking about?"

Yolanda shook her head. "Nope, but I'm sure it's a lot. Another family has sued the company for wrongful death as a result of the crash."

"Damn, Bernard," I said, shaking my head. "So, what are you driving Tanya around in?"

"Claude leased a minivan for me. It's so much more convenient than a car, since she's got equipment and stuff I have to haul from time to time." It was hard to imagine Yolanda driving a minivan.

It was even surprising to see Yolanda in public wearing slacks. I thought hard and couldn't remember ever seeing her without a dress or skirt on. I had seen her in jeans, but not in regular slacks.

The waiter reappeared. Yolanda grabbed the check, looked at it quickly then reached in her purse. She pulled out a fifty dollar bill. "Here," she said to the waiter.

"Keep the change." To me, she said, "Just chill out, my hero. I invited you to lunch remember. If there's a next time, I'll let you pay, ok?"

I smiled. "Ok, Miss Walker. If there is a next time, it's on me."

Yolanda looked at her watch. "I'm sorry. I have to go Rome. I got to get across town to pick up Tanya and then take her to her doctor appointment."

"No problem, Yo. I have a class to get ready for, anyway."

We rose to leave. Yolanda hugged me tightly. When she pulled back, I could almost swear her eyes were wet. My throat was tight.

"Bye, Rome and thanks for everything," she said emphasizing the word, 'everything'. "I'd like to meet your new lady friend someday."

"That is entirely possible. If we're still hanging out together, and we're invited, she'll be my 'plus one' at your wedding. I'm glad we got the opportunity to have lunch with you and catch up. We've been there for each other. Let's stay in touch every now and then. And try to get some rest, ok?"

Yolanda nodded tightly then left the restaurant. I sat and drained my water glass. The waiter reappeared with a pitcher of water. "Beautiful lady," he said looking at me. I half-smiled. "You know what Prince said," he continued. I looked at him quizzically. He smiled. '*The beautiful ones always manage to hurt you—*"

I held my water glass out to him in a mock toast. "*—Always, every time—,*" I said completing the line from Prince's song. The waiter clapped me on the shoulder and walked away.

After draining my water glass again, I got up and walked out into the cold afternoon air. It felt like a drastic change in the weather was coming. I pulled my collar up around my neck and walked to my car.

Clearly, me and Yolanda were done. While a part of me was glad, some of me hurt. I had sacrificed my marriage partially due to my obsession for Yolanda. As I walked to my car I, it hit me, no Yolanda, no Akeba, no house and only scheduled time with my daughter.

Reaching my car, I groped for the roof to steady myself. I closed my eyes and breathed deeply. I had sacrificed almost everything that was important to me. Looking up to the darkening sky I pleaded for relief. For forgiveness. For help.

"You ok, mister?"

I turned to find a squat, gray bearded black man in a tattered coat holding a shopping cart filled to the top with various items and wrapped with twine. His pants were tied with a piece of rope and the dingy sweater he wore was zipped up to the neck. His fingers peeped out of the open fingers of grimy gloves that may have been white at one time.

"Yeah, I'm ok. Just a rough day," I responded.

"Uh-huh." We both stood silently measuring each other. "You got a couple dollars, young blood?" he asked, finally. I didn't move or respond.

"Look," he said. "Give me a couple dollars and I'll give you something you can use."

Intrigued, I reached in my pants pocket and gave him a five dollar bill. I watched as he carefully folded it and placed it inside the fold of the toboggan he wore. He nodded and began to move away pushing the cart.

"Hey!" I yelled out to him. The old man stopped and turned to face me. I continued, "you said you would give me something I could use."

The old man limped back toward me pulling the cart behind him. He looked at me with his rheumy eyes. He turned his head and spat, then wiped his sleeve across his mouth leaving a streak of spittle across his gray bearded chin.

"I just did, boy," his parched voice said. "Don't you feel better?" I shrugged my shoulders as I watched him, transfixed by the light in his eyes that seemed to burn through the film that covered his pupils.

"You see? Life ain't all about you. No matter how much you want it to be." Then without another word, he turned and pushed his cart away from me. Faintly, I could hear him humming tonelessly and the squeaking of his cart's wheels as he walked away.

Not sure what to make of this encounter, I got in my car to return to school. Before pulling out, I checked my calendar for the day and noticed the one word note I wrote, 'tuxedo'. I needed to pick up my tux for the ball, which Lahti and I planned to attend in a few days.

I took a long look at myself in the rearview mirror. Just as the cold rain began to fall, I looked out the windows of my car to see if I could see the old man, but he was gone.

With a deep sigh I pulled out of the parking lot of Caswell's and headed back to work, the old man's words echoing in my mind.

THE END